READ ME

Questmyre

Book One

"Robin's Awakening"

By   HaaJar Johnson

DEDICATION

To my father; O'Dell Lea Johnson, Jr. You were and will forever be my biggest supporter, my greatest fan and a star that shall forever shine in my soul. AND For all those who feel like they are on the outside looking in...

ACKNOWLEDGMENTS

I would like to extend my heartfelt gratitude to the following people who made the completion of Questmyre, Book One, possible: To my sister, Aisha Johnson, for helping me make Questmyre into something the whole world will come to love. Her tireless attention to detail and enthusiastic love for the saga kept me moving in the right direction.   My nephew, Jamil Gambari, who let me read the first drafts of Questmyre to him. He gave great feedback and encouraged me to bring the story to a global audience. And my little sister, Katrina Reavis, who helped market both, Questmyre and Tweedopplin with energy and   passion.

A great big thanks to my friends, Karina Marino and Craig Groshans, for helping me during my darkest hours. For their critiques, helpful edits and inspiration; I am eternally thankful!

CHAPTER 1

"Always on the outside..." Robin muttered to herself as she walked along the edge of the dirty street curb. Her skinny brown arms were spread at her sides for balance. Thanks to her above average height, her silly antics had begun to annoy a few grim faced pedestrians as she was taking up a substantial amount of the sidewalk. She, however, had no care for anything or anyone around her. If someone wanted to get past her they would have to find their own way, just as she had always done. The old cobbled stone sidewalk and cement streets were littered with gold and bright red leaves that swirled like fire around her and crunched under her worn gray sneakers. Somehow the idea of her walking through fire seemed to fit perfectly as that was exactly how she felt. It was an odd idea, yet Robin could not help but think her entire life had strategically led up to this moment in time. Her old blue skinny legged jeans had a few holes at the seams and fringes at the bottom where the material had rubbed against the ground far too many times. Her small thin cotton jacket had once been a bright, cheery green but was now darkened with soot as was her plain thin lavender t-shirt beneath it. Robin had never been a slave to fashion so she did not mind the looks of ridicule she received from the more fashionable young girls she passed on the streets. As they held their noses up, giggled maliciously and flung their long silky tresses in the autumn wind she ignored it all. With a deep indrawn breath, she continued to trek forward despite the feeling that she always seemed to be struggling against the tide in the stormy sea of life. "Never on the inside looking out, but always on the outside looking in..." She whispered sadly. She did not mind talking to herself in public since no one ever paid her much mind, anyway. As she took each step forward she felt her spirits sink deeper and deeper into a black abyss. Robin had never felt as low as she did at this very moment. "Help me..." she whispered into the cold air, knowing she would receive no answer or aid. She could remember too many times she had asked that very same question in the deep of night; tears streaming down her cheeks and not once was she answered. Without realizing it, Robin's thoughts were transported back in time. The dead orange leaves at her feet, the yellow taxis, the stone-faced New Yorker's all meshed into a swirl of color then vanished altogether as she relived a moment in her past.

Robin found herself standing in the dirty yellow and orange colored kitchen of a tiny apartment in Brooklyn. "You lazy, good for nothing little n-" Her foster mother's cruel words were stopped short when her live-in boyfriend yelled from somewhere in the next room. "For christ sakes, leave her alone Vicky! Just tell her to clean the bathroom and leave off all the hitting. Last thing we need is that Social Worker getting on our case again for crying out loud!" His loud baritone nearly shook the apartment and made Robin tremble inside. She was relieved he was taking her side for once. Thankfully he seemed to be more passive than Mother Vicky. Robin could not imagine him being the one hitting her. She would be in a hospital for sure the day he decided to take his girlfriend's place as her tormentor. Vicky was short; no more than five-foot four inches. However, if she wanted to, Vicky could do some serious damage as she was heavyset with hands that looked like meaty mallets. Mother Vicky hardly ever left the run-down apartment so saw no need to wash or dress up. She wore only two types of outfits; muumuus and large sweatshirts with sweatpants. Her double chin sported tons of errant hairs and her greasy light brown skin left oil marks wherever she went. She always wore flip-flops no matter what the season and never cared to get a pedicure to make the sight of her bare feet less upsetting. Vicky had made it clear to Robin, in her nasal voice, that she took her in solely for the money and free labor. Nothing more. "Don't tell me what to freaking do, Dwaine! You're the one that makes this place into a nasty pigsty in the first place! And what the heck do you think you're doing taking her side, huh? What's that about? You like her or something? I swear I'll kill you both if I find out anything is-" Before Vicky could even finish her sentence, Dwaine stormed into the room with a fearsome look contorting his face. She finally quieted; her eyes wide in fear. It was plain to see that she was thinking that perhaps she had gone too far this time. Dwaine stood at least two feet taller than his girlfriend. He was black where she was yellow in complexion and generally did not show much emotion until she pushed him to his limit with her whining. In Robin's mind they appeared to be complete opposites. He was skinny, tall and completely bald whereas she seemed to be covered in hair. The only thing the couple seemed to have in common was their shared laziness, perpetually unemployed status and inability to wash themselves more than once a month. Robin closed her nose against the plethora of smells coming from the angry duo. She was starting to wish she had cleaned the bathroom this morning before going to school like she had been told. That way instead of standing between these two elephants she could have been sitting in the small closet, they called the "children's room", blissfully curled up with a book. "What the heck is wrong with you woman?! See how you nitpick and push me to my limit?! I swear to God, I should leave you right now! How could you dare even think something like that? And to say it right in front

8

of her... what if she tells her case worker that nonsense? Especially after she already had a situation like that in her last home..." He looked angry enough to hit Vicky. Seeing this, Robin slinked even further into the shadows near the dingy yellow refrigerator hoping they would forget she was even there. "Oh please, you know that was a freaking lie, who would even want to touch that scrawny child? She was just lying and trying to get attention!" Vicky yelled back at Dwaine then turned towards Robin with a glare. "You go right ahead and try to make up some stupid lies about us like that and just see what I'll do to you, you little stupid-" She grabbed Robin's arm and pinched as hard as she could, "little nothing! Here take the mop and this sponge and get the bathroom cleaned now or else!" she shoved the materials at Robin then slapped her on her back to get her moving.   Robin did not let Vicky's actions hurt her or make her cry. Dry eyed she made her way into the decrepit bathroom and began to clean. The tears only began as she heard their continued conversation in the kitchen. "She's a little liar. Nobody would touch her." She heard Vicky say loudly. Oh, but they would and they did... Robin thought as the memories flooded and the tears fell unbidden.

"They did..." she mumbled to herself. She was back in the present and her muttering was cut short by a passersby's abrupt words, "Watch where you're going kid!" a man in a crisp blue business suit screamed. He shoved roughly past her outstretched arms. Robin stumbled slightly from his forceful push and her tiny shoulder length braids fell over her forehead in disarray.

Yes, she was definitely back in New York and back from her trip down memory lane. Her face remained stoic, nothing and no one had the power to hurt Robin anymore. She had seen and heard it all. She simply smoothed back her braids and continued on. Unperturbed by the strangers animosity Robin did not slow her stride or exhibit any guilt over her own selfish actions. The smell of New York City cart pretzels and hotdogs wafted past her and the bustling sound of car horns, thousands of conversations, laughter, footsteps... it all seemed so much louder than usual. These everyday sounds all but attacked her now, whereas they were normally overlooked. What was it about this day that made the past come alive in her head and the present seem extra colorful and clear? She could not put her finger on it, but she just knew that something out of the ordinary would happen; and soon. She decided to prepare for the worst for that was all she ever seemed to get. Ignoring these odd feelings, the skinny young girl focused on annoying all the city people as they brushed past her without a care for either her or her sorrows. A small child with a beautiful sky blue dress with a pink hemline and dirty-blonde curls held back with a sapphire colored bow was making her way towards Robin. She skipped ahead of what appeared to be a stern-faced nanny pushing an infant in an expensive looking stroller. The little girl gleefully ignored the nanny's pleas spoken in a thick patois which clearly showed she was a foreigner.   When the girl came within a few feet of Robin and took in the dark image she made with her dirty unkempt clothes, beat up sneakers and old frizzy braids; the poor child stopped short in fear. Mouth agape she turned and ran back to her caregiver and hid behind her long jean skirt. "I'm scared." She said while peeking at Robin fearfully.   Robin was not sure if she felt hurt or humor at that very moment. Staring at the child who had all the benefits and opportunities Robin had never had and never would; Robin became angry and wanted nothing more than to torment the little girl. Walking towards the trio she screamed, "Boo!"   The girl screeched and raced around her nanny and hid behind the stroller. The nanny looked at Robin with a grimace, although part of her was happy to see someone could put the child to task. With a sharp eyed glance, the nanny shooed Robin away.   "Get away child! Just keep moving you!" She said before taking the little girls' hand and pushing both her and the stroller in the opposite direction.   Robin laughed aloud. She could hear the little girls' cries echo as they disappeared from view and made their way to whatever rich and immaculate condo her parents owned.

The residual echo of her cries took Robin back...far away in the past... but not another apartment...she was in a house this time. A green house with wood shingles and a basement that was chilly year round. It was in that basement she and two other foster children slept. Besides the small three metal cots, there was an old wooden crib right besides Robin's bed. There would apparently be a new addition to the "family" today. For the life of her, Robin could not imagine what sane adults would allow yet another child, let alone an infant, into the care of her current foster parents. She was no more than eight years old but was well aware that this place was not fit for kids. "Robin, get up here!" Sue screamed from the basement door at the top of a short flight of wooden steps.

Robin wore plain black stretch pants and a dirty white t-shirt with a picture of a cartoon bird on it. She started searching frantically but could not find her white flip-flops. With an exasperated sigh she gave up and ran up the wooden stairs barefoot. Her foster mother, Sue, grabbed Robin's arm when she got to the top of the stairs and dragged her into the kitchen. Sue was very dark skinned with piercing black eyes and a large mole on her chin. She was of medium build but was somewhat tall for a woman although she still was shorter than her husband who stood at six foot three inches. She always wore white and would cover her hair with a white scarf while at home. Robin was sure she was some sort of witch but kept that idea to herself so as not to feel Sue's wrath. Sue was extremely concerned about her public appearance and reputation was everything to her. She ensured she made it to church every Sunday and would have killed anyone who called her a witch. In an effort to seem above reproach she always dressed in the finest clothes and kept her house clean and tidy. The decision to move the children to the basement had been made in an effort to keep the rest of her home spotless. Robin had often dreamt of the day she would leave that house. Her dreams always included gallons of red paint and hours of breaking everything in sight. "The baby is coming in today. Now, you're the oldest girl here so you'll take care of it for the rest of the summer. It'll probably be gone by the time school starts... but then... for that matter you're behind will probably be gone by then as well..." Sue let her gold manicured nails dig into Robin's skin and stared at her painfully. The old woman's brown eyes shown with pain as she looked at the little girl before she whispered, "You think I don't know what you've been doing... I promise you, you'll pay. Every day until I can get you off my hands, you'll pay you little hussy!" She shoved Robin to the floor forcefully. Tears began to fall from Sue's eyes; giving away the true depth of her feelings.

Breathing in deeply, Sue wiped at her face to brush the tears away and pushed back her long mane of hair. Most of her heritage was from the Caribbean islands and as a token she sported a beautiful head of wavy hair. "I gave you a home and this is how you-" Before Sue could finish, the doorbell rang. She looked up in surprise. "They're early... Go back downstairs. When they leave I'll give you the baby. Go now!" She yelled again. Robin walked off with a sigh and could hear Sue answering the front door with a fake smile and a "Hi, how are you?!" "What did she want?" Before Robin could fully make it downstairs she heard Vick's urgent question come from under his cot. This was their secret hiding place so it did not seem at all odd to her that he was there. Vick had a light brown complexion and was obviously of mixed race. No one was entirely sure what he was mixed with exactly but his light brown eyes, yellowish brown complexion and almost dirty blonde hair told a story all itself. He had quickly become her best friend in the house and somewhat like a brother. They were from the same agency and she had seen him there in passing however this was the first home they shared together. He wore a pair of black sweatpants and a green tank top. His hair was a small curly afro since it had not been cut in months. Smirking a little she made her way across the red painted cement floor and slid under Vick's cot against the wall.

Since the ground was very cold they had placed an old blue rug under the bed to keep them from catching a chill. "She wants me to take care of the new baby. I guess it's here now." Robin said without any real emotion. "A baby? You don't even know nothin' about babies." Vick looked at her in question. "Nope. Not really. But I guess I'll figure somethin' out." Robin said without much concern. Vick grew quiet while staring at Robin. "What?" She finally blew up and glared at him. "What happened... last night?" He asked with a small quiver to his voice. Robin stared at him with pain etched across her face. She saw it in his eyes. He already knew what had happened. Vick just wanted her to say it aloud so he could go and do something stupid to avenge her. He would get them both thrown out on the streets. She could not let him get hurt over her. "Nothing. Nothing happened so just stop asking!" She yelled vehemently. She began to push herself out from under the bed. Vick grabbed her hands to stop her. "Just tell me... Please! We can leave here you know. I'd go with you. We could go anywhere we don't need them!" He said with a tear slowly peeking its way from his eyelid. "No, just please stop. We're too young to go on our own. We'd never make it. So just leave me alone Vick! It's none of your business anyway!" Robin tried again to pull away from him but he held on. "What did he do to you? I swear I'll make him pay for it! Just tell me Robin!" He cried all out now, tears and mucus dripping and combining across his small face. "You know what he did. He took me upstairs and..." Robin could not finish the sentence because by saying it out loud it would become a reality. Up until now, Robins' foster father's nightly visits were just in her head after the deed was done, but if she said it aloud and shared it with another person... It would truly make it real and something so ugly should never be allowed to exist in reality. Robin grew quiet; deathly so. "Say it!" Vick said. Robin did not respond. In fact she remained silent for the remainder of their time in Sue and Baron's house. She spoke to no one. She took care of the tiny infant named "Jessica", went to school, came home, did her chores and went through all the motions of life without truly living. It would be some time before she started speaking again, because it would be some time before her foster father's crimes ceased. Robin had blocked out so much from her time in that house. The only thing that stayed with her were Jessica's infant cries resounding in the middle of the night while she was far away from the basement, upstairs... Crying like a baby, as well; but with no one to save her. Shaking her head to purge the past from her mind, Robin returned to the present. She could still hear the young girl in the blue dress. Finally her cries echoed into silence. Robin did not feel even an inch of guilt over her

16

behavior. She had always known that her only means of expression in this world was to "act out". Perhaps if she acted wild enough she could draw attention to herself and get the world to finally notice her. That was the philosophy she and her old friend Vick had come up with years ago as they played on the floors of their foster agency's building. The very first day they met, they had become fast friends and ended up staying at the same home for five years. It took five long years before their unwise social worker had discovered their caretaker was not fit to nurture animals; let alone, small children. By that time Vick and Robin had grown in ways that could never be dismantled, erased or fixed. The only thing that had saved Robin during those hard five years between child and young adult had been her friendship and eventual kinship with Vick. They had grown tough together and in time, decided they would be wild, loud and unpredictable; together. They each believed this tactic would make the world see them; help them; heal them. If there was one thing Robin was sure of, it was that people were by nature; very selfish. If Robin and Vick could make their problems, everyone else's problem; maybe someone would finally lend them a hand. A bus horn blared, the chill wind grew a bit stronger and pushed her lithe body forward but her memories went in the opposite direction; backwards... "You know, it's the only way to get any real attention." Vick had told Robin one day long ago. Robin had to agree. She realized that acting 'out' was the only way the world would ever notice them and see just how broken they were inside. It was what the world expected of them; two minority inner city orphans. Robin was quite smart and loved nothing more than escaping in books. However, she found through the years that school was a waste of her time. No matter how hard she tried she felt she could and would never get out of poverty or move past the misery that she had been born into. And God knew she had to work overtime, juggling both her sketchy personal life and the demands of public school. While she was and probably would always be a bookworm, using books as an escape from her existence; Robin eventually took Vick's advice and just stopped trying so hard. She finally gave in and decided to just be what the world expected: A bad, loud and unruly inner city kid. Robin and Vick had set their plan into action. They would grab the world by its collar with their wild antics. Once they had the world's undivided attention, they would sit everyone down and tell their audience how many years they had been in the foster care system. Everyone would see how many bruises they bore due to unkempt conditions and abusive foster parents. The world would know about the hurt Robin felt every time she had been moved from home to home. The world would be able to see

18

the darkness of her past, the corners and places in her mind that she could never show to the light. Then, when the world had seen its share, it would reward Robin, Vick and others like them, for their courage to endure it all and still retain even an ounce of sanity. This was her ultimate dream; her own personal 'heaven on earth'. On that day, all Robin and Vick's dreams would come true, one by one, and they would have a home; a family to call their own...forever. "A real 'Happily Ever After', not just the ones for golden-haired princesses and sweet singing mermaids from magical kingdoms. No more slipping on the edge, I'd be part of something...something real. A family. I'd be loved and..." Robin slowed her gait and finally brought her gaze up from staring at her feet.

Central park was to her right and its large shadowy trees called to her wild spirit. She almost felt as if there were a song in each old trunk singing to her; beckoning her into the only semblance of nature amidst the concrete jungle of New York City. Since her earliest years, Robin sometimes imagined angels, nymphs and fairies were watching over her to offer protection during her darkest hours. This was, in fact, one of those times. Before she knew it her mind was pushing her back to the very first time she had created an imaginary confidant. In her minds' eye Central Park disintegrated and in its place sat another, much smaller city park. Robin found herself in the center of a desolate city park in the middle of the night. All the lights were shut off to keep trespassers out after dusk but that had not stopped young Robin. She had no other choice after two gruff little hoodlums on the corner had tried to grab her into their parked car while she wandered the streets for a place to sleep. She had left yet another foster home in the heat of the moment and after punching and kicking the two guys off she had run to her favorite neighborhood park and slumped onto a swing. That's where she was now, head down, tears streaming, left eye swollen and her lip busted with a trickle of blood dripping into her tears. "Stupid Shanta... I hate her!" She said aloud into the cold silence. Robin was definitely not dressed for the sleek and bitter chill that was creeping across her frame. The winter was coming and she had raced out of the apartment too quickly to pick up her small jacket. She only wore a bright red long-sleeved turtleneck and brown corduroy pants. Her hard black school shoes were still biting into her feet for she had had no time to change before her foster sister Shanta had started up yet another fight. When Robin came in the front door from the school bus, Shanta was already there waiting. She was three grades above Robin and got let out before her. Shanta's short wiry hair had come out of its haphazard ponytail during one of her many brawls in her special education class during the day. Her white shirt and black pants looked dirty and disheveled. Overall, she made quite a picture. "What you looking at Stupid?" Shanta had caught Robin staring for more than she would have liked and she went straight into offensive mode. "Nothing, I'm just tired." Robin said hoping it would get Shanta off her case. She started moving past Shanta through the kitchen and towards their shared room but Shanta put out her foot to trip Robin. "You think you so cute but you not! That's why your mama was a-" Robin did not let Shanta finish. She had heard this particular comment too many times for her liking. While Robin had simply held it in before and saved the tears for the middle of the night, she had finally reached her breaking point. Robin lashed out with her fists and her feet then tackled a surprised Shanta to the floor. "I told you don't talk about my mother you-" Robin had the upper hand for only a second before Shanta, being the bigger and more experienced fighter of the two, began to pummel Robin until she lay in the fetal position to deflect the vicious blows. "You two stop it! Just stop it!" Their foster mother, a matronly old woman who had been nothing but tolerant and patient with them ran towards the scuffle in the kitchen. She tried her best to pull the two young girls apart and ended up with a few scratches and bruises for her efforts. "Animals! That's what you're acting like fighting each other like this!" She said

21

breathlessly once she was able to separate them. Tears were in her eyes, her gray hair in disarray from the tussle and her kind large brown hands were scratched up by the two girls. "How could you do this after all I've done for you two? I swear I don't think my heart can take any more of this..." She fell to her knees in defeat. Robin took one look at the one care-giver she had actually opened up to and felt was genuinely decent. Seeing the pain in her hazel eyes, Robin decided she would not allow her poison to hurt the kind old woman. Without a word, Robin grabbed her book bag off the floor and raced out the front door, out of the apartment building and eventually found her way to the park she now cried in. "I don't need her, I don't need anyone..." Robin whispered dejectedly. The wind blew again and she shivered. Robin pulled her red turtleneck up around her mouth and ears to get a little warmer. She could not for the life of her, understand why she had reacted so violently towards Shanta. She had been living with the troubled girl for over a month now and knew she had some serious problems. From what she had overheard her caretaker Mona say over the phone to her friends, she could clearly see why. If Robin thought her life had been hard, Shanta's had been even harder. Her parents had both been heavy drug addicts, her mother had left her on the side of the street after giving birth. From that point on Shanta had been in and out of foster homes and abused for most of her life. To top it off since her behavior was so violent and she was getting too old, Shanta would be in a group home by her next birthday. Robin had known this and thought, given both of their not so cheery backgrounds they could perhaps be friends but Shanta took Robin's niceness as slyness. She had beaten down Robin's every attempt at friendship. Robin could not deal with hearing anymore slights against the mother she had never known. She too had been found on the street and had thought for years that perhaps her parents were wonderful people who had just...somehow lost her. Shanta would not allow her to believe in such a fairytale and had told her straight out that her mother was probably nothing more than a streetwalker who had thrown away a useless baby. Robin sobbed at the thought and held her arms around her middle to take away the ache she felt there. She had never wanted much in life, but the one thing she had wanted was to be loved, protected and feel the secure feeling a child feels when wrapped within the love of their mother or father. 'That's all I ever wanted..." Robin said softly. She had never ached so much with the pain that desire lit in her. She needed a hug; a loving hug or she felt she would die right there in that lonely park on that solitary swing in the dark. She saw a light in the distance near the entrance of the park. It glowed and grew brighter as it came towards her. Before she knew it Robin saw the light slowly transform into a matronly old woman with beautiful gray hair, soothing green eyes, noble nose, smiling mouth and a beautiful pink cloak about her sturdy body. She smiled and made her way to Robin then walked behind her swing. Before Robin could turn around or say a word she saw the woman's hands wrap around her in a warm embrace.   She hugged Robin close. "I am here my darling baby. I am here, don't worry. You are safe." She whispered as she rocked Robin's swing gently in the breeze. Robin could almost feel the warmth of her breath and the strength of her arms around her.   Just when Robin felt the safest she had ever felt, her fairy godmother disappeared into thin air. The bright light coming towards her shone harshly in her eyes and an abrupt voice spoke from behind it, "Where are your parents little girl? What happened to your face? Get up. Come on, you're coming with us..."   It was the police. Robin stood up sadly and followed the officers. She walked away from the swing, away from her fairy godmother and back into the black abyss that was her nightmarish life. Another cold wind brushed past Robin's cheeks and brought her back to the present. She was standing at the entrance of Central Park. Although, she was past believing in fantasies and knew without a doubt how cold and brutal the 'real' world was, she could not help but revert to her childhood safety mechanism. Without realizing that she was doing it, Robin began to create a beautiful forest guardian in her minds' eye. Her guardian was a woman with caring motherly eyes; large and violet in color. Her long flowing hair was a lighter shade of purple and was frizzy and unkempt. She wore long shimmery robes of blue, green and lavender and her tanned skin glittered gloriously with fairy dust. She smiled at the entrance to the park as she sung a beautifully haunting song of joy. Her long slender silver ringed fingers moved like butterfly wings in the air as she motioned for Robin to join her in the park. Taking a deep breath Robin walked towards the entrance intent on seeing her hastily made plan through. She would start here tonight, at Central Park. She would not return to her foster home but sleep here protected by her very own forest guardian. Robin would sleep beneath the trees tonight and let tomorrow and tomorrow's tomorrow do as they may. She could not take the starvation, the yelling, the cursing, the... everything. And if this was not enough to push her to run away, Robin had heard her counselor mention that she was now at the age where she would have to go into a group home. Adoption was of course no longer an option given her age and foster homes would soon be off-limits. Robin could not imagine living with a group of kids with as many or even more emotional and mental problems as she herself had gained over her traumatic childhood. It felt like she was being condemned to jail or hell rather than a youth home. Shaking her head to push back the tears, Robin forced herself not to think about the future or what awaited her at her current foster home. She swallowed hard, shook her head sharply and forced her feet forward towards freedom... The sun was slowly leaving the city and the park dwellers began to leave the main gates in a wave of movement. Robin swam against the current of energy feeling lost and empty, but this was nothing new to her. She walked staring at her feet for the most part but then came across one of her favorite statues in the park.   The Alice in Wonderland montage stood before her, shining eerily in the glow of the setting sun. She looked at Alice woefully. Robin had spent many nights and days wishing to be like Alice or Cinderella or Snow White or pretty much any beautiful girl in a fairytale. She was not picky; she would take Alice's life before or after the rabbit hole. Living in an estate with nothing to do but read in petticoats... Robin thought to herself and laughed, yeah nothing at all difficult about that. She stared at the rabbit, the mad-hatter and sighing, leaned against one of the metal mushrooms while looking around her.

Everyone was leaving the park...everyone was leaving her...nothing at all new about that. She would never be Alice or Cinderella or anyone important. She was just...Robin. Shoving off from the mushroom, she continued walking down the path and deeper into the park. Pushing aside the dark void growing in her heart as she watched the smiling strangers brush past her, she focused on conjuring up her made-up forest guardian once again. The beautiful woman came back together in a flurry of color and particles. She smiled at Robin and led her deeper into the recesses of central park. Like a child following their mother with pure faith and confidence, Robin walked in her guardian's footsteps. Part of her knew it was sad she had to create a parental figure such as this but Robin was a survivor through and through and knew she needed extra support to get her through this potentially rough time. She was finally setting forth into life all by herself and could only hope she would not end up like the many half-crazed, dirty homeless men and women skulking in the shadows of the city that never sleeps. Before she had gotten halfway through the crowd of people walking on the pathway, she was assaulted by a fit of coughs that violently wracked through her body. Once again her midnight black hair, which sported a shock of purple dye over her right temple, fell across her forehead. Agitated, she swiped it away. She had been ill the past week due to the coming winter weather and the poor conditions of her bedroom at her current foster home. Some nights it felt

27

as if there were no walls surrounding her, as the cold winds swept through holes and slits and made their way over her barely covered body. Once the coughs dissipated Robin continued on her way. When she got past the bulk of bicyclists, joggers, strollers and happy, privileged children skipping beside their parents, she searched for the darkest path she could find and slinked into it. The leaves of the bushes and trees all seemed to change color with the growing loss of light. From bright vibrant reds, oranges, yellows and purples they began to dim until all looked blue, gray and black through her frightened eyes. Her forest guardian had forsaken her at some point during the long walk deep into the park. No matter how hard Robin tried she could not re-imagine her. She was too busy staring frantically into the dark shadows and imagining less friendly characters waiting for the right moment to pounce on her. "Keep it together, Robin. There's nothing to be afraid of. It's just darkness..." She whispered fearfully. Robin began to lose some of her nerve and bravado as her eyes strained to make out her darkening surroundings. Squeezing her cold and numb hands tightly she began to whisper the song she had made up years ago. She always sang it when she felt extra afraid or confused. "Twilight pours on your tear soaked face and I cry; I cry with you. In a house; not a home, I watch you stand all alone and I watch; I watch you. Don't think you're on your own because I'll never go. I'm near; I am near you. You have a friend.... to depend...til the end...together we will win. I'm here for you; I am here... for you...I'll be there for you for-ever." She ceased singing when she came across a short black iron bench hidden amidst a crop of deep green bushes. Robin sat on the hard cold metal and leaned her head back to stare at the heavens above. She let loose a huge sigh that turned into a tiny sob. The sun was nearly gone and Robin was finding it hard to distinguish any of her surroundings.

"Twilight pours on your tear soaked face..." she sang softly into the growing silence of the night.

"I'm not scared. Nothing scares me. I'm good. It's all good. I'll just sleep here tonight and worry about tomorrow... tomorrow. Then, I will go and find Vick wherever he's staying and see if he will ... If he will..." She faltered, not knowing what she expected Vick to do. How could they survive alone on the hard streets of New York City? She did not know exactly; had not thought it all out and she definitely did not have all the answers. All she knew for certain was that she did not want to be alone. Not like this. Robin pulled off her small green jacket and draped it over her upper body for a blanket. She knew her efforts were in vain, however since her flimsy denim jeans and purple t-shirt would not keep her warm through the night. Looking down she took notice that even her sneakers had a few tears in them. Resting her hands on the hard bench like a pillow, Robin laid her head on her hands. With her makeshift blanket and pillow positioned, Robin begged herself not to cry and to fall fast asleep. Only one of those pleas was answered...   As she slept, her cheeks sparkled in the glow of the moon and only a nearby night owl was witness to her silent weeping.   That night Robin slept within the deepest slumber she had ever experienced. It was as if she had fallen into a bottomless well and even the opening had blacked out into an endless darkness. Her head tingled with a cold more frigid than she had ever known and her body felt weightless and insubstantial.   When Robin awoke she had no idea where she was and how she had gotten there. Her first thought was to find what had pulled her from her dreams. Opening her eyes was the first feat Robin had to undertake. It felt as if her eyelashes had melded together in the night and her eyes would never again have the privilege to greet the morning sun.   "Oh my God!" Robin proclaimed as she leaned up from her sleeping position and continued to struggle to open her eyes. Bringing her hands up to rub at her eyelids, she began to work in earnest wondering how something as simple as opening ones' eyes could have become such a challenge. "What the heck?!" Robin proclaimed as her eyes stretched out of whatever odd film had restrained them. Blinking the sleep from her eyes, Robin struggled to bring the world into focus. When everything finally came together Robin screamed and shook with pure horror. She was not where she had been when she fell asleep the night before. Gone were the bench, the bushes and the leaves. In fact, all of Central Park had disappeared overnight!

CHAPTER 2

Robin found that instead of lying on the hard metal bench she had fallen asleep on, she was now crouched in a corner. Her head was leaning against a wall coated in thick royal blue paint.

The overpowering smell of dust filled her lungs which already felt weighed down as if this was her first time using them for the purpose of breathing. Her small green jacket which she had used as a make-shift pillow the night before lay limp in her right hand, she quickly put it. She began vigorously wiping at her eyes to get past the fog which seemed to cloud her vision. When she could see clearly her heart came alive, pumping blood frantically and adrenaline began to soar throughout her body. She was not at all where she belonged. "What... Where am I?" She whispered fearfully. There was really only one explanation for what had happened. At some point during the night, some sick creep had picked up her sleeping body and transported her somewhere else. Robin's hands and knees shook with the enormity of her situation, "Oh heck no! I've been kidnapped!" She finally spoke the words aloud and stared incredulously around her. This sort of thing could only happen to her, she thought sardonically. Robin began to search the room she found herself in. She moved with lightning speed knowing that the quicker she got out the better her chances of survival.

Her heart beat against her chest as if it were trying to flee. Robin had been in some extreme situations in her life but she had to admit this was her very first kidnapping. Well, no, come to think of it that was not entirely true. There was that time she had tried to run away from an extraordinarily abusive foster home. When her guardians had finally caught up with her she had been locked in the basement for three days.

Thankfully child services had for once come to her rescue right on time. On the third night of captivity, she had heard a commotion in the room right above her. Seconds later the basement door had been unlocked and her latest inept social worker had been standing there with a look of both surprise and guilt plastered across her face. Robin had nearly forgotten about that particular memory as she tried her best to push her blackest moments into the shadows of her mind. She had run away last night in the hopes of changing her luck for the better. In her mind, when she awoke this morning, the perpetual darkness of her life would burst with light and all her worries would be a thing of the past.

However, in its usual fashion, her life had thrown her yet another immense obstacle to tackle and get over. Sighing deeply, Robin blinked her eyes, shook her head, gritted her teeth and let her brain take control. She would find a way out of her current predicament. She was Robin, she was strong, and she was indestructible. At least she hoped so... Glancing around frantically, she searched to see if her captors hid in any of the many shadows scattered throughout the room. She was alone and so decided it best to slow down enough to analyze her situation. Robin perused her surroundings. She was standing in what appeared to be some sort of study or perhaps a sitting room. She could not be sure for two reasons. One; she had never been in any home big enough to have a study or sitting room. The second reason being; her fear was so overwhelming she could barely remember to breathe let alone determine how best to categorize her surroundings. Robin surmised it must be such a room, based on various television shows she had seen and books she had read. Having had such a troubling childhood, Robin was and had always been quite an avid reader. She dove into books at public libraries, at school and pretty much anywhere to keep her mind off of her life. It was so much easier to ignore reality and just focus on the fun-filled adventures of more fortunate individuals. Nearest to her was the only window in the dark and dingy quarters. With escape, her biggest concern at the moment, Robin moved towards the glass window. She hoped she could climb out of it without being caught by her captors. Robin ran her hands over the dirty and chipped white painted wood of the window frame and wondered at how dirty everything seemed to be. The only exception was the actual glass of the windows which were impeccably clean. Apparently whoever owned the house was afraid of pine sol but not Windex, she thought sarcastically. Robin brought her attention back to the matter at hand. Her breath

34

caught at the absolutely stunning sight outside her prison window. The sky appeared as she had never seen it before. In fact, she knew in an instant that she was not in New York City anymore. Where the heavens above had once been dark blue and littered with bright white stars, what she saw now was a dark hunter green expanse of night sky. Where there should have been a sun, stars or even the moon, all that hung in the empty space between the ground and the heavens were spiky clusters. She noticed these white orb-like objects were semi-translucent and glowed with an odd light. They were way too close to be stars and did not appear stationary but bobbed to and fro across the sky like floating balls in an ocean. To Robin, they looked like badly fashioned spiked paper-mache spheres idly thrown up in the sky and long forgotten.

"Oh my..." Robin heard the whispered exclamation come from just below the window, which she surmised was situated about two stories from the ground. Squinting, Robin searched the area just outside and below her to see who had spoken. She prayed fervently it had not been one of her captors but rather someone who could and would help her escape. She knew too well the average New Yorkers' penchant for ignoring pleas of help and deftly 'minding their own business'. Robin could only hope that if she were still in the city that never sleeps, some naïve and helpful tourist would come to her rescue. In a flash, Robin found the source of the voice, standing within a cluster of bushes below and to the right of her current position. It was a young boy, about her age, with eyes huge and golden-brown with dark pupils. He stood with a sky-blue rock held timorously in his hand. He looked at her as if he had seen a ghost; his mouth gaped slightly open in surprise. Robin could not see much more than his lean silhouette and light colored eyes as he stood in the shadows. Robin stared back for a moment wondering at the boy's appearance. There was something different about him that she could not quite pin-point in the heat of the moment. "What the heck am I thinking? Focus girl! You have to get out of here now!" She shook her head and pursed her lips in determination. Waking from her dazed stupor Robin tapped on the window and called out to the boy, "Hey you! Can you help me?! I need help getting out of here! Can you please call the police or something?" The boy continued to stare as if frozen in place. Robin rolled her eyes in frustration and began trying to pry the window open. Just her luck, the dumbest boy in New York City, was her only hope for escape.

"Oh, dag! It's stuck!" Shaking with fear now, Robin tapped frantically at the window trying to wake the boy from his trance. "Hello! Can you hear me? Can you see me? I need help!" She screamed at him. Her breath quickly fogged the window. The boy shook his head as if to wake himself from his own shock then motioned for her to leave the house. Robin looked at him incredulously, "Didn't you hear a thing I just said? I need your help! I can't just walk out of here! My kidnappers are probably waiting just outside the door!" He continued to motion for her to leave and his waving became increasingly frantic. "Okay, I guess I can try to just walk out. Maybe they're amateur kidnappers and left me here by myself." Robin mumbled to herself as she turned away from the window and refocused on the small room behind her. The dark midnight blue color of the painted walls made the room seem even smaller than it actually was. Robin noticed a single green door at the other end of the quarters and quickly turned towards it. However, before she had taken a single step something stopped her in her tracks. Robin paused feeling the hairs on the back of her neck stand up. "Wait... Something's wrong..." She whispered softly as she finally took a good look at her surroundings. There was a dusty old brown velvet couch, and tall wooden wall library at the rear of the room. As everything was caked in dust, Robin realized she was in an expensive yet rarely used room.

Everything in the room appeared ancient, from the worn wooden floorboards to the massive blue velvet drapes. It did not take long for Robin to realize what had gnawed at her conscious and put her ill at ease. "Dolls..." She looked around incredulously. "Thousands of dolls..." What was most incredible about the room was what filled nearly every crevice of it. While everything else in the room was dirty, dusty or falling apart from misuse, thousands of wooden dolls no taller than four inches in height stood on nearly every available surface of the room. Not one of them had a speck of dust on them and it was clear whatever psychopath owned this place, was a bit particular about the cleanliness of their dolls.

Robin had to watch where she moved because the room was filled to the brim with these miniature figurines. They were littered across the floor, some lay on chairs, on desks, in front of the books of the library, on lamps and atop boxes. They each had distinct faces etched with precision however their bodies were all identical with the basic limbs all carved in soft brown wood. What was so odd about their placing was the fact that while the surface they stood on was packed with dust and debris, the dolls themselves were immaculately clean. Robin had almost knocked over a few of them when she turned to leave. She wanted with all her heart to stop and study the perfectly sculpted dolls but the danger of her situation did not allow for any more dallying. She made her way carefully through the room, trying her best not to knock over any of the figurines for fear that if she did she would bring her captor's attention to her escape. It felt as if each moment that passed by was a decade long. Her heart beat so hard against her chest, she was afraid it might burst free. Despite her fears Robin continued to move forward; one step before the other. When she stood before the green door she tentatively turned the ornate brass doorknob expecting it to be locked. To her surprise, the door opened effortlessly and Robin cautiously poked her head out to see what awaited her on the other side. The air in both the room and the hallway was musty and she felt as if she would sneeze at any moment. Robin feared if she did, she would be found out and her escape; thwarted. On either side of her, all she saw were countless closed green doors along the same midnight blue colored walls and an old worn dark brown hallway rug. Small dim recessed ceiling lights made a pattern of light along the hall. Not wanting to allow her imagination the chance to run wild and freeze her with fear, she quickly exited the room. As she stepped into the hallway she went with her gut instinct and decided to go towards her right. She walked with caution, trying her best not to make a sound as she passed a number of shadowy doors. As she passed each one she was overcome with the fear that some monster; man or beast, would jump from behind it and drag her within. She finally came across the stairway leading down to the first floor. Robin you're a fighter and a survivor, just keep putting one foot in front of the other and do whatever you have to do to get out of here alive! She told herself forcefully. Robin took one step and nearly screamed at how loud the old wood creaked beneath her sneakers. Holding her breath she waited to see if anyone came running or moved about in the house. Nothing... She mouthed the word, "Okay" then slowly; painstakingly made her way down the stairs and towards what she surmised should be the front of the house. All along the floors, the windows, shelves and side tables, she noticed the same tiny wooden dolls were apparently scattered all throughout the old house. She was sure that whoever lived here had a creepy 'thing' for dolls and she was not too eager to meet them. When she finally made it to what she figured would be the front door of the house, Robin heard the sound of someone slowly walking down one of the long corridors just above her on the second floor. Their hard bottomed shoes slid against the floor in an eerie rhythm and the sound nearly scared Robin to death. She paused in complete and utter fear. All of a sudden the footsteps stopped, apparently somewhere near the room Robin had left, or so she guessed. The entryway was bare of any tables, mirrors or pictures on the wall. All she saw atop the wooden floor boards were hundreds of thousands of the same wooden dolls, all fairly identical in form. All she could discern in the dim light of a dusty brass chandelier right above her, were the four windows facing the front of the house. Each was covered in dark blue velvet curtains so she could not see outside. Robin looked ahead of her and noticed the front door just a few feet away. She gulped hard and felt as if she had to forcefully fight her body to do her bidding, as she was frozen with fear. While the walls were painted a deep dark blue, the door was bright red and made of wood. Robin inched towards it and stretched her hand to grab the doorknob. Once she grasped it, she slowly turned the knob to see if it was locked. To her relief, it was not. As she pulled it open, Robin heard the sound of someone knocking incessantly on a door above her. In her heart she was sure it was the door to the room she had just escaped. Not wanting to find out what would follow that knock; Robin ran out of the house, across a gray colored porch and down a short flight of wooden stairs. She turned towards her right; straight towards the bushes where she had seen the young boy standing. He was still there in the shadows and motioned for her to come towards him. Before Robin came too close to the boy she slowed to a cautious walk and called out, "Who are you? Where am I? What is this place?" She whispered loud enough for only him to hear. "Shhh... You must not wake the butler." He said as he began to back away from the house and deeper into what appeared to be a dark forest, which surrounded

41

the house. "The butler? What butler? What do you mean? And why are you-" Robin had been walking tenuously towards the boy as he retreated into the trees but stopped in her tracks. She now noticed something peculiar about him that she could not have discerned from her previous position at the window. "No time for questions outsider. You must follow me and I will keep you safe. But please do be quiet or the butler will... come for you." He motioned for her to follow him then turned and started to disappear into the forest. Not sure what to do or who to believe, Robin stared back at the house she had left. It was very wide for a two-story house. The outside façade was gleaming white and made of wood paneling. Although it shone bright and white it looked somehow sickly against the backdrop of the hunter green sky.

The windows were dark and she could just make out the small doll figures within. Some stood precariously on the window panes and she was sure there were many more littered about in various rooms throughout the house. On the very front of the dwelling, just above the red front door was a white sign with black lettering that read, "The House of Intrigues". Before Robin could wonder more on the sign and its meaning her eyes caught onto something. In the window of the room where she had once stood, a flurry of movement caught her attention. As Robin strained to see through the window, she saw the silhouette of a large man move to stand before the same spot she had been when she first awakened. He wore a black and white butler tuxedo with a black bow tie at his neck. His hands were encased in pristine white gloves.

She could not make out anything other than this, as his coloring and face seemed to be hidden in the shadows. He did not look at her but used his hands as eyes as he moved them over the dolls on the window sill as if he were surveying them and mentally counting each one. All of a sudden his hand stopped in mid-air as if he had finally realized something was missing. Robin shivered in fear and wrapped her skinny arms about her middle. Not waiting to see what happened next, Robin turned towards the spot where the boy had disappeared and ran after him. Her old gray sneakers beat against the hard ground. With each step she scattered rocks, dislodging sky blue dust which swirled in the air behind her.

Robin's frantic yell echoed throughout the dense dark forest, "Hey wait! Please wait for me!"

CHAPTER 3

Robin ran like the hounds of hell were at her feet. Everything passed by her in a blur of colors and sensations. Her focus was solely on the back of the young boy who was now her only connection to normalcy in this strange new world. Leaves swiped past her face, branches and twigs scratched at her legs and arms. She nearly tripped twice but was able to right herself just in time.   Thankfully Robin was in pretty good shape and had ran track for a few years while attending school. She had been addicted to extra-curricular activities as they allowed her to stay away from her countless "homes" as much possible. Robin had joined any team or group that would take her. Running was something she had found to be mildly therapeutic.   While running, her body and spirit seemed to slowly separate. While her legs and feet held to the rhythmic pattern of the forward motion, her mind would slowly slip away into a blissful cloud of whiteness. She loved finding this ethereal place where time, space, pain and hurt did not exist. Here, Robin could just float without worries. That is where she was slowly going as her feet pounded over rocks, logs, branches and other forest debris towards the young boy who held all the answers to the questions she needed answered. "Please wait!" she said breathlessly as she followed where he led. It seemed to her that he was going to run forever. Just when she wondered if she could keep up their wild pace, he began to slow down and then stopped altogether. When Robin finally caught up with the young man he was standing beneath a large tree breathing heavily from his run. She doubled over as well as she gulped down mouthfuls of sweet oxygen. As soon as Robin regained her composure she dived straight into interrogation mode, "Who are you? What is this place?' The boy stared at her as if she were some sort of miraculous creature that had fallen down from the heavens. His eyes were wide and his lips gaped slightly open in surprise. "I can't believe it. You are here... finally here standing before me. I never dreamed this could happen. I don't even understand how...it must have been the rocks... I threw some rocks at the window to... I'm not sure why I did it actually... I mean, I guess I just wanted you to stop crying but I suppose maybe the rocks hitting the window somehow dislodged your doll and... I just don't know what I was thinking..." He continued to mutter to himself while Robin looked on in both annoyance and growing frustration. She blinked her eyes and stepped back from him praying her rescuer, was not a raving lunatic. Robin put up her hands in a sign of surrender to show him she was completely confused, "Hi, Hello! Will you please slow down and just...I mean, what the heck are you talking about? I asked you who you were, and what this place is and you're talking about dolls? Are you alright?" She rolled her eyes to the heavens only to get another glimpse of the strange dark green sky spread out above her. Her breath caught in her throat and her slightly slanted brown eyes opened wide in wonder. The spherical orbs hanging in the sky reflected in her eyes and she licked at lips which had suddenly gone dry. Robin could not help but shudder in fear. She slowly let go of her tough façade and in defeat let her eyes drop from the sky to look down at her feet. This did not help matters as she finally noticed that the ground beneath her, both grass and dirt were an odd shade of light blue. The tree they stood beside had a green wooden trunk and glowing light blue leaves which waved in the wind. All about them similar trees swayed to and fro as if laughing at her look of absolute confusion. Robin swallowed hard to keep from getting hysterical. "Please... I am very scared right now. I don't understand this- this- place. Please just help me. Please..." Robin finally broke down. Her false tough front crumpled from bricks into dust as the reality of her situation seemed to fall all at once on her thin shoulders. She heard his soft, mellow voice pipe up beside her. "I am sorry. I too am confused by all of this. But I will endeavor to explain what I do know." The boy seemed to have calmed down marginally although he still looked at her as if she were an alien. Robin smiled at his sincere words and nodded for him to continue. A few tears she had not known were there; fell as she moved her head up and down. She wiped each away quickly, hoping he had not seen them. Robin could not afford to appear weak in front of anyone; especially not a stranger. She had been taught that particular lesson far too many times to count. Feeling a little more at ease with Robin, the young man cleared his throat and began to explain, "My name is Roami. I am from the Tinktu tribe. This place that we are now in is called 'Source One'. It is the main world of all the worlds in all the galaxies. Some would even say it is the center of existence." Robin looked at him in complete shock. Before he could utter another word of nonsense she put up her hand to stop him. "Whoa! Wait. Stop right there! You're kidding me right? Wait..." Robin's head began to swim and her fingers tingled oddly. Before she knew it, she was hyperventilating. She bent over and took deep breaths to calm herself down. The tough inner-city girl, who had been through nearly every extreme situation a person could be in, had finally met her limit. When she had steadied her breathing Robin stood up to stare at the boy standing before her. She wanted to believe that he was lying or just plain crazy but his physique alone told her that he might just be right. In the frenzy of the run and the insanity of his disclosure, she had not been looking at anything properly. Or perhaps it is more accurate to say that she had been looking with her eyes but her mind had been unable to process much of what she was seeing. Not until that very moment. Robin finally realized what had seemed 'off' about her young companion. Her body felt as if it could take no more of these shocking revelations. She felt dizzy and wondered if she should sit down on the ground before she had no choice and crashed into it in a dead faint. Without a doubt Robin was definitely not in New York City anymore. "Well, no... it could still be New York City. There are all types of crazies in Manhattan but this is definitely not...Earth." Robin said to herself and laughed shakily. "I'm sorry, what is that you said?" Roami asked politely. "Nothing. Just talking to myself... I do that when I'm nervous...or scared out of my mind...like say... now." Robin looked over at the young boy named Roami. This time she truly looked at him with open eyes and mind. She was absolutely amazed that she had missed this initially. He looked like any other boy her age except that his skin was a brilliant shade of royal blue. His large eyes were slanted exotically and they were golden-brown in color; without a doubt they were the most beautiful eyes she had ever seen. His ebony black hair was curly and coiled handsomely against his sculpted and angular face. His body build was slight and yet toned. She knew this because what he wore was quite flimsy. His shirt was a soft woven brown t-shirt that left his arms bare and a matching pair of shorts which stopped just above his knees. His legs were slightly muscled and on his feet he wore dark brown sandals with thick soles. "You're blue." she stated with a blank look on her face.   Roami looked at her as if she were not too intelligent. "Yes. I know". He replied with a bit of question in his voice. He stared at her now with a hint of concern, "Are you okay? I know this is a lot to take in all at once." "No, seriously... You're blue. Absolutely, blue. Is that paint?" she asked as she leaned forward and swiped her index finger over one of his long slender arms.   Roami jumped back as if she had scalded him with her touch. "No, it is my skin. Have you no blue skinned people in your world?" He seemed slightly annoyed by her shock.   Robin laughed for the first time since she could remember. The sound was a bit rusty and she was sure she would have to do it a few more times to get the hang of it. "Heck no there are no blue people! Well, at least not by nature." She said with laughter in her voice as she thought of a few blue skinned guys with spiky blond hair and body piercings she had once saw running and howling through the east village one night. At the time, she had been kicked out of her latest foster home and ended up walking through the streets of the city looking for a place to sleep for the night.   She had seen tons of very odd people enacting unimaginable actions that night before finally sleeping on a park bench in Union Square. Shaking her head she tried her best to focus on this odd dream that had apparently become her reality. "Oh..." Roami said. He continued to stare at her as if she were a mythical creature from a storybook which had just jumped out of the pages and into real life.

"Well here in Source One we have every color there is. We have some browns in the likeness of your shade. I think it is very beautiful... your skin pigment." He said softly. He looked away nervously. "Thanks..." Robin said off-handedly and turned to look back in the direction they had come. "What was that house I was in? There was a sign in front that said 'House of Intrigues'." Roami nodded his head, "Yes that is what it is called. No one knows how it originally got its name. It is something that has been around almost before the idea of time itself. In fact, The House of Intrigues is one of the greatest mysteries of Source One." Robin's forehead crinkled in question. "Source One? You keep mentioning that. You said it's the center of existence... but... I still don't get it. What is it exactly?" She asked.   Now it was Roami who looked confused. "How could you not know what..." He drifted off into thought then piped back up, "Oh well, I suppose you would not know, being locked up in the House of Intrigues for so long. Source One is everything you see around us. It is the world of all worlds. The... source... of everything." He chuckled to himself, "I am sorry. It is just... I am not sure how to explain it. You see, to me it is so basic and fundamental. I cannot find the words to express what just 'is' to me."   "But please try... I'm sorry I just realized I haven't told you my name. I'm Robin." She smiled at him as best she could. Robin was not really one for smiling and could not remember the last time she had looked at anyone with anything more than a blank stare, sarcastic smirk or deep frown. For some reason she could not help but act out of character with this boy. He was one of the few people Robin had met who seemed genuinely.... 'good'.   He smiled back a bit sheepishly, his gold eyes twinkling in the semi-darkness. "Now do you think you can explain everything...from the beginning? I really need to know what I've gotten myself into here." Robin pleaded.

"Okay. But first let us sit down and find a comfortable spot to talk. This explanation may take a while." When she nodded at his request, Roami led Robin through a copse of blue trees and into a small clearing of sea-blue colored grass.   As they walked Robin took in her surroundings trying her best not to completely freak out. "Great, the sky is green and the grass is blue and the trees are... blue and you are... blue and... I-I...oh my goodness... I think I really need to sit down." Robin felt dazed and out of sorts. Her head pounded and her palms were sweaty. "Yes, of course. I just wish there were something for us to sit on besides the damp ground." Roami said as he looked around for a secure spot to rest. He bit his lip as he searched about for an ideal location. "I explore the forests often so I just have to get my bearings to figure out where we are exactly." He explained. "I'm usually pretty good at this but... right now... I seem to be a bit..." He looked at her oddly and let his words fall off with no conclusion. Robin returned his odd look with a sardonic lift of her eyebrows. The longer she was in this new world the more comfortable she got and could not help her usual safety mechanisms from taking over. She focused on helping Roami and also looked around the small clearing. "You know what? Forget it. We can just sit on the grass here and-" Roami moved to sit cross legged on the grass. Before he could finish the thought Robin spotted something black as ebony, jutting from a few bushes nearby. It gleamed against the dim light of the spiky orbs in the sky. Walking towards it she swiped at the tree branches covering it. It was a small black metal bench. The back of its frame swirled into beautiful circles and diamond shapes. It looked sturdy enough to hold both of

them.   "Hey, here's a bench right here." Robin sat down to test its durability then motioned for him to come sit beside her.   Roami looked surprised and got up from the ground to sit beside her. "I don't recall ever seeing that before..." He looked at the bench in confusion but quickly left off his investigation of the bench as he felt Robin's stare burning into him. She was obviously eager to get some answers and was not about to wait a minute longer. "Yes, so...Source One..." She prompted him as politely as she could muster despite her desire to just scream out, Tell me everything now or else!
"Yes, so...Source One is... everything. There are countless worlds in countless universes. While they may be light years away from one another and appear to have no contact between each other; this world can act as their one true connection. Source One is like a network of wires all tied to alien lands and exotic places you could never imagine. It is also a very finicky, shifty sort of place. One must be careful what one says, or does; touches or even thinks because the invisible lines that connect Source One to all of these worlds, are very sensitive and have no rhyme or reason." Roami paused to catch his breath and looked off into the distance as he recalled a particularly unbearable memory.   Robin took advantage of the moment to stare at Roami. She took in his beautiful golden eyes, the thick long black lashes, his pert

blue nose, full lips, glossy black hair and strong yet lean fingers. He looked absolutely amazing to her. When he looked up from his thoughts and into her eyes, she blinked then looked away, embarrassed for having been staring so intensely. He swallowed hard, his adams' apple moving in response. She could tell from his determined expression and furrowed brow that he was about to delve into a somewhat painful memory. Robin was all too familiar with those and so prepared herself for what was to come.

His soothing voice piped up again, putting an end to the uncomfortable silence. "For instance... when I was younger, I had a friend named Tobias. He was a corky and fun fellow and we were inseparable as children. One day we went out to play in Gilaboo Forest which surrounds my village. His bearer and mine told us repeatedly not to play 'Hide and Seek' that day for they felt a sneaky mist was in the air. My people call any ill feeling they have, a 'sneaky mist' because that is how Source One can shift on you...very slyly. One day the links to the other worlds can be very weak and the next day, it can be so strong that the air crackles with the intensity of it. When the links are strong a blue colored mist can be seen floating through the air." He explained.   Robin found she had unconsciously moved closer to him on the bench. She was perched precariously on the edge of the seat and watched his mouth move eloquently, with each second giving her information that was shattering all that she had thought was real and true in the world. He was effortlessly changing her very foundation of what was and what was not, reality. Roami fiddled with his fingers as he delved into the story; reliving each moment as if it were only yesterday. "That was how it was that day. I remember it clearly. Usually, on such a day we were told to stay indoors and our parents would cover our mouths and make us stay in one spot until the sneaky air passed us by. But on this day Tobias had begged and pleaded to be allowed outside. Tobias was his bearer's favorite child so she finally gave in. And my bearer-" Robin interrupted his story by asking, "Wait, Bearer? What is that exactly?" She had never felt like such an apt pupil. She wanted to know everything there was to know about this place she had been thrown into. Knowledge was after all; power. She would be better off if she knew what everything and everyone was. There was no telling when she and Roami's paths would part; she had had a lifetime of abandonments to know not to rely on anyone but herself. She would glean as much information from Roami as she could before he left her alone in this strange world called Source One. "Oh, sorry I guess you do not use that term in your world. A 'Bearer' is someone who gives birth to another being. I believe the equivalent on earth would be-"

Roami was cut off by Robin. "So, it's like a 'mother' then?" Robin nodded in understanding. "Okay, go on." She urged him on as she was now itching to better understand this strange place. Just as she was thinking this, an odd looking creature no larger than a bee flew past her face. It moved too quickly for her to see anything but a flurry of purple.   A moment later it flew past Roami but without a thought he grabbed it and popped it into his mouth and began to chew.

Robin's mouth gaped open in shock. "What the..."she said this slowly and in complete astonishment.   Roami looked at her a bit perplexed then laughed and explained, "You really have to prepare yourself for just about anything Robin. Everything is new to you. That was a Pickery Pea. They are not truly living organisms but sort of like..." He stopped to think of the best way to explain it to her, "They are like flying food. They can only be found in the forests of Source One as many travelers get lost here and sometimes need sustenance. That is why they fly so slowly, they actually want to get caught and eaten. When I was younger my mother said that when you eat a Pickery Pea, somewhere in some far off world a new baby is born. I am not sure how true that is but it is a nice idea at least." He said with a smile.   "If you see another one, catch it and try it. They're actually pretty delicious. Even though the morsel is small it fills you up for a few hours and each has a different sweet taste." Roami swallowed the last of what was in his mouth and looked around to see if there was another one flying about. He noticed a small green one a few feet away. He got up and ran towards it and quickly grabbed it in the palm of his hand.

Walking back towards Robin he noticed her grimace and could not help but laugh out loud. "Don't be afraid Robin. I'm a friend. I would not steer you wrong. Taste just a piece and you will see..." He said as he took her right hand and placed the flying creature in her palm then brought her left hand over her right to encase it.

Robin could feel the fluttering wings tickle the inside of her hand and laughed a little at the sensation. She could not fight the curiosity to see what it looked like. Bringing her clasped hands up to her face she peered into the small opening her thumbs made. Inside she saw the Pickery Pea up close and personal. It glowed slightly and the inside of her palm shone with a small green light. It did not have a face, eyes or limbs as she was afraid it might. Instead it was nothing more than a plump circle held up by two small thin wings. She was not sure why but something about the circular fruit made her mouth water and Robin could not help but lick her lips.

Roami was watching her closely and laughed when he saw this gesture. "Eat it if you like. I'm sure you must be hungry. It will appease your appetite for a while." He said. Robin was never one to give into peer pressure. In fact she could remember countless instances when she had said 'no' to drugs. She had seen the ugly side of drug addiction and would never allow anyone make her into the type of mindless zombie drugs could create. She had a gut feeling that Roami was not lying to her and that the Pickery Pea was food, just as he had said. Pushing aside her fear, Robin put her hands to her mouth and let the Pickery Pea plop onto her tongue. There was an instant when it fluttered at the top of her mouth but then she bit down and tasted what could only be described as pure heavenly bliss. Robin's eyes closed in pleasure and her mouth cried out a silent thank you. She had never in all her life tasted anything so absolutely delicious. Just a moment before she moaned right out, Roami laughed and brought her back to the here and now. "See, I told you! It's just food and it is probably better than anything you have ever tasted on earth huh?" He smiled showing his strong white teeth. "Mmhmm..." was all Robin could say as she nodded and chewed and tried to keep her eyes from rolling back in her head. Once she was done savoring the delightful morsel, she swallowed and shook her head to regain her focus. "Okay, back to your story." She said bossily and yet with a hint of humor. Laughing, Roami continued with his story, "Well now... where was I? Oh, yes." He grew serious again. "So, my bearer always does what Tobias's mother does because she is considered lucky in the village. All of her sons are Motlings and therefore she is respected. And that is how it happened; how we were allowed to go out despite the obvious danger that day posed... So we went into Gilaboo Forest which was not far from our village. We played every game you can think of. We played Twilight's Scissors, Ruman's Cave and lastly, the game popular in all the worlds; Hide-n-Seek. We played for some time and it seemed as if the blue winds would pass soon so we became less careful in our play. We said what we wanted and we even went so far as taunting the mists to take us into galaxies with creatures we could not even imagine. I remember stopping the game for a moment because all of a sudden, the mist had turned a deeper blue and could be seen growing in intensity. I begged Tobias to end the game so we could return home. However, he wanted to hide just one more time. So we decided we would play one last round. He swore I would never ever find him. He hid and I counted with my eyes closed. All the while I could feel the mist gathering and growing stronger. The pungent salty smell of it nearly burned my nostrils as I stood and counted down to one. By the time I had finished counting the mist had disappeared completely and I could see every detail of the forest clearly. Tobias however, was nowhere to be found. The mist had taken him with it... I searched and searched. It was not long before I was certain that Tobias had been taken into one of the sub-worlds and that I would never see my friend again." Roami glanced at Robin who sat beside him staring sadly at the sky above them.

"Oh my..." she said with tears brimming in her eyes. As she listened to the story she thought of losing her only true friend in the world, Victor, like that. The thought nearly killed her and made her wonder if she had in fact lost him already anyway. Who was to say if she would ever get back to earth? She pushed these morbid thoughts away and focused on Roami whose head hung down sadly. "You must miss him so much. Do you think there is any way to find him?" Roami shook his head. "No one ever finds someone who has been taken by the mists. Everyone knows it is near to impossible. Who knows where he is or how to even connect to that particular world if they did know which one he was in? It is absolutely impossible. If there were a way, believe me I would go in an instant. Tobias's bearer is so sad now... I would do anything to bring him back to her. But as it is, I can only hope that he is okay in whatever world he has been in all these years." "Yes... I guess that's all you can do. Dag... Roami, have you ever thought about what you'd do if you were sucked into one of those worlds?" Robin asked sadly. She wanted to place her hand on his to soothe that sadness away but that was definitely not Robin's style. In fact, she was amazed the thought had even crossed her mind. "Yes I have. We all think about it some time or another. And we all know there is only one thing you can do. You must figure out the riddle to the world you have been sucked into. Then and only then, will you be able to return to your original world." "Huh? What do you mean?" Robin looked perplexed. "I mean. Every world has a riddle; something that must be learned from the experience, something that is meant to be taught. If and when you figure this out you may return to your home. That is part of the reason I worry about Tobias so much. I know that he has still not learned the lesson to whatever world he was sent to. He was always very cocky and prideful. It's possible he is ignoring all the signs and thinks solving the riddle is beneath him. If that is the case he may never return home."

Robin grew quiet as she thought this all over. She watched as Roami went back to fiddling with his fingers nervously. A question popped up into her head and she blurted it out without much thought. "Hmm... So, what about Source One then?" Robin asked. "What do you mean? What about Source One?" Roami asked distractedly.

"What is the riddle for Source One? You say there is a riddle for each world so... what if you figure out the riddle to Source One... then where would you go?" Robin asked her ingenious question and waited for Roami to respond. At first he glanced up from looking at his hands and looked at her in shock. He let the question swim about his head and was quiet for some time before he finally said, "I don't know. That's... That is a crazy question..." Robin looked at the troubled look on Roami's face and realized he was very uncomfortable thinking about this particular topic. Not wanting to upset her only friend in this alien world, Robin quickly discarded the question. "You know what, it's not that important. Just forget I even asked." She said this aloud however, promised herself she would ask someone else in Source One the first chance she got. Roami heard her docile words but they did not mirror the soft twinkle in Robin's brown eyes. He could only imagine the potential mischief that sort of look could bring about in a place as tricky as Source One...

CHAPTER 4

A soft wind rustled the sky blue leaves of the trees surrounding their little bench. Robin could not help but stare at them in awe. She noticed the thin dark blue veins running through each one and the way they swayed back and forth as if clapping at some secret joke. The breeze blew her braids across her face and while she raised her hand to push them back she heard an odd

whistling sound. It took her only a moment to realize the sound was being emitted from the leaves as the wind swept across each one of the blue tear drop shapes. Robin looked at Roami to see if there was cause for concern but he seemed not to have noticed anything out of the ordinary. Robin could only assume this like so many other things in Source One was second nature to him and something she would have to quickly get used to. Robin hugged her arms around her middle in a protective gesture. She shivered and looked around her in fear. "This place seems way too scary and...confusing. If I decide I want to... How do I get back to Earth?" she ran her fingers through her shock of purple braids to push them back from her face while deep in thought. Before Roami could answer her she piped up with yet another question, "And speaking of Earth, what does it have to do with the House of Intrigues?" Roami seemed upset by something she had said. Pursing his lips slightly together, he glanced at Robin with his soulful golden eyes, "Would you really want to go back in there? If you had the chance, would you really return to that dark place? A place where you were an outsider with no one to lean on..."
Robin paused for a moment and really thought about his question, "I don't know. I guess you're right. There was nothing really... for me back there. I did have one friend... I mean, I do have a friend back on earth named Victor. I would miss

him, but... nothing and no one else." She shrugged her shoulders nonchalantly and tried her best to swallow the hurt her seemingly perpetual loneliness caused her to feel. Roami stood up from the bench and began to pace back and forth in front of her as thoughts raced through his head. He stopped short and stared up at the sky above, his face contorted with some unseen struggle. Robin remained quiet, waiting for him to speak up. He finally looked down from the sky and directly into Robin's eyes as he said, "Well, truth be told...there is no need to worry about returning to Earth, Robin. You have no real say in the matter. In just a short time you will be returned to the House of Intrigues and back to your planet; whether you want to or not. That is the way it is done when someone leaves the house before their time..." Robin glared at Roami, "What do you mean? I can do whatever I want to. If I don't want to return then guess what? I won't!" She had unknowingly scooted to the edge of her seat, ready to pounce if necessary. Her automatic response when confronted had always been to fight for survival. 'Old habits die hard' or so she had heard the saying go. Roami rested his hands on his hips and looked down at the ground in defeat. This pushed Robin's ire down a bit as he did not look as if he desired an altercation at all. He sighed heavily and replied, "I am sorry but it does not work that way Robin. There are rules for

64

everything, even if they are rules without reason, there are still rules. And the rule for the House of Intrigues is that only those who have died a true death on Earth can awaken in the House of Intrigues and enter Source One. If by any chance someone is awakened prematurely, they are to be summoned by the butler of the house. The butler will summon the person three times. First, he will knock on all the doors of the house, then he will ring a bell, finally he will utter the persons' name and no matter where that person is they will be drawn back into the House. They will turn back into doll-form and will remain that way until their true death on Earth." Robin had been listening to Roami's every word intently. She piped up when she realized there was something missing from his explanations. "Wait! If what you say is true... then somebody or something woke me up too early, right?" Robin asked cautiously. "Well... yes." Roami, who still stood near the bench, began to take a few steps away from Robin's inquisitive stare.

"And how was it that I was awakened too early Roami?" she glared at him and left the bench to stand behind him with her arms crossed over her chest. She could not wipe the accusatory look off of her face as she looked at the back of his head. Roami turned around to face her and bit his lip the moment he saw the determined expression on her face. His eyes did not meet hers straight away as he searched for the best

way to explain the situation to her.   "Well...
when I say 'awakened' I mean that your doll
form must have been... uh... disrupted. If a doll in
the house is moved or disturbed in any way, they
wake up. And um... another thing I forgot to tell
you," Roami continued, trying his best to change
the subject and Robin's line of thought, "is that
each doll is placed in the room of the house that
best represents their personality, their station in
life or the way others on earth perceive them. As
these conditions change, the butler will move
each doll to their rightful position. By the way,
the butler is the only being who can touch the
dolls without awakening them. So for instance,
dolls placed in the living room of the House of
Intrigues usually are part of large families on
Earth, they are outgoing and loved. Dolls placed
in the kitchen tend to be-" "I was on the window
sill..." Robin said the words so quietly; Roami did
not hear her at first. "What did you say Robin?"
Roami was not sure if she had spoken or not, her
words had been uttered so softly. "I was on the
window sill." She repeated with more force.
"Oh... yes. Well... that is... um... I know." Roami
said. He looked more and more uncomfortable
as this particular conversation progressed.
"And what does that say about me Roami?"
Robin asked the question while already knowing
the answer. Her brown eyes began to glisten
with the tears she fought to hide. Although she
wanted nothing more than to stick her head in

the ground, she forced herself to look him directly in the eyes to ensure she received a straightforward answer. Sighing, Roami replied, "You were an outsider on Earth. That is what that particular position means." When she heard the words aloud Robin gasped and swallowed hard to stop herself from crying. "Yes. I guess, that's exactly what I was. What I always was…" Roami moved towards her as if to comfort Robin but she moved away and began to walk deeper into the forest. She needed to change the topic desperately before the tears that fought so hard to fall; eventually got their wish.   As she walked towards no particular destination, she called back over her shoulder loudly, "But you know… you still have not answered my first question." Robin accused him as she sank further into the darkness of the trees. She felt edgy and raw, overwhelmed with the pain her life back on earth always seemed to drown her within.   It seemed that being in such unfamiliar territory and under such odd circumstances made it easier to look at her past from a bird's eye view. Robin definitely did not like what she saw. She desperately tried to push the images away with each step she took into the sea colored forest. Not only did the forest look like an ocean of blue but it was just as suffocating. Robin felt as if each one of her steps was bogged down by unforeseen currents and she found it harder to breathe with each passing

67

moment.   She knew however that she could not blame the trees or bushes but her emotions were in fact the culprit. Gulping in deep breaths she fought to get her thoughts under control. "Okay, okay. If you must know I was the one who... uh... disrupted your doll. I-I-" Roami realized he was stammering and so stopped speaking to gather his wits. He struggled to find the right words to express himself and yet not give away too much of his personal thoughts. He did not want to scare Robin away. She had already been through so much; Roami could not bear to be the cause of any additional stress or heartache. "You did what?" Robin prodded as they both began moving through a sea of blue bushes, trees and leaves. Once she had gotten her feelings under control and pushed her past back where it belonged, she felt less burdened and found it easier to breathe.   Robin looked around thoughtfully. She was slowly getting used to the blue forest and felt she rather liked it. It felt like they were swimming in a dry ocean. They moved further into darkness, further away from the House of Intrigues. Further away from all that she had ever known. Roami continued to chase after Robin while trying to explain himself, "I had seen you day after day on that window sill and you just... you looked so sad out there alone and I just couldn't... I mean... I-I wanted to save you from whatever sadness haunted you on Earth. So I would sing to you some nights when I came here and-" Robin stopped in her tracks and stared at Roami. "You'd sing to me?" No one had ever done anything quite so nice for her. She was completely taken aback and looked about as uncomfortable as he did in what had quickly become a painfully awkward moment.

Wanting to fill the now electric air with words she quickly asked, "What song did you sing?" Before she knew it an odd thought came to her but she squelched it in order to focus on his response. Roami took a deep breath and replied nervously, "I actually... made it up. I used the melody from a song my Bearer sang for me, many nights when I could not sleep. It goes like this: Twilight pours on your tear soaked face and I cry; I cry with you. In a house; not a home-" Before he could finish Robin screeched aloud at having had her odd thought confirmed. "So it was you! I didn't make up that song long ago... it really did just pop in my head... I can't believe this!" She stared at Roami in absolute surprise. She could not help herself but began to sing as if to test out the truth, "Twilight pours on your tear soaked face and I cry; I cry with you. In a house; not a home-" Roami softly began to sing with her. Together they sang, "I watch you stand all alone and I watch; I watch you. Don't think you're on your own because I'll never go, I'm near; I am near you. You have a friend.... to depend...til the end...together we will win. I'm here for you; I am here... for you...I'll be there for you... for-ever." When they came to the end of their song, the two stopped and stared at one another with seemingly new eyes. Robin could not help but smile softly at her newfound friend who was apparently not so new after all. "Oh my goodness! This is too crazy, I can't believe this! I swear, this is all too much!" Robin was brimming with so much emotion, she felt as if she might faint at any moment. "Believe it, Robin." Roami started walking again and Robin let him take the lead. She followed him in a daze. "I threw a rock at the window tonight. I was so tired of seeing your pain. I just didn't think about the consequences, I just... acted and now here you are; standing right before me." He said it as if the full reality of the situation had just hit him. "Right,... so what now? What am I supposed to do? If what you say is true then this butler guy will be searching the house for me and I will be pulled back to Earth, no matter what. And I just... I just don't think I want to go back. At least, not yet..." Robin stared at Roami hoping he somehow had all the answers to the questions rushing through her head. "Well, I don't know Robin. There is no way to stop it; you will have to return eventually. But until then we will wait. You can stay with my family and I. We will all take care of you." Smiling Roami gently took Robin's hand and led her deeper into the forest in the direction of his village. As they walked, both were lost in their thoughts. They barely heard the crunch of their feet against the dry blue grass, the whistle of the wind or scurrying of forest creatures. Unbeknownst to both Robin and Roami, a strong blue mist crept over the tree tops and began to descend menacingly to the ground below. *** Source One's night was slowly transforming itself into day. The sky changed from a dark hunter green into a lighter, minty shade of green. Robin was all eyes despite her lethargy. She felt like a newborn babe, trying to capture every little sound, sight, smell and taste for thorough inspection. She had never felt so brand new in all her life. Even as a child, having been thrown into adulthood so quickly, she never had a chance to truly be innocent. It seemed there was a time for everything and this was hers...finally.

After walking for some time Roami realized that Robin appeared unnerved and out of sorts from the physical exercise as well as the new reality she had to quickly get accustomed to. "I believe we will stop here for a spell, Robin." Roami took her hand and guided her towards a large tree. When he saw her look at it in wide-eyed wonder he laughed and stated, "It is called a Nommo tree. I've passed this particular one many times on my way to the House of Intrigues when I came to visit..." When he realized what he was divulging, his words trailed off shyly. Robin just turned away to hide her own secret smile. She had never felt so special in all her life. To think that during all of her hardest times, when she had felt so completely alone, there had been someone watching over her. Through it all there had been someone hoping she was safe and happy. Having never felt protected in her entire life, Robin did not know how to properly respond to Roami's kindness. She let the awkward silence grow as they prepared to sit and rest near the Nommo Tree. The tree was huge with leaves nearly as big as Roami himself. Their color was bright green unlike most of the blue foliage surrounding them. The magnificent tree's large trunk which would have taken minutes to circle, had a deep purple pigment with flecks of glittery silver dust coating the hard purple wood. Overall it seemed to shine like a beacon in the forest and Robin was sure it must contain some sort of magical power. She could not help but run her index finger across the rough trunk to test out her theory. When she pulled her finger away it was covered in the same beautiful silver glitter. However, her theory was proven incorrect as she did not turn into a frog or grow a fishes' tail. No magic here, she surmised. Robin stood staring at the tree for some time before her shock at its appearance began to wear off. Roami could not help staring at her each time she stopped to stare at their surroundings in wonder. She was incredibly cute when she let her guard down, he thought. Too bad that was a very rare occurrence.

Knowing what he did of her past, he could not blame her for her series of gargantuan shields and protective armor. She turned and caught him staring at her. Robin could not help but feel uncomfortable with the puppy dog look in his eyes. She quickly covered her own emotions with a protective shield then spoke, "Our trees don't look like this on Earth." She said softly as she sat to lean against its trunk. Robin wore a numb expression on her face. "Everything is just so... different here." She said the words so softly Roami could barely make them out. "Yes, that is true Robin. But you can get used to anything. That is how life is. We can all program ourselves to deal with anything life throws at us." He stood beside her and leaned down slightly to pat her shoulder softly to reassure her that everything would be okay. "I don't know about that Roami. I mean... my God! The sky is green and this tree is purple and you're ... you're blue!" She stared at him as if for the very first time, taking in every detail of his physique. Their eyes met for a little longer than expected. Robin felt as if everything were going in slow motion and had to force her eyes to leave his and look back out at their surroundings. "You're blue..." She repeated, with a look of wonder on her face. "I wonder how you managed to be that color. Are all of your people blue like you?" She asked.

Roami stood up abruptly and turned to face the Nommo trunk with a look of consternation. "I'm sorry. Did I say something wrong?" Robin quickly asked with concern. He looked more preoccupied than offended. "Oh, no. Nothing at all. I will answer your question in just a moment, my friend. But first I must contact my Bearer or she will be distraught." He said as he began to move his lean blue hand over the purple trunk as if looking for something. "What are you doing Roami?" Robin began to feel slightly uneasy as her only friend in a strange world, was acting a bit peculiar. She pushed up from her seated position and moved to stand beside him. Her arms made their way around her middle in her usual protective gesture. "I am looking for an access point. Nommo trees in Source One... well, I guess they are like communication devices. We Tinktu use them to connect with our homes and our tribes. While we cannot connect to someone in another world through this device, it is still handy to keep track of our family and loved ones who are in Source One." He finally found what he was looking for. Robin moved closer to see him move his hand over a small circular groove in the wood. Roami kept his hand glued to the spot until the circle began to glow with a silver light. Robin stood and watched Roami in awe. "What are you doing now?" She asked when she saw him pause with his eyes closed. It amazed her that one could have so many questions to ask and new things to see. She had become so jaded by life on Earth. Here she felt an energy she had

74

never known before; she was revving with excitement and ready to discover all the mysteries of Source One life whereas on Earth she had drowsily struggled to get up each morning. "I am speaking to my Bearer. I use only the voice in my head and she too speaks to me from her mind. I need only think of her name and the tree connects our sub-conscious so that I can assure her I am well." He scrunched his forehead in concentration. "Ah! There she is... and my Guide is there also." Roami opened his eyes for a moment to see Robin's forehead creased in confusion, he smiled and said, "I'm sorry, I forget there are some differences between us. My Bearer and Guide; they are what you would call on Earth, my "mother" and "father"." Roami closed his eyes again and appeared to be receiving a message. He opened his eyes once more and said, "Hmm... They are very upset. Please give me a moment so that I may concentrate and speak to them." He grew quiet and Robin watched as he communed with his parents. While he stood before the tree focusing on his conversation, Robin walked around in the semi-dark of the early morning and had a better look at her surroundings. The spiky glowing balls which apparently passed as stars in Source One had slowly floated higher into the sky so that they were now only tiny specks. They no longer glowed as brightly against the minty green expanse of sky above her.   Robin glanced back to see if Roami was still busy. He stood with his head down and his hand still held against the tree trunk so she figured she would continue her exploring.

They were standing in a very small clearing in the forest where at least eight feet of short blue grass surrounded the Nommo tree. Outside of this parameter were crops of small sky blue and midnight blue bushes situated at the base of the forest trees. The trees here were so tall they nearly blocked out the sky. Robin walked towards a few of the bushes, wondering at their unusual color.   As she grew closer she noticed an odd whispering sound. To be more exact, she heard the sound of nearly thousands of whispers and they all seemed to be coming from somewhere within the dark blue bushes. She could not imagine how this made any sense and therefore could not prevent her curiosity from pushing her ever closer to inspect the small mass of shrubbery.   Her slender brown hand slowly reached out towards the bush then pushed aside the leaves. Robin's first thought was that maybe someone hid within the bush whispering loudly. When her hand touched the leaves, she pulled it back quickly upon feeling a tickling sensation.

"Whoa!" She cried out. Robin looked at her hand to ensure it was unharmed. It was. She leaned in once more to look at the leaves; on each small leaf she saw what had tickled her. There were hundreds of small mouths, one on each leaf, speaking all at once.   Robin's eyes opened in shock. "What in the world..." She muttered as she stepped back cautiously. When she realized the bush would not attack her she moved closer slowly while perking up her ears to listen to what the leaves had to say. As soon as she was able to discern one of the leaves' words, she could not help the smile that lit her mouth or the laugh that escaped her.   "Oh my! Hahahaha!" she was crying laughing before she knew it. Robin never knew a bush had so many jokes to tell. She soon realized that each whisper was an extremely hilarious joke.   Wiping the laughter tears from her eyes, she leaned in closer to hear yet another one. This particular one made her laugh so hard she fell back from her squatting position and sprawled out on the ground beside the bush. Moments later Robin was rocking back and forth with spasms of laughter.   As her revelry died down, she wiped away the laughter tears. Robin happily sighed for it had been some years since she had laughed so hard or felt so good. Before she could get back to her feet she looked up and noticed a large flower hung over her head.   It was so beautiful Robin could not help but remain right where she was and just stare at the amazing artistry of the plant. Each petal was nearly translucent except for a hint of purple and blue, while the center of the flower was a vibrant orange that nearly glowed. The blue stem as well as each petal glittered like diamonds in the light of day and Robin was sure she had never seen anything quite so lovely.   The flower's head was nearly as big as her own and seemed to dip farther and farther down until the petals nearly kissed her lips. Robin's breathing began to slow as the orange glow within the flower began to grow brighter. She began to feel lethargic and her eyes seemed to be glued to the orange center.   She slowly forgot her body and even forgot to breathe.   Within moments the orange glow became so bright it blinded her to anything but the beaming light. That is when the visions began. Robin began to see her life, from its very beginning and moving towards the present. But not every moment was illuminated; just the saddest most painful moments were brought to light.   Given Robin's background there were countless moments to relive, none of which she had ever wanted to deal with again. She saw flashes of a mother abandoning her infant baby girl. Robin's dreams of a wonderful, benevolent mother losing her daughter against her will were all but shattered as she finally saw the truth of the matter.   Her birth mother had been strung out on drugs, letting the destructive chemicals take over her in an effort to smother her own disturbing past. It appeared her mother's demons had not only destroyed her but in a classic domino effect had dashed Robin's life into a pit she was still trying to climb out of.   Next

Robin saw each foster home and all the horrible things done to her behind closed doors. Robin cried as she saw herself from a birds' eye view; saw her nights filled with tears while knowing there was no hero out there to save her. She saw her countless classmates making fun of her; saw the times she had been laughed at on the streets or in parks by little girls and boys who had everything and yet were still so very mean to the less fortunate.   Robin could not stop the massive flow of tears careening down her cheeks as she watched her life as if for the very first time and realized how brutally sad it all had been.

The images would not stop. Next, she saw one of her darkest moments. It was the moment she had been rejected by a boy she had had a schoolgirl crush on. He had laughed in her face when she confessed her feelings. Then to top it off he had told her she was too black; and not good enough to be his girl. "Robin! Robin! Close your eyes! You have to close your eyes!" She heard this as if from somewhere very far away but was too busy watching the tragic movie of her life to investigate its source. "Robin! It's me, Roami! Please, you must close your eyes now!" She heard this again and felt someone shake her body. With the violent shake Robin recalled that she did indeed have a body and had eyes which could close off all these ugly images. Robin forced her eyes to close although it seemed an impossible feat. They finally shut.

Blackness... The images stopped and the orange glow receded. "Oh, thank you..." Robin whimpered. She kept her eyes shut but sighed in relief; happy to have that particular torture end.

"It's okay Robin! It's okay, I'm here..." Roami held Robin's limp body in his arms and rocked her back and forth. They both knelt on the ground near the large flower which was quickly withering into dust. Within seconds it was nothing more than silver dirt which blew in the wind. Each speck held a seedling which would spread across the ground and create ever more of the same flower. Roami saw this and frowned, "Stupid Sad Sally Flowers...I've never understood why they even exist..." He muttered to himself then looked down at Robin who still lay in the crux of his arms with her eyes shut and her cheeks glistening wet with tears. "It's okay, you're safe. You can open your eyes now Robin." He said softly while wiping the tears from her face with his hand. Robin sniffled and opened her brown eyes to look up at Roami. She swallowed hard and shuttered as she forced herself to breathe in deeply. She felt lightheaded and as if she were floating. His arms around her seemed to help her to stay grounded. "What happened?" She asked as she stood up and moved out of his embrace a bit defensively. Her arms made their way around her middle as she hugged herself where he once had. "You found a Sad Sally Flower. That's what they are called here in Source One. They hypnotize you and show you all the sadness in your life. My Bearer says they were created to help purify people of their old sadness but I never truly understood the need for them. It seems like they just make things worse..." He looked at her swollen eyes and wet cheeks and grimaced at the thought of the pain she had just gone through. "I should have been here for you. I was so busy speaking to my parents, I did not realize what-" Before he could blame himself Robin shook her head and said, "No, it's my fault. I started...exploring and at first it was fine. I saw those blue bushes and they started cracking jokes and-" Roami glanced at the blue bushes and said, "Yes, those are Wildo Bushes. They collect the funniest jokes from all the worlds and whisper them to keep travelers entertained. They are pretty harmless." He said. "Yes, they were fun but...that flower..." Robin looked a bit traumatized. "I tried so hard to forget so much...but it brought it all back and..." She looked down at her feet. "I'm so sorry Robin. I know that must have been horrible for you. We can only hope that what my Bearer says about the Sad Sally's effects is true...that maybe it helped purge you of some of your old sadness..." Roami sighed heavily as if he too held part of Robin's pain in an effort to unburden his new friend. Needing to change the subject, Robin wiped away the last vestiges of her tears and said, "So, um... what happened with your parents?" Roami cleared his throat, "Yes, I told them about you and everything... While they are angry with me for messing with the order of things, they have no ill feelings towards you. They say they will gladly accept you into our home during your stay here in Source One." Roami walked back towards the Nommo tree and sat down near the base its purple trunk on a mound of tiny sky blue rocks which appeared to encircle the tree. Robin returned to Roami's side quickly, still feeling a bit uneasy after her ordeal with the Sad Sally. While she stood over Roami near the tree trunk she could not help but look at a few other strange organisms near the base of the tree. There were odd red and yellow striped heart shaped mushrooms that emitted a beautiful harp-like sound. The sound was so soft she would need to put her head to the ground in order to hear it properly. After her last experience Robin had no desire to do so. She let the mushrooms' song forever remain a mystery. Near the mushrooms were a few pink colored berries that were translucent and had green juice swirling within their circular encasements. They reminded her of her favorite starburst candies and she had to stop herself from popping one into her mouth. "Remember, this is not New York City, or even Earth. Those berries could be dangerous." She whispered to herself. Robin returned her focus to Roami,

"Great, I can't wait to see your parents and your people. Now will you answer my question now? Are all the people of your tribe, blue like you?" She asked as she sat down cross-legged on the sky blue ground besides Roami.   Sighing and leaning against the Nommo trunk. Roami glanced over at Robin and finally answered her question. "You definitely are obsessed about color. It must be very important on Earth, I suppose... Well, in answer to your question, my people are not all blue like me. We come in every color ever created and we even get some new colors here and there."   When Roami heard Robin's gasp of surprise he continued on, "In my village... my village is called Ryt by the way. Well, in my village we Tinktus are all born without color. And by that I mean we are the color of... of a space where all color has been sucked out. We are like... your hair, the color of your hair..." He said excitedly when he found an example they both could understand.   Robin ran a hand over her braids, her hand stopping on the shock of hair she had dyed purple during one of her more rebellious periods, "Purple?" She asked in shock.

Roami laughed, "No. Black." He laughed again when he noticed the shocked expression on her face. Continuing, he said "Yes. You see, we are all born that color so that there is no difference between us and we can see each other for what is on the inside. We play together, we learn together and there is no difference that our eyes

83

may see, which could turn us against one another or make it hard to see the person beneath... you understand?" He asked, looking at her with his penetrating golden eyes. "Yeah, go on. I mean... Continue please." She prodded. "Well... uh... that is the way it is until our 'Going On' ceremony. This ceremony usually occurs after nine cycles of the planet Pur. At that time we are old enough to decide what color we feel fits our personality and also, how we want the world to view us. On my 'Going On' day, I thought about which color I would pick, for the longest time and I... well, I had always been interested in the House of Intrigues. I had heard all the stories about Earth, from people who had left it naturally and came into Source One. One of the things I loved the most about it was the night sky and I realized I would love to be that mysterious deep blue color. And that is why you see me as I am today." Roami smiled at Robin. "Wow. That's... without a doubt...the dumbest thing I've ever heard..." Robin said staring at him as if he had completely lost his mind. Roami looked perplexed and somewhat hurt by Robin's abrupt words. "Huh? What do you mean by that?" he asked. "Exactly what I said! I think that was a really stupid choice. I mean... you seriously just threw a great opportunity down the drain. So, is there any way to change your color after you've set it? Sort of like an in-store return?" Robin looked both confused and angry.

She did not look directly at Roami but stared at her feet while she spoke to him. Roami however, glared straight at Robin, "How dare you!" he asked with a hurt expression. "I dare because I can! It's stupid; plain stupid. I can say how I feel." Robin said with conviction. She once again turned defensive, opting for a pre-emptive attack rather than be anyone's victim. Roami fumed and brought his face to hers and spoke slowly, "Take it back Robin." "No." Robin said incredulously and stood up to walk around the circumference of the Nommo tree. She was a native New Yorker; an inner city kid. If he thought she was going to back down, she was about to school him on a couple of things.

Roami followed her with an exasperated look on his face. "You know you're totally ungrateful. I can't believe-" He began to dive into a full blown tirade, but she cut him off. Turning to face him, she marched towards him, "I'm ungrateful? Me?! You are the one who is ungrateful and didn't see a blessing when you had it right in your hands!" She was so angry she was near to crying right there in front of him. She, Robin; the girl who never let anyone have the satisfaction of seeing her cry, had done so too many times in front of this particular boy. She was not about to let it happen again if she could help it. Seeing her eyes glisten as tears began to form, Roami decided to back down and let her win this one.

"Robin... Please, I don't want to fight with you.

Tell me... What is really the matter?" he asked softly. "I am... sorry Roami. That was wrong. I shouldn't have said that... the problem is that you and your people are given such a wonderful gift; the ability to change your color and then you just threw it all away and it just makes me so angry because I know that... if I had been given that opportunity I would cherish it. I would have made the right decision..." She said sadly. Roami was confused by Robin's admission. "I honestly don't understand Robin... What is it you think I did wrong and what would have been the right decision?" he asked softly. His hands itched to take her in his arms and hug away all the sadness he saw within her. He fought the urge knowing that such an action would definitely scare her away. Glaring at Roami again Robin looked at him as if he were absolutely insane, "You threw it away because you had the choice of any color. Any color! You could have had it all and yet you picked such a dark, dreary color. If I had a choice I would have been...light... I would have been...white..." Robin closed her eyes and sighed blissfully at the thought. Now Roami stared at Robin as if she had lost her mind. "White? There's nothing wrong with white... but out of the whole rainbow spectrum... why would that color have been the right one to pick?" He asked gently. Sucking her teeth, Robin opened her eyes and stared at Roami. "If not white, I would have been a nice light color... a beautiful pastel or something. Then, maybe the world would love me; would smile at me when I walked by and my life would be so much lighter and brighter and... just... good." Robin looked delighted by the thought and Roami grew even more confused by her odd logic. Upset by Roami's inability to see why his choice had been the wrong one, Robin placed her head against the trunk of the tree as if the sight of him was too much to bear at the moment. "I just wish that... sometimes I just wish that--" Robin grew quiet as if making a soulful wish.

"Oh no!" Roami had been so intent on their conversation he had not been paying any attention to their surroundings. To his dismay, he now realized that clouds of dark blue mists had been steadily circling them for some time unnoticed. It had grown so thick they could barely see the sky or even the rest of the forest clearly. Grabbing Robin's shoulder, Roami yelled, "Stop it Robin! You must be careful of your words and your wishes, I told you-"

Before he could finish his sentence it was, without a doubt... Too late.

CHAPTER 5

Robin opened her eyes and was about to tell Roami he could not give her orders. He was not her boss and she had some pretty creative ideas about what he could do with his commands... Before she could even form the words in her head she saw that she had; indeed made a huge mistake. The trees that surrounded them were slowly disintegrating, turning into just swirls of color. It was as if they had been nothing more than water-colored drawings someone just doused with a bucket of water. An odd crunching and crumbling sound blared so loud it seemed to shake Robin's very insides. It was the sound of a world breaking apart and collapsing in on itself, or so she surmised. The sky too, was changing from green into a deep reddish brown and the blue grass was rapidly flooding with cool salty smelling sea water. Gallons of gray, murky liquid poured in from some invisible source and began to cover their feet, their legs and eventually reached just below their chins. Mere seconds later the ground beneath them disappeared altogether. "Roami! Oh no! Roami what's happening?!" Robin screamed and began to grab at both him and the Nommo trunk for support as the ground fell away and left them floating in a watery abyss. What little trees that were left quickly sunk beneath the water's surface with apocalyptic speed. Her fear was so intense; Robin had no idea how to react to the incredible events transpiring in real-time around her. "Oh no..." Was all Roami could say as he too fought to find something to clasp on to for support. The two teens thrashed around frantically and were soon completely drenched from head to toe. Robin's sneakers and jeans were soaked and their weight seemed to drag her down with each passing second. Mere moments later, the changing environment stilled and they found themselves suspended in a foreign water world. The only thing that remained familiar was the huge Nommo tree. They grasped onto its purple trunk as if their lives depended on it. Both ignored its rough texture and errant splinters as the tree was their only support at the moment. Other than that all they could see was dark red sky above and miles of gray sea spreading far into the distance. Water surrounded them for what appeared to be eternities. "Roami... please... tell me I didn't just do what I think I did..." Robin hugged at the tree trunk and let her head fall limply against it as she sighed and shivered in fear. Roami looked at her to determine her emotional state. He could not be sure if it was sea water or tears that fell unbidden down her cheeks. Given what he already knew about the tough New York City girl he assumed it was the former. He fought to find the right words to help her calm down even though he himself was just seconds from losing his own composure. Nothing like this had ever happened directly to him. Roami could only hope they would be able to meet this challenge victoriously or at the very least; alive. He breathed in slowly and deeply to compose himself. Taking yet another moment, he cleared his throat to ensure his voice was strong and would not crack when he spoke to her. "Do not worry. It is not your fault. We both did this... It is my fault as well. We will find a way out of this world if we just work together, use our brains and be patient." He said as he tried his best to stay afloat. "But Roami... you don't understand." Robin said with terror in her voice. "There is water all around us and I can't... I've never had the chance to learn... I mean... I can't... swim." Roami now stared at her with open fear in his eyes. "Oh, please don't say that Robin. You can swim... I mean, you have to know how to swim!" He said with force; as if by saying it adamantly, it would become fact. He knew without a doubt that there were large bodies of water on Earth. In fact, the planet was comprised mostly of that particular element... How on Earth could she not know how to swim? Roami could not help but wonder about this. Knowing they were currently in dire straits he decided not to worry about the how or play the blame game at a time like this. They had to figure out the best way out of this situation and fast. "No. I can't! I can't!" She screamed emphatically while pushing her wet braids back from her face and gulping down air in an effort to calm herself down. Robin's voice was filled with intense fear. Her hands grabbed desperately at the Nommo trunk and she saw they were beginning to bleed slightly as they scraped against the rough purple wood. "Stop it! Just stop it. Do not panic. You can do anything you want to. You can swim, I promise you." Roami said as he moved closer to her. He used his body to push her up against the tree trunk to ensure she would have the added support she needed.

"Thank you..." Robin said breathlessly. She huddled against the tree trunk in a near fetal position while trying to control her breathing. Her supple lips pursed as she took long, deep breaths to calm herself. Roami's broad shoulders at her back and the strong beating of his heart helped her get her emotions in check. She turned a little to look up at her new friend. His blue face was drenched and his curly black hair lay plastered to his angular face. She was amazed at how quickly she had gotten used to his seemingly odd physique. In fact, she marveled how she could have thought his blue skin was bizarre. Looking up at Roami, she wondered if she had ever seen anything more beautiful. Or more controlled. He did not seem to be freaking out half as much as she was. If he could handle this then so would she, Robin forcefully told herself. The water which had at first felt slightly cool was now becoming uncomfortably cold. Robin looked at her pruned fingers and shivered in Roami's embrace. She did not voice the obvious; that they would die of hyperthermia if they did not quickly figure a way out of their predicament. She was sure he was thinking the same thing from the look of gloom on his face. "Robin, look at me..." he waited until she did just that then continued, "I won't let anything happen to you. I promise. We're in this together and together we'll figure a way out of here. Now... we must remember what was said and thought before we were sucked into this world. It could hold our clue to this world's riddle." He said as he searched his brain for what they had said and what significance it may have on their current situation. Robin wracked her

92

brain, what should have been a simple request seemed harder under their current duress. She was an inner-city teen who like so many others had never had the chance or need to learn how to swim. Now, through an odd twist of fate, she was now suspended in a water world on some godforsaken planet. How could anyone problem-solve while under such unreal circumstances, she wondered frantically. "Okay, okay..." She forced herself to focus as best as possible, "Um... we were arguing about your decision to be blue and about what color I thought would be best and then I started to wish that..." Before she could finish her sentence the Nommo tree began to tremble slightly. It started as a gentle rumble and the trembling soon became a violent shaking which cast them away from the huge tree and into the water surrounding them at every side.

Robin screamed as they were instantaneously swept away by a strong current. "Ahhh! Oh God, oh God, oh God!" She cried as Roami fought to hold her as close to him as possible. The last thing either of them needed was to get separated on top of everything else they were dealing with. The water viciously twisted and swished around them with no apparent cause. But just as soon as it began, it ended. In an instant, the strong current died out and they were left suspended in still water. Not one ripple marred the ocean . It was as if the turmoil of the previous minutes had never even occurred.

Robin and Roami's heavy breathing and traumatized expressions were the only proof that the odd quake had ever transpired. "Look Roami..." Was all Robin said as she wrapped herself around the front of his body and nodded her head towards the Nommo tree. They could see the Nommo was now miles away from them in the opposite direction of the moving current.

Roami could feel Robin's thin body shiver sporadically against his. She made a small whimper before whispering, "So this is it... This is how we're going to die..." "Stop it, Robin. We'll be fine. I won't let you go, I swear. I will tread water and hold you." She ignored his words and only shook her head in dismay. He nudged her head up with his to force her to look directly at him. His chin was set determinedly.

Robin looked up into his gentle golden eyes, "Yes, but for how long? You can't do it forever, Roami. You know that... You will get tired at some point..." Staring up at the ruby red sky for strength Roami said, "I will do it for as long as my body will allow." he promised her then clenched his jaw with sheer determination.

They stayed that way; holding each other and drifting in their new water world for what seemed like lifetimes but which may have only been the equivalent of a few hours on earth. Robin knew the exact moment when Roami had no choice but to give in to his body's exhaustion.

Roami looked at Robin, his face sallow from

lack of sleep, food and rest. "Robin... I'm sorry... It is time." He said sadly while his blue tears fell down from his face to mix with the gray water around them.   Nodding her head while she whispered her thanks softly in his ear; Robin rubbed Roami's back to comfort him before they died.   She did not know what words were appropriate for the occasion of imminent death and so did the first thing that came to her mind. She sang their song... "Twilight pours on your tear soaked face and I cry, I cry with you..." she paused to gather her breath and all along rubbed his back soothingly. She caressed him the way she had always dreamed of being held, touched and soothed those countless lonely years between infancy and adolescence.   His face was held against hers in exhaustion but upon hearing her beautiful words, he smiled against her cheek. With his last breaths he sang with her.

Together they began, "In a house; not a home, I watch you stand all alone and I watch; I watch you. Don't think you're on your own because I'll never go. I'm near; I am near you. You have a friend.... to depend...til the end...together we will win. I'm here for you, I am here... for you...I'll be there for you... For-ever."   Slowly as Roami's legs stilled and stopped treading water, the two slowly drifted below the water's surface.   Robin closed her eyes and did not open them for fear that she would have to watch as gruesome sea monsters ate Roami and herself alive.   When their feet hit the bottom of the sea and still nothing grabbed them, Robin spoke up timidly, "Roami? Why haven't we been eaten?" she asked in bewilderment. "I am not sure Robin…" He paused for a long moment then continued with a slight smirk, "but perhaps you should ask yourself another more important question." She heard his voice clearly at her ear but refused to open her eyes just yet. Breathing in deeply Robin asked, "What do you mean? What question?" She hated when he spoke in riddles. Especially at a time like this when their very lives were at risk and time was of the essence. Laughing a little, Roami smiled and gave her waist a little squeeze before saying, "How is it that you can breathe, speak to me and hear me so clearly under water? That is the question you should probably be asking yourself, my dear friend." Robin opened her eyes. She could not believe what she was seeing. As she moved out of Roami's arms she wore a comical look of shock painted across her face. Robin now realized that she could in fact breathe and hear as well as she had above water; if not better.   Beside her, Roami had already checked out their surroundings but he waited for her to get adjusted before they began to investigate this brand new world.   Below the water's surface, everything looked so clear and vivid. Unlike the water on earth, it did not distort objects or make their surroundings seem wavy.   "How is it we can breathe under water?" she asked Roami while she continued to look around in awe at all the exotic sights, colors and sounds. It was without a doubt the oddest sensation Robin had ever experienced; being under water and yet not feeling at all wet or suffocated. She looked down at her brown hands and splayed them out in front of her looking at them in wonder. Everything seemed crystal clear and the colors seemed enhanced. Robin felt as if she were watching a television show which had gone from analog to high-definition in a split second. Roami glance at her and could not help but laugh at her silly antics. Robin looked up at him to see what was so funny. When she realized she was the source of his amusement; she glared, rolled her eyes and returned to focusing on their surroundings. The soft sand beneath them was a deep red color, similar to the shade of bricks back on earth. Robin noticed it was very dusty and her shoes were quickly turning a reddish color where the sand residue had settled on them. There was not much to see beyond acres of red sand. Just a few colorful sprouts of small plants and gray coral looking rocks and boulders were scattered haphazardly. Recalling her question Roami replied, "I don't know how we are able to breathe under water. From what I have heard, most times when someone is sent to another world they are given the capacity to survive in it. This ensures they have a fair chance to discover its riddle. I had assumed the world above water was the true world we had been sent to. However, it seems this is where our riddle may be hidden." He said. As he spoke Roami began to walk in the direction of the Nommo tree whose trunk was some distance away. The purple obtrusion could be seen descending as far as the sea bottom.   "Where are you going? Are you crazy Roami? We don't know where we are, what lives here or if it is even safe? We should stay right here and find a place to hide for a while." Robin said as she trailed behind him haltingly. She bit her lip and looked around nervously. "No. We will never figure out the riddle and get back to Source One if we are too scared to move about and-" Roami looked annoyed for the first time since she had met him. Sighing in exasperation he turned to look at her then said, "Please just come on, we don't have time to argue about this." He said as he motioned for her to follow him.   Whereas back on earth Robin would normally have argued until she was blue in the face, she realized she was completely out of her element. At the moment, Roami was her only foundation on which to stand. She sighed inwardly and let him win this particular battle. However, secretly she waited for the moment she was better equipped to survive and could once more be the independent Robin she had always been. Robin followed   Roami   while   looking   around apprehensively ready to defend them if they were attacked. Looking up, she saw that the surface of the water, like that on earth, rippled with waves that distorted images. The perpetual movement of the surface water made the reddish brown sky above look choppy. Kicking at the sand below her feet, Robin noticed it seemed to be softer than any sand she had ever felt. There were quite a few plants and trees sprinkled about the area and they were all made in painfully vibrant colors. As they passed one such young tree, that had a blue trunk complete with red and pink leaves, Robin noticed it bore the most exotic looking fruits and flowers she had ever seen. The flowers were bright green and seemed to glow from their centers while the odd yellow fruits looked like large plump closed eyes. As she drew nearer to get a better look and reached her hand out to pluck one such fruit, she nearly screamed in terror as the fruit indeed opened like an eye and shined a bright green light on her. "Ahhh!!!" She instantly had a flashback of the golden glow of the Sad Sally Flower. Robin screamed and ran to hide behind Roami. "Robin! What did I tell you? Stay close to me and don't touch anything! You'd think after the Sad Sally incident you would have learned your lesson!" Roami fumed angrily. Robin had never seen him so emotional. It truly looked as if he had been scared for her safety. Feeling slightly chastised, Robin nodded took a deep breath and continued to walk at his side without venturing too far off to explore. Despite the dramatic moment, she could not help but look around her in awe. Robin felt as if she were in an underwater wonderland. "Do you see that?" Robin squinted her eyes to better make out what she thought she saw near the horizon. "There are little people waiting there in the center of what looks like a city Roami!" She pointed to a cluster of brightly colored coral houses and an ever growing crowd of green skinned people standing at its center. They were all staring at them in awe. Robin immediately felt uncomfortable by the acute attention. She stopped walking and started searching the ground with a determined expression on her face. "Why are you stopping? What are you looking for Robin?" Roami asked in confusion and with a hint of frustration. "I'd think it was kind of obvious. We need some sort of protection in case they try to kill us or eat us or something." She found a large sharp red rock and stood up with a smile on her face as she gingerly placed it in her green jacket pocket. "Okay, I'm ready. Let's go." She said nonchalantly. Roami shook his head, rolled his eyes in exasperation and continued walking towards the growing crowd. They stood a few feet in front of a bright green wooden sign on an archway. It was apparently the city's entryway as the red path began there. The sign read in bright yellow letters: The City of Fitz. Robin and Roami stopped once they were about ten feet away from the odd looking people who all had dark green skin, fuchsia colored hair in various styles and large piercing eyes. It seemed like a silent standoff until a small jolly looking man waddled to the forefront. Robin noticed he had an exorbitant amount of jewelry covering his clothes and body. Roami decided it best for them to preemptively make their declaration of peace in order to avoid being mistaken as a threat. He stepped protectively in front of Robin and beamed out, "Peace and Greetings! We are visitors in need of food and shelter. Are you willing to take us in?" Roami asked with an open smile on his face to show that they meant no harm. The short, yet hefty man spoke up, "You are from the sky so you must be sent from the great almighty one!" His green velvet clothing was of a finer grade than the others and gave him the air of royalty. His elaborate robes were made in varying shades of green with shiny flecks of what looked like light green jade encrusted throughout. He wore mounds of emerald jewelry; rings, chains and even numerous earrings. His eyes were dark green, very large and stood out against his shocking frock of fuzzy fuchsia colored hair. He had a neatly trimmed goatee in the same fuchsia color. Roami quickly surmised he must be the king of this particular world. He guessed this by the man's overdone appearance along with the fact that two very large men flanked him at both sides. Both guards sported expressions that looked perpetually dour, towered at near to seven feet tall and wore gem-studded armor. Robin and Roami took a better look at the king and his people as they slowly moved forward and began to gather around the two kids. Whereas from their initial vantage point, the people had seemed tiny, Robin was now sure that had been an incorrect assumption. Most of the people were very tall and Robin deduced they were between six and seven feet in height. Even the youngsters were tall and a bit lanky; with large feet that seemed made just big enough to keep their lithe figures balanced. Robin could not help but wonder that they had picked such a short man among giants to be their leader. The king looked to be no more than five feet tall and both Robin and Roami had to look down when addressing him. The people's pigmentation was a deep shade of green that appeared similar to the color of pine needles on earth. Their eyes were large and seemed to be the biggest feature on their faces. Robin quickly realized that most had either light blue or light green eyes. Their noses were tiny things and their lips puckered up as if they had eaten something sour every day of their lives. She was not sure what was most shocking; all of these attributes or the apparently identical brilliant shade of fuchsia hair they all seemed to sport in various styles, lengths and textures. Altogether Robin thought they were the strangest looking creatures she had ever seen.   "No, we are not great or anything like that. We are just travelers. Lost travelers." Robin said, trying to clear the matter up. The King chuckled boisterously and made initial contact by clasping both Robin and Roami's hands briefly in a show of acceptance.   Smiling he said, "You are most humble Sky-Ones. I am King Hurtz; ruler of this great city of Fitz. We shall of course, take you in as honored guests and give you the best, for you are definitely heaven sent beings. Would you be so kind as to follow our local Disposer? His name is Thister. He will take you into his home and ensure your needs are met."   Before Robin or Roami could reply to the King, he motioned with his hand and several more armored guards appeared deftly out of the crowd of people. "Escort them at once to Thister." He commanded and with a unified nod the guards made their way towards Robin and Roami.   The sentries were all about seven feet tall and wore black clothing while their chest, legs and arms were covered in armor made of smooth polished jade. They wore no helmets and apparently the only weapons they had were long green clubs dangling from their waist on jeweled belts. They positioned themselves on either side of Robin and Roami. "By the way... You may visit my royal palace at

your convenience once you are both settled in."
With that said the king was escorted away by his
two personal guards. In respect, the crowd of
people knelt to their knees as the King made his
way back through the crowd and towards the
city. No one stood until he had reached his home
which was apparently very nearby. The trio
made their way towards the shortest coral
building in sight which was just feet away from
the city center. It was nearly half his size in
height. Robin thought it looked similar to a ranch
style house on earth except made for a tiny elf.
The architects had put more attention on the
design of the structure as opposed to ensuring a
livable height. There were slanted parts of the
roof as well as circular structures next to square
shaped segments. The actual home took up
much more horizontal space than vertical. Robin
surmised it would take quite some time to walk
the entire parameter of the estate. The house
was surrounded by beautiful trees similar to the
ones she saw littered about the land; with their
dark green trunks and bright lavender colored
leaves. The only exception was that the trees
surrounding the royal home held fruits which
looked like large pears made of pure jade.
While the home's exterior material was porous
like coral it was painted hot pink in color. The
windows were all triangular and looked like
blown green glass, lightly frosted for privacy.
Overall the effect was both magical and comical

given the ridiculously diminutive height of the structure. Robin and Roami watched as the short king was led into the even shorter mansion. He had to bend slightly in order to enter the gray metallic, green gem studded front door. Robin nearly laughed out loud at the sight but caught herself just in time. "That's strange..." Robin began but was cut off by Roami's warning glare. Robin sighed and grew quiet knowing he was right to censor her. They should keep their thoughts to themselves until they were alone and out of earshot of others. With the king gone, the people surrounding them stood up from their kneeling positions. Some members of the crowd quickly left to return to their daily tasks while others continued to stand there and stare at the sky-ones with open curiosity. Robin took a moment to stare back at them with just as much inquisitiveness. She noticed they all wore very similar looking clothing. All of their outfits were made of the same type of material. Not the green velvet the king had been draped in, but a rough woven thread similar to that which Roami wore, except that theirs was dark hunter green. Some wore shorts, skirts, pants, turtle-necks, tunic shirts, t-shirts; all made of the same fabric but cut into various fashions to allow for some individuality.

It was only the king and few others who seemed to be considered royalty among the crowd. This superior group of citizens sported velvet and silk garments with a larger assortment of colors and patterns. Robin lost her frame of thought as she realized it was time to stop staring and start moving. The guards motioned Robin and Roami forward and led them around the group of citizens. They had not walked more than a handful of steps when a man raced towards them as if he were late. When the guards stopped in front of him; the man struggled to catch his breath. Robin and Roami guessed he must be Thister; their new host.

Thister; the Disposer, turned out to be the shortest person among the group; standing at about four and half feet tall. He had a kind face, pudgy cheeks and a ready smile to offer them. He too was dressed in dark green velvet clothes; a large tunic and pants with green sandals. He however, did not wear any jewelry at all. "Sky-Ones, sorry I am late. I tried to get here as soon as I heard the news of your arrival! I am honored to have you stay with me. I believe the king has given me the privilege to watch over you due to my important status here in the city of Fitz. I am the local refuse disposer, or as many call me; The Disposer. This is a very important position here, you see, as we like to keep our land as clean as possible. You will stay at my home, and I hope you are not displeased with my humble abode. Come! Follow me, I am afraid my occupation forces me to have such a tall home, but I assure you, the luxurious accommodations make up for the somewhat unpleasant height." He spoke nonstop as he ushered them down a small red stoned street which would apparently lead them towards his home. Robin noticed that he had pointed towards what appeared to be the only sky-scraper in the entire city. While most of the houses were two or three stories high; the king's large palace had been only one story but very expansive in width. The Disposer's home however was nearly thirty-two stories high!

Roami looked up at it in amazement. He had never come across a structure so large in his own village or during his explorations throughout Source One. Robin, having come from New York City was not shocked by the size at all. She quickly glanced at it, then looked around for the next new piece of excitement. All the homes, no matter how tall or short, were made of the same gray colored, hard porous material. There were not many windows in each home but the few they did have were tinted green or covered in decorative glass art in odd geometric designs.

The actual structures were not identical. Some looked similar to the standard ranch style house Robin remembered from earth. Others were connected to one another like short apartment buildings or the brownstones Robin remembered from Harlem and Brooklyn. Some, she noticed, stood alone and looked like roughly put together shanty town shacks. The overall look was breathtaking as each home was painted in nearly every color one could imagine. In front of each stood a bright orange bush. Robin thought this a bit peculiar and so could not keep her eyes off of the odd looking plant. When Roami discovered what had caught her attention he whispered, "That looks like it may be a Yaru bush. It is not found in Source One, but I have heard stories about its existence in a few other worlds." Roami glanced toward Thister and asked, "Am I right? Is that a yaru bush? " "Yes, sure is! It's the official flower of the city of Fitz. They grow like weeds out here in the city but despite the quantity they are still valued above all other foliage. Like to know why? You see the yaru bush-" Before Thister could explain, Roami cut in. He did not mean to be rude but was so used to explaining everything to Robin it had become second nature to him. Roami looked at Robin as he spoke, "It produces a flower called the PomPu flower. This flower bears a single fruit within its bulb before it blooms, dies and withers away; all in the same day. Inside the PomPu fruit is held whatever the planter wished for most strongly during the planting process. Sometimes one may find a wonderful surprise in one of these. However, if you are not careful what you wish for and think of something negative it too will also appear within this fruit once the flower has bloomed." Robin continued to stare at the yaru bush in awe. She vehemently hoped to one day plant one of her own. Thister harrumphed at having been cut off. He cleared his throat uncomfortably. Noticing this, Roami turned from Robin and faced Thister with a guilty expression. "Sorry about that. I just got a bit excited about showing off a bit of my knowledge. We are ever so grateful to have you as our host and guide, Thister." Roami saw from the slight greenish blush covering Thister's face that he had been appeased by this apology.

"Yes, well. No worries. No worries at all! Let us get moving towards my home and get you two nice and settled in then." Thister turned and continued walking while Robin and Roami oohed and aahed over all they saw around them. Robin quickly got over the idea that she should be seeing fish floating about her or crabs scurrying at her feet. This was unlike any ocean she had ever known. Everywhere they went they were stared at and Robin quickly went from feeling uncomfortable by the scrutiny to feeling like a celebrity. These were not stares of fear, or stares signaling that she was not wanted or out of place. They were clearly stares of reverence. Without a doubt she had never, in all her life, experienced such a rush. They passed the city center with beautifully landscaped trees, red cemented paths and quaint coral stores with vibrantly painted facades; meshed one beside the other. Each store front window was covered in the same tinted green glass they were getting used to seeing everywhere they looked.

Children flew by them on what looked to Robin to be electronic sea horses made of silver metal but decorated with green jewels. As they puttered by Robin wanted nothing more than to get closer and ask for a quick ride but Roami's strict look made her second guess that particular idea. Before they knew it, they were nearing the end of the commercial district and were only a few feet away from the gigantic skyscraper Thister called home. "Look Roami! His place almost touches the waters' surface!" Robin whispered excitedly to Roami as they finally stood before Thister's home. It too was made of the coral-like material and was painted a bright shade of golden yellow. Robin and Roami surmised Thister must be a very important person. Why else would he be the only person with a large home among a city of short huts? Oddly enough, even the king of the land squatted in a tiny domicile while Thister's home apparently towered over everything and everybody. Thister had been rambling on about the city and historic sites the entire walk towards his home and continued speaking hurriedly, "I can assure you, you will have rooms on the very first floor so there is nothing to fear sky-ones." He promised. "Fear?" Robin and Roami said at the same time. "Yes, of course..." Thister said without inflection. He ushered them into the huge metallic front door of the building he called home. The door was silver like so many others they had seen during their walk. It sported a small crescent window at the top made of green glass. Tiny stars of jade jewels were embedded across most of the door. Robin ran her hand along the jewels as they passed the threshold. She could barely hold in the excitement she felt at being in yet another new world she had never thought could possibly exist. While Robin and Roami stood in the entry way looking around them in wonder, Thister continued speaking rapidly. Robin got the feeling he wanted to get them situated quickly and return to some important business he had left off. "You may have the room to my left, brown Sky-One." He said to Robin. "And you blue Sky-One; you may have the one just beside hers. I will have food brought to your rooms and will allow you this day of rest. Tomorrow I will show you about our city and answer any questions you two have." Outside a loud bell rang and it appeared to have come from somewhere near the city center. Thister looked slightly startled by the sound. He became even more rushed in his words and actions in an effort to get away to some important business. "Right now I have work to attend to and garbage to dispose of. I-um... Just ring the bells in your room if you need assistance and you will be seen to by my numerous servants. Do not worry, they only show themselves when they are needed." Smiling at them briefly he turned back towards

111

the front door, rushed out and left them to marvel at their surroundings. The floors were made of green marble while the walls were constructed from the same yellow coral as the exterior of the building. The entry way was littered with all sorts of decorative items, exotic flowers in vases, an emerald chandelier hung from the ceiling above the entryway and colorful glass art covered nearly every window. Right in front of them was a large elevator framed in jade with dark green painted doors. It appeared all the doors were painted in the same shade. Robin was the first to speak after carefully perusing their surroundings. "This place is freaking amazing! I've never lived in any home this... I don't even know how to describe it. I think I'm speechless." Robin twirled around in a tight circle while taking everything in. Roami chuckled while looking at her, "You speechless? Yes, I believe that would be a first." Robin glared at him playfully then rolled her eyes before stifling an unexpected yawn. "Dag, I didn't realize how tired I was." Robin said with yet another long, hearty yawn. "Yes, I too am a bit exhausted but we must inspect our rooms to make sure we are truly in no danger here." Roami said with an identical yawn. "Okay, sounds like a plan." Robin said with a sleepy smile. They moved into her room first. Roami looked over the furnishings, checked beneath the large golden framed bed with downy purple comforters, and tossed around elaborately embroidered pillows. The room was quite expansive and Robin noted it would take her some time to fully investigate her new quarters. Everything she saw was so colorful it nearly hurt her eyes. There were at least five sofas, ten chairs, a few tables and even a device which looked similar to the radios found on earth.

Green apple colored walls and a matching rug lent a cozy feeling to the room. The soft carpeting made Robin feel as if she were floating on clouds. Looking down she realized that the idea was not so farfetched. The rug and apparently the purple window curtains were all covered in white cloud and star patterns that moved perpetually; drifting and then disappearing only to return again. Robin knelt down to touch the soft fabric beneath her feet to see how it felt and ensure she was not seeing things. "You're really seeing that effect. You must prepare yourself to see the unexpected. We are in a new world after all Robin." Roami said while stifling yet another yawn. Robin had never been more excited in all her life. To think that she; plain old Robin, was sitting in such a luxurious setting and it was all there just for her to enjoy! She had never been so pampered in her life, not even close in fact. Robin could not help but recall the last place she called her "bedroom". It had been a tiny five by six foot attic room with slanted walls in a small house in

Brooklyn, New York. She had not initially been relegated to the attic as the child care agency would never have accepted such unsafe conditions. Initially she had slept in a room with her foster sister in the Reynolds' home.   The Reynolds had been one of the best care-givers she had ever had, which was of course not saying much given her seedy background. She could not have asked for more. They did not hit her, curse at her or worse. She had finally felt as if she had found the perfect home for her. While it had taken about thirteen or so years, she knew happiness was always better late than never.

Things were fine until her fragile looking light-skinned foster sister with the long kinky breaded pigtails and beautiful dresses, decided she was not going to share her parents love and affection. The moment she saw them treat Robin as part of their small family, Jasmine had declared a silent war on Robin.   She destroyed items and blamed it on Robin. She started fights and said Robin had attacked her. Jasmine did just about anything she could to discredit the unwanted newcomer. She enacted her plan with gusto until Robin's foster parents began to question their decision to bring her into their home.   The first step away from their love had been the attic after Jasmine had claimed Robin assaulted her in her sleep. Robin had spent three long weeks in the chilly and drafty quarters before she met with her Social Worker. During that critical meeting Robin had found that just after her next birthday, in just a months' time, she would be taken from the Reynolds' home.

They had decided not to adopt her and being of an age; Robin could no longer be placed in additional foster homes. She would be forced into a place called a 'diagnostic'. There Robin would live a life similar to a prisoner until finally making her way into a group home filled with all manner of disturbed, traumatized and problematic youngsters like herself. This was akin to hell on earth for Robin and was the sole reason she had decided to run away that fateful day in Central Park. The night that had changed her life forever.   Just thinking about how much that one decision had changed everything so drastically, nearly took her breath away. To think one moment she had been sleeping on a park bench worrying about her next meal; then in the next moment, found herself standing in a doll filled house in another world. Talk about anything being possible. And she was proof of that; she thought as she looked around her at the beautiful quarters which were indeed fit for a princess. Robin decided to shake off her melancholy thoughts of the past and found it much easier than it had ever been. She noticed the sights, colors and sounds of her most recent flashback seemed more faded and muffled than her usual memories. Perhaps the Sad Susan flower had truly had an effect on her past grief.

She smiled hopefully. Robin decided to cease daydreaming and help Roami with his safety check. She moved towards a dark green door and pushed it open thinking it was yet another walk-in closet. To her amazement, Robin saw with a turn of an odd looking circular light-switch that it was in fact a very large and very exotic looking bathroom. The floor was covered in smooth red pebbles similar to that which was outside and there was a beautiful rainbow colored coral tiled shower. A large copper colored bathtub sat in the room's center. It was filled with water and blue flowers drifting on the surface. Robin moved closer to the tub and noticed something peculiar. The water shimmered in a rainbow of colors that, like the effect on the carpet and curtains, seemed to ebb and flow in a perpetual pattern. "This is so rockin'..." Robin had no adequate words for all she saw. The sound of soft lilting harps and violins played continuously in the bathroom. No matter how much she searched, she could not determine its source. Finally, giving up her mission to determine how everything 'worked', she walked back into the main bedroom to find Roami still searching for danger in every crevice of the room. At the moment he was checking an ornate jewelry box made of jade. "Find any murderous toy ballerinas in there?" Robin asked with a smirk. Roami merely glanced in her direction and continued his search on the other side of the room. The extraordinary comfort of the quarters along with her lack of sleep was a dangerous combination. Robin tended to get very silly when she was tired. In order to stir up some trouble and shake up Roami's perpetually serious demeanor she slipped into one of the large walk-in closets while Roami moved about the room seemingly deep in thought. When Roami came to investigate the closet she hid in, Robin jumped out growling and shaking her arms in the air wildly. "Ah!" Roami screamed and jumped back fending her off with his arms lashing out in response. Robin laughed hysterically then jumped onto her large, amazingly soft bed. When Roami realized he had been fooled he scowled and marched over towards the bed. Picking up the nearest and biggest pillow he could find, he threw it at her while she laughed for what seemed like the first time in way too many years. "You've lost it, you know that? Anyway, it's all clear in here. I'm going to check out my room now." He stalked out of the room glaring back at her but with a telltale smirk on his face. If truth be known, Roami was happy to finally see Robin with something other than a frown on her face. He found his room looked nearly identical to hers. After he had made sure that everything was as it should be Roami decided to freshen up as he assumed that was what Robin was doing as well. He took a quick shower in his luxurious blue coral covered shower stall. When he was refreshed he realized his clothes were a mess from their journey but was unsure how to go about cleaning them.

With a sigh, he resigned himself to wear the interesting looking outfit laid out on his bed by some unseen servant. Roami picked it up and let the clothes dangle in his hand as he looked them over quizzically. The silky blue and green colored pajama pants suit, soft green velvet undershirt and matching silk green and blue robe were of the highest quality. He was amazed at how beautifully the garments had been made. Realizing he wanted to catch up with Robin before she had a chance to leave her quarters and get into any mischief, he threw on the clothes. Once dressed he slipped on the simple green velvet slippers lying at the foot of his guest bed. When he was fully clothed Roami returned to Robin's room and tapped lightly at the door. "Yeah, come in." She said distractedly. He walked in and found she had already changed into the long green and purple colored pajama dress and robe that had been left for her as well. She smelled sweet and fresh. He noticed her skin looked brighter and her braids; still wet from her bath, curled against her face.

Robin loved the feel of the soft silky material which cinched at her tiny waist with a wide green velvet, gem studded belt. The supple cushioned green velvet sandals felt like heaven on her feet. She thought the colors were astounding. She had never felt at all like a princess, but she had to admit that is exactly what she felt like at the moment. Twirling about the room in her long gown, Robin was so excited she wanted to bask in the feeling forever. It was then that she decided she would discard her old dingy pair of jeans, t-shirt and small jacket for the clothing of the Fitz. She figured, it would be easier to forget the old Robin she had been on earth if she could dress the part of a fairy princess every day. Roami still stood at the doorway staring at her with an odd expression on his face. She had been too busy twirling about and sashaying dramatically before her dresser mirror to notice him at first. When she realized he had not said a word since he entered, she looked at him with a quirked eyebrow. "What's wrong with you?" She asked. Realizing how odd he must appear, Roami shook off the affects her image was having on him. She looked like a fairy princess and he was sure he had never seen her look as beautiful. The sight nearly took his breath away. But so as not to scare her, he coughed slightly and quickly whispered, "Nothing. Just tired I guess." She rolled her eyes and returned her gaze to the dresser mirror in front of her. Robin could not help but feel as if her new appearance had wiped away her previous sleepiness. She was now revved up and rearing to go. "Wonder how we get food around here. I'm starving!"

Robin said while Roami still stood at the door staring at her despite his attempts to look a bit more inconspicuous. Flinging herself on her bed and laying on her stomach, Robin mumbled into the soft covers, "Starving and sleepy. Sleepy and starving. What I wouldn't do for a burger and fries right now. La, la, la, la la! I'm lovin' it!" She sang out and ended with a giggle once she realized she had been singing an old fast-food jingle from back on earth. Roami stopped looking at Robin with wonder and his expression quickly moved towards something a bit more comical. He stared at Robin as if she had completely gone insane. Roami began to wonder if all the dramatic world changes had somehow messed with her brain. Shrugging his shoulders, he decided to worry about her sanity at a later time. At the moment they did indeed need to get some sustenance. He walked towards a large golden bell set against the wall near her bed and gently pulled at the black rope dangling within. Robin peeked up from the covers and stared at Roami. "What are you doing?" she asked. "I believe this may be a service bell..." Before he could finish speaking a light green servant tapped at the door then walked in. He had gray colored pants and shirt. Robin noticed his feet, however, were bare. His fuchsia colored hair was shaven so low there was just a hint of the brightly colored hair stubs on his head. His eyes were the bluest Robin had ever seen and his face was very gaunt and angular. Without a doubt he looked painfully thin. Bowing the servant blandly asked, "What is your wish?" "Cool. We even get room service!" Robin stood up and began jumping on the bed. "This is so cool! We should get stuck in new worlds more often Roami. We're being treated like royalty! How cool is this?!" "Robin you really should not get so excited about these things." Pulling her down from the bed and to his side he whispered, "Worlds can be very tricky. There is something that we must learn from this experience so we must be cautious and remain attentive at all times. We also must be careful of what we say and what they hear us say. We don't know who can be trusted just yet." "Well my world on earth was just as tricky and dangerous. In fact, New York City was probably even worse than anything they could think up here." Robin pulled away from Roami and sat on the edge of the bed sighing with exasperation.

"I'm tired of being cautious, I just want to enjoy this great new life for as long as I can. Is that wrong?" she asked with a pout to her lips. She walked towards the servant eyeing him quizzically. "Now... When you say 'what is your wish' do you mean we can have whatever we want? I mean...anything we want?" she asked with hope filled eyes. The servant eyed her with a blank expression. "Yes, Sky-One. What is it you desire?" "Ah! Yay, yay, yay!" Robin began hopping about the room and nearly knocked Roami and the servant over in her excitement.

"Okay, okay, I know what I want!" She cried. "I'd like a strawberry shake with whipped cream and a large strawberry on top. Um... and some steamed carrot sticks with a side of hummus. I just love carrots and who doesn't like Hummus?! Let's see, what else? Oh yes, with a side order of french-fries and a huge chicken sandwich and..." Robin stopped mid-sentence and stared at the servant, "Wait... do you guys have chicken here? I mean... I'm sure I didn't see any chickens outside and... oh well, you did say I could have whatever I wished so...add a chicken sandwich with lettuce and tomatoes, hold the mayo. Oh, and while you're at it, I'd like the newest Nintendo handheld game and a few word games and... and... I guess that's all for now." Robin said breathlessly. She sighed dreamily with a giddy smile plastered across her face. So this was how kids who have gone to Disneyland feel? She had never been there but she had always guessed she would feel just as she did at that very moment. Robin sighed happily then plopped on the bed; exhausted from giving her order. The servant gave a slight nod of his head and turned to Roami, "And you male Sky-One? What is your wish, sir?" Roami stared at Robin who was sprawled out on her bed with a silly grin on her face, "I'd like some water and a putrin rock nut, please." The servant nodded his head again and vanished from the room. When the door clicked shut behind him, Robin got up from the bed slowly. The air nearly crackled with kinetic energy. Roami was absolutely sure she had something on her mind and that something was about to explode. Her eyes blinked in shock and her mouth gaped open in disbelief. It was obvious she was not happy with him...yet again. "Are you out of your mind Roami?" She asked slowly. She put her hand to his forehead to check his temperature, "No. You're not sick. So I don't know what possessed you to totally waste the chance to have your every wish granted just two seconds ago!" Rolling her eyes she stepped back and stared at him as if he were a puzzle she just had to figure out. She shook her head back and forth incredulously. "Who are you Roami? Ya know... I wonder what makes you tick... You seem way too serious all the time and that can be dangerous to your health, you know." She began to poke him in the chest. "Does this bother you Roami? Hmm? Where I'm from this would really tick someone off... I mean, they would be so upset they couldn't help but just scream and chase after me like a madman." She said while continuing her attack. Roami did nothing but cross his arms and stare at her as if she were insane. Realizing she would need another tactic, Robin appeared to sober up and made her facial expression identical to his. She then continued to poke him even harder. Finally Roami blew up and screeched, "Ah!!!" Laughing, Robin ran to find cover. Roami chased after her throughout the room until he caught her and tickled her unmercifully. They both fell to the floor in a fit of giggles. "You're crazy." he said between his bursts of laughter. "Yes, well... I have to make sure you don't kill yourself with seriousity, somehow or another." she giggled. Laughing Roami asked, "Seriousity? Is that really a word on earth?" Robin shook her head and said, "Nope. I made it up just for you." Sobering up and wiping the laughter tears from her eyes Robin lay on the soft green rug and stared up at the beautifully painted blue ceiling. "It's been a while since I've been happy enough to laugh and play like this. Sometimes things got so sad and heavy I felt I would explode from the weight of it. I don't want you to ever feel the way I did...you have to let go every now and then..." She turned to look at her friend beside her. One last tear fell; this one not from joy. Roami looked at her and wanted nothing more than to bring back the laughter. He opened his mouth to speak but was interrupted. "Your wish is served." The servant had entered the room unannounced and beckoned them to follow him to the serving hall which was on the same floor but in a room just beside the elevators. When they entered the large green double doors of the serving hall the first thing they noticed was that it was very long. It was filled mostly by a large emerald table lined with soft red velvet cushioned golden seats. The tabletop was covered with green crystal glasses and golden utensils. A large emerald chandelier hung above the center of the table and the walls were lined with multicolored glass art covered windows.

Everything Robin had ordered sat magically on the dining room table and she screamed with delight. "Oh! Let's stay here forever Roami! We don't need to think of any stupid riddle with all this here for us!" She said before diving into her food and presents. After Robin had eaten her bounteous dinner and Roami swallowed his simple meal, the two returned to their rooms. Within minutes both fell into a deep and restful sleep. For Robin, it was the first in quite some time.

CHAPTER 6

The next morning light from planets in the oxygenated skies above their water world beamed down on the colorful Fitzian rooftops. A dark orange glow spread across the city signaling the dawning of a new day. The inhabitants began to wake and the city slowly buzzed with life. Robin and Roami awoke to find new sets of clothes awaiting them on their beds. Instead of robes there were woven pants, sleeveless tunic tops and hard soled green sandals. Robin tried her outfit on. To her surprise there was a trendy difference between the male and female garments. In addition to her straight legged hunter green pants, there was a mint-green skirt that snuggly wrapped around her thighs. This along with the purple sleeveless v-neck woven top studded with emerald stars and silver glitter made for an awesome effect.

Altogether, Robin thought she looked cooler than ever, in her new attire. Having had times when things were so rough she had been forced to wear just one outfit for weeks on end, she felt even more convinced that in this new world she could truly be a princess. A thought that, of course, given her reality back in New York City, had never even remotely crossed her mind.

After dressing, Robin and Roami met in the hall then made their way to the serving hall which was just a few feet away. When they reached the large and magnificently decorated room, they found Thister already sitting at the table. He appeared to be in very good spirits. However, neither paid him much mind as they made their way towards their seats. The two young adults could not seem to get their eyes off of one another. Robin's eyes roamed over Roami. She saw to her delight that he wore a matching outfit, purple top and dark green bottom minus the mint green skirt, of course. Roami, however, did not seem to like his current outfit. There were way too many jewels, glitter and flash for his tastes. He would have voiced his discomfort but was too preoccupied with staring awestruck at Robin. Roami thought Robin's brown skin nearly shimmered against the beautiful symphony of colors she was wearing. Her toned and slender physique made the outfit truly come alive. Her black and purple streaked breads were pulled up with a purple ribbon into a neat bun at the top of her head. To add effect two single braids fell on either side of her face. Roami's mouth nearly gaped open and his eyes shone with wonder so strong they nearly sparkled. Not at all comfortable with this amount or type of attention, Robin woke from her own stupor and glared back at Roami. Seeing that his presence had gone unnoticed long enough, Thister politely cleared his throat to gain their attention. "Well, hello again Sky-Ones!" His loud welcome nearly made Robin jump out of her skin. She made a mental note to tell Thister sometime later that she was not really a 'morning person' per se and that loud noises tended to make her reflex...violently. But for now she just smiled at her short and annoyingly happy host then made her way to her seat. She sat at the middle of the table just across from Roami. "I had quite a time at work the other day, but good results for sure! Good results to be sure!" He motioned for them to join him at the table where once again their orders were taken by soft spoken; nearly invisible, pale green servants. During the meal, Thister carried most of the conversation with stories about the city of Fitz, the odd but funny quirks of the Fitzian people and listed all the exciting landmarks and tourist spots where he would take them. All along, Robin and Roami nodded politely between bites of food. Each of the teens appeared deep in thought.   Roami's thoughts were filled to the brim with possible riddles for their current world and he tested potential plans and intricate schemes to escape the City of Fitz. He had not forgotten their main goal was to return to Source One.   Robin on the other hand...simply thought about how delicious the food was; how magical her room turned out to be; how cool the water had been during her morning bath; and how great it felt being treated with such respect and reverence. Finally, looking up to meet Roami's eyes for a split moment, she could not help but wonder why he looked at her the way he did or why those long gazes made her feel such immediate shyness. When they finally completed their breakfasts, Thister rested his hands on the table and beamed at them, "Well, it is best that I take you two around and teach you about our great city of Fitz. We'll take a water buggy and I'll point out all the sights. Then we'll visit a few places like the town center, the amusement park and maybe we'll even get a little rustic and visit the village." Robin and Roami noticed the odd way he said "village" as if just saying the word left a bad taste in his mouth. "That sounds great!" Robin said and nearly knocked Roami over in her excitement to leave Thister's home and begin their tour. She was no longer afraid of their new world and with each moment felt as if leaving New York City and falling prey to the blue mists might have been the best thing that had ever happened to her. Robin felt like a celebrity and like a princess. She was no longer some dirty, poor and forgotten girl from the harsh ghettos of the greatest city on earth. Roami did not appear as excited or trusting. He glared at Robin each time their eyes met, urging her silently to keep her wits about her. She blissfully ignored him and tried her best to do something she had never had the chance to do before; enjoy life. They made their way out the front door then stood on the sidewalk to await the carriage. The water buggy was brought around to the front of the building by two servants. Robin had to stop herself from jumping up and down in excitement. She had never seen anything so spectacularly magical as the vehicle now standing before them. It looked very similar to her idea of what Cinderella's pimped out pumpkin might look like. It was made of bright blue painted coral and had dark blue wooden doors on either side of the circular enclosed carriage. The coral had been elaborately etched with designs of various geometric shapes and studded with emerald and jade stars and moons. It glimmered with sprinkles of what Robin could only describe as diamond dust. She noticed a small silver megaphone sat on the roof of the vehicle. Tied to the front were two large sea horses made entirely of green crystals. Robin assumed those too were cut from emerald. "What is it about emeralds and jade here?" Robin wondered aloud as she eyed the fantastical looking vehicle in front of them. Thister heard her question and spoke up with pride in his voice, "They both have special powers here. Only a few among the Fitz are allowed to have these gemstones in their possession. As you can see on the water buggy, the emerald sea horses make the buggy hover above ground and move in all directions. I will show you the steering lever inside which is programmed to direct the crystal horses and move the entire buggy with ease." Thister explained with a broad smile as he motioned for a servant to open one of the dark blue side doors and allow them entry into the vehicle. They stepped into the carriage. Robin and Roami were seated beside each other on the soft velvet blue cushioned bench. Thister settled in opposite them in a single seat. His back would be to them as the seat faced towards the front. Robin guessed that was the driver's seat. Thister showed them the large emerald lever at the center of the coach. Robin thought it looked very much like a joystick. He swiveled around while in the drivers' seat to see if his two young guests were comfortably situated in the long indigo colored bench behind him.   "Great. Well, we're on our way then!" He proclaimed this loudly then turned back to face the front of the buggy. Right in front of him was a small square of clear glass cut into the coral. Robin and Roami saw that there were small circular glass windows on either side of the buggy that they could look through as well as they coasted through the city of Fitz. In seconds, the group were on their way to the city center.   Once there Thister urged them out of the water buggy and eagerly introduced the 'sky-ones' to a number of passing citizens. They met affluent businessmen, bakers, teachers and store owners. All possessed the same dark green skin with fuchsia hair; despite various other differing physical attributes. Robin quickly grew bored with the introductions as she found them polite yet not "real" enough for her tastes. It seemed like all the people they met through Thister were of the royal or upper classes. They each were so worried about "appearances" they did not let their true personalities shine. Robin wanted excitement; she wanted to see who these people truly were underneath their well made disguises. She was sure given enough time and opportunity she would unearth just that. At the moment, they stood in front of a dentists' office talking to the dentist, a lawyer and a store owner. Thister was going on and on about his last visit there to get a root canal. Robin stifled a yawn and took a moment to look around them.

The entire city center was covered in red cement for the sidewalks, and large maroon colored cobbled stone paths for the streets.

Robin quickly noticed that some parts of the streets however, were paved in gray cobbled stone. These gray patches made alternate pathways on the outer edges of the city. She could not help but wonder what their purpose was. Robin was about to interrupt Thister's boring monologue with this question when she saw him follow her line of vision and nervously coughed before quickly saying, "Ah well, enough of my old stories. Let's get these two back in the buggy and continue our wonderful bout of site seeing. Good day fine citizens and thank you for your time!" He shook each of their hands in turn. With uncharacteristic speed he then rounded Robin and Roami up and ushered them quickly into the waiting buggy. When they sat behind Thister in the cozy carriage and it began to move, Robin whispered to Roami at her side. "Did you see those gray pathways Roami?" He nodded. She continued, "Do you think maybe it's some sort of game? Like a life-sized board game or something? I can't imagine what else it could be..." She looked out the window and stared at the gray pathways they were currently passing.

"Perhaps it has something to do with the riddle we must find..." Roami said softly. "Maybe we should just ask Thister." Robin said. "No. They're hiding something. I can tell from their body language. He saw you looking at the paths and then got nervous. This is something we should figure out on our own in time. Just be patient Robin..." Roami squeezed her hand to comfort her. Robin looked at his large blue hand covering her brown slender one. She looked up at him and he smiled reassuringly. He hoped his smile said the words he was too shy to say aloud. That he would always be there for her; and she was not alone in this strange and potentially dangerous new world. Robin nodded in response to his plea to be patient. She then turned to look out the window closest to her.

In an instant she forgot all about their somber conversation. Robin screeched aloud in excitement. "Roami look! There are people running next to our carriage. Someone even has a home-made sign!" Robin moved closer to the window to make the words out, "How cool? It says 'Welcome Sky-Ones. We Heart You!!' Oh my god! I can't believe this! They treat us like we're celebrities!" Robin said in wonder while enthusiastically waving at the city people as they passed by. Her eyes glittered and it was apparent to Roami that she was not accustomed to such praise. He feared her inexperience would make her more prone to become drunk with power. Roami just nodded somberly in response, looking extremely uncomfortable with the attention. "In my village only the Motlings get this sort of attention. Robin, you and I have done nothing spectacular. We are not worthy of the adoration we get here. False fame feels like heaven for a while but always ends up badly. Just try and don't let it get to your head, okay? Remember why we are here and how we must get back." He said abruptly. Robin rolled her eyes. She set her jaw stubbornly and vowed to enjoy her new status despite Roami's dower expression. Peering out the window as the buggy began to move forward, Robin whispered for Roami's ears only, "You know something else I've noticed is that they have two different classes. They all look very similar but you see those people over there, they have four emerald earrings in their left ears and their skin is dark green. Now look over there at that group standing in front of the soup shop, they have only two emerald earrings in their left ear and they are lighter green, like the servants back at Thister's home. I guess the ones with four earrings must be the upper class from the way the others treat them as if they are better than everyone else. See the light ones won't even look the others in the eye when they pass. They even bow slightly right before they speak to them." As Robin shared her findings with Roami, the light in her eyes seemed to fade slightly. Sighing with a hint of her old melancholy, Robin looked away from the glass window and her sight-seeing. She stared at Roami, "I guess some things are the same everywhere." She returned her gaze to the passing crowds of green people with sadness in her eyes. Roami's only response was to pat Robin's hand soothingly. He was not sure why but he needed desperately at that moment to rejuvenate her spirits. Picking up on something she might like, he pointed to an area of the city where a large festival was underway. Streamers, flashing rainbow lights and neon signs could be seen. "Hey, Robin look! There's a huge carnival or festival over there!" He said enticingly. Robin's eyes lit with excitement as she leaned over Roami to look out of his window and see what had caught his attention. There was indeed a festival underway. Several in fact. "Wow! How cool! We have to check this out! I don't think I've ever seen so much happening in one place. It looks more interesting than even Time Square!" She whispered in awe. She could hear Thister's soft chuckle from the driver's seat as he listened to her go on and on about the festivities. "I think there's a bunch of festivals happening all at once. And look; each festival area has a special name. See, look over there! That one has a sign that says "Coming of Age Festival" and the one across the way says "Friendship Festival." Roami pointed at each one hoping to rev up Robin's excitement. While her cockiness, just minutes before, had been annoying her sadness was absolutely unbearable to him. "Yes, yes Sky-Ones! I told you our city was a great place to be! We have festivals every day and for every occasion. I will be sure to bring you two back here another day. It would take more than a day for you to properly see each festival. Believe you me!" Thister said matter-of-factly then went back to whistling some tune he had been humming during most of the ride. Robin looked at each of the festivals they passed with excitement growing steadily in her eyes but by the fifth one she once again became disheartened. "They're nice festivals, Roami... But look who attends them... only the upper class. None of the lower class are actually joining in on the festivities. Can't you see they're either serving the food or doing some other menial labor." Roami had not noticed that. He sighed as he realized his efforts had not only failed to bring her happiness but seemed to have made her even more melancholy. All the while they spoke, Thister had bounced between humming happily to himself or screeching over the silver loudspeaker attached to the top of the roof. He held the microphone to his mouth and yelled out for all citizens to hear, "The Sky-Ones are coming through here to see our fair city on this fine day. Come out and see them and greet them! Please be on your best behavior my fellow Fitzians!" In between his boisterous dialogue on the loudspeaker he pointed out important monuments and buildings. Without a hitch he told Robin and Roami the history behind each in minute detail. "Now coming up next we see the fantastic Fitz City amusement park!" He said with pride. This woke Robin from her stupor. She sat on the edge of her seat trying to take in all the sights and sounds presented before her. The amusement park was huge and brimming with games and strange rides Robin could never have imagined. It seemed like a small city within itself. "Oh... my... goodness! We have to come back here and try out those rides Roami!" Robin screeched with excitement. "Did you see that?!" She could barely sit down and pressed her face against the glass trying to take in every single detail before the carriage left it all behind. While Robin could not see much she did see a few rides. There was one that spun people around in large spheres of orange water. Another one looked like a maze of mirrors; mirrors that appeared to allow one to walk straight through them and change clothes magically. Lastly, before the massive park was no longer viewable from the buggy she glimpsed a haunted house that nearly reverberated with horrified screams. Moments later, they left the amusement Park behind and it became no more than a myriad of small dots in the distance. Robin sat back in her seat with a sigh and a gleam of absolute joy in her eyes. Roami just stared at her with a small smirk twitching at his mouth. She did not care what he thought of her actions, she was in pure rapture. Just thinking about the fun that could be had there made her heart skip a beat. Robin simply stared back at Roami, shook her head joyfully and mouthed the words, "I-Love-Amusement-Parks!". She followed this off with a muffled scream to show her extreme excitement. Roami chuckled and shook his head but before he could respond, Thister's voice boomed once again over the loudspeaker. "We're at the outskirts of the city and are now nearing the village. This is where the common folk live and I daresay that if you don't want to be so near the stinking lot of them we can just bypass Hartan Village altogether. It's a rotten sewer if you ask me!" Thister grew very serious and slowly brought the buggy to a complete stop. He turned around and waited for their directive. Robin and Roami looked at him in astonishment, wondering why he had to broadcast such disparaging speech over the speaker. He could have simply turned around and asked them face to face. "No!" Robin and Roami said simultaneously. Thister looked confused by their outburst. "No, you don't want to see it or..." "No, we would like to see Hartan Village now, please." Roami clarified. Nodding, and with a quirk of his brow, Thister spurred the buggy forward. The path of concrete and cobbled stone was completely gray in this particular area of town. There were less trees, less flowers and not many stores to be found.

All Robin and Roami could see on either side of them was red sand in the distance, orange sky above them and gray cement below them. When they drove up a slight hill, the two were able to finally see Hartan Village just at the base of the incline. It was very small, the roads narrow and overall, everything looked cold and drab.

"Okay then. Well here it is; this cesspool of a place. Hartan Village. We do try to keep it clean and keep all the garbage out as best as can be expected... So you shouldn't see anything worth upsetting you, if you know what I mean." Thister turned back to glance at them with a wink then chuckled good-naturedly. Robin and Roami looked at each other in confusion. They had no idea what he meant by these cryptic words but decided to overlook his strange comment. The two were much too focused on staring at the raggedy and poorly made coral houses which made up the village. Each stood about four or more stories high. While the village looked despondent due to the cracks in the houses, the pale and patchy paint jobs on the coral houses and the very few plants, trees or shrubbery; it was still very quaint and clean. Nothing was out of place. In fact, they saw very few if any people walking about the small zigzag of gray cobbled stone streets that ran through the tiny village on the outskirts of Fitz City. "Well, that's enough of this sludge bucket! I'll be about returning you both to my home so that you can rest and clean yourself of the stench of Hartan Village." He said while sniffing against an imaginary odor. Robin breathed in deeply to determine what smell Thister spoke of. "What stench?" Robin asked Roami in a whisper. Roami just shook his head and shrugged his shoulders in confusion. Speaking up, Robin said, "Um... Actually... We'd like to walk around here for a while if you don't mind Thister." Thister looked at her as if she had lost her mind. "Well... I can't imagine why you'd like to do that miss. Oh, wait... I get it! You want to go out to put your nose up at them. Ha ha! I understand perfectly little miss. I will just," suddenly a bell sounded across the city and Thister looked up with a grin. "Ah! That's my work calling me for sure. I'll just get to my job and then return for you two in a bit if that is okay with you?" He asked quickly. "That's fine." Robin said with a bright but false smile. "Okay, so that is the plan then." Thister said as they left the water buggy and shut the door behind them.

He sped away as soon as his guests' feet touched the ground. "Woa! He must really love his work..." Robin said as she stared at the blue water buggy flying down the road back towards the main city. "Apparently." Roami said dryly while dusting off his clothes. Seeing his actions, Robin laughed hysterically. "What?" Roami asked. "Nothing." Robin said while trying to keep her laughter inside. "It's just that... you're dusting yourself off... under water." She pointed out. Roami thought about it for a second and then smirked despite his attempts to keep a gruff outward appearance. "Well anyway. Let's go meet the locals." Robin said then began to walk along the extremely narrow street ahead of them. The smooth cement they had rode on through most of the city ended near the village entryway. From that point on everything grew increasingly shoddy. Robin noticed there was no real difference between sidewalk and street as everything was made of the same sloppily constructed gray cobbled stone. The two quickly perused the village's coral cottages. To their surprise they noted that while the homes were very skinny in width, they appeared to each be much taller than any of the other buildings in the city. Aside from Thister's abode, of course. Furthermore, the exterior of each home was painted in dull shades of grays and white pastels. There was not a single drop of emerald to be found on any of the furnishings and décor.

"Hey, there are no yaru bushes Roami. Do you see any?" Robin asked as she looked around for the magical bush. "No. You're right. They seem to be missing. But if these people really are the peasant class I guess that is to be expected. The upper classes would not want them to have their wishes fulfilled. That's what yaru bushes do after all..." Roami looked at Robin and noticed she had lost some of the silliness which had lit her up just moments before. She appeared sad once again. He sighed; knowing that pretty much everything they saw in Hartan Village would prevent her from smiling. The two friends walked side by side, through the tiny maze of streets. They had to stop every now and then as loose gray pebbles found their way into their sandals. For the most part it seemed as if they were in a ghost town. When they finally came across a few of the tall, lanky, light green villagers, with fuchsia hair, Robin and Roami grew increasingly uncomfortable. They did not fear for their safety but were not used to the overwhelming praise they received. The people would either bow so low they appeared to have lost their legs, or they fell to the ground deep in full prostration. Not one of them ever once looked the Sky-Ones directly in the eyes. Robin and Roami tried to get them to stop all their reverence but to no avail. While Robin had loved the celebrity attention in the city; here in the village, she felt more and more guilty with each bow. Finally they made it to the last home in the small village. It stood at the end of a dead end street which was blocked off by a protrusion of the grayish, uncut coral material the houses were all made of. Robin could smell the scent of what she now knew to be fresh 'sea bread' cooking somewhere nearby. She and Roami had heard all about it while visiting a bakery that sold it earlier that day. Sea bread was apparently a staple food for many of the people of Fitz for it was very cheap and easy to make. The royals, however, never ate it as it was considered the food of common folk. All this and more, Robin and Roami had learned during their day running around the city. "Mmm... I wish we could go in there and get some of that." Robin said wistfully. She quickly determined the lovely smell was wafting from the last home in the village. They stood in front of it and she could not help but stare beseechingly at the open window. "Yes me too. I am quite hungry." Roami said as his stomach growled in confirmation. All of a sudden a little pale green woman poked her flaming fuchsia covered head outside of the open glass window of the home.

"Oh my! It's the Sky-Ones!" She screamed and comically fell to her knees in prostration. Because she was inside the house it just appeared as if she disappeared altogether from Robin and Roami's vantage point. All they could see now was her curly hair bobbing slightly near the window. Lifting her head up slightly, the woman screamed, "Boonie! Come outside with me to praise the Sky-Ones!" She raced from the front room of the house and out of her pale green colored front door to prostrate at their feet. She wore a simple gray dress with a white apron over it. Her feet were bare and the bottoms were stained red from the sand. An identical looking man raced from the house with his fork and spoon still in hand as he bowed before them as well. He wore the usual clothing of most of the servant class; a simple pair of woven gray trousers and a matching gray sleeveless shirt.

At this point Robin and Roami were tired of all these unnecessary antics. Robin stepped up to finally do something about it. "Would you please just stop it!" Robin screamed. Boonie and his wife, Beenie froze in place. Shaking in fear; they glanced up at Robin. "I'm so sorry female Sky-One. Whatever we have done to anger you, we are so very sorry." Boonie said with his mouth quivering. "We only ask that you not harm us since I am expecting a child and..." he let his words drift off not sure what to say next to plead their case. Realizing Robin may have scared them with her outburst, Roami quickly chimed in, "We have no intention of harming either of you. My companion and I, only ask that you stop being so submissive. We just want to come into your lovely house and share a meal with you if that is okay." He spoke in a kindly manner, in an effort to show they came in peace. The husband and wife stared at Robin and Roami as if they had gone mad. "Yes. Yes, of course! If you will not be insulted by our lowly home, then... of course, you are most welcome to be our guests, Sky-Ones!" With that said, the couple stood up and motioned for Robin and Roami to follow them inside. Robin and Roami were directed up the short flight of cement stairs and through the front door. Their hosts led them directly to the kitchen where all the wonderful smells were originating. The first thing they noticed was that the interior furniture was very slender to accommodate the structure's narrow width. The wooden floorboards were painted gray and creaked as they entered. All of the furnishings were simple and yet quite colorful. This particular fact came as a surprise to Robin since the exterior was so very dull. As they passed the entry hall and living room on their way towards the kitchen, Robin and Roami noticed they could count all the furniture on one hand. There was a deep blue couch with worn edges, a curtain that was gray on the outside and pink on the inside. Lastly, splayed across the living room floor, there was a rainbow plaid rug beneath a simple coral crafted coffee table.

Robin and Roami were offered wooden seats at the small kitchen table and Beenie rushed to serve them food. "Mmm... smells delicious!" Robin said with a delighted smile. Boonie smiled with pride, "Yes. Tonight we're having Snails eggs, Sea bread and a side of Hryg's Shadow pudding. We do hope you enjoy our lowly meal." He said humbly with his head bowed low. "I'm sure we'll love it!" Robin said. She smiled delightedly as she and Roami waited for the feast to be served. Roami looked the couple over in confusion. They looked like so many others in the serving class with their two silver hooped earrings in their left ear, pale green skin and very simple gray clothes. "So you two are expecting a child. That is what you said, correct?" Roami turned towards the kitchen counter to address Beenie. Beenie continued pulling out plates and collecting the food items without a hitch. It was Boonie who responded to the question. "Yes, it is due any day now." Boonie smiled politely although a shadow passed over his eyes. Roami quickly determined that this was an uncomfortable topic for the couple. Robin did not see this and so continued questioning them on the subject. "Wow! I hope we are here to see the birth of the baby. Wait... How are the babies born here, anyway? I mean..." Robin quieted for a moment as she glanced over to the kitchen counter where Beenie was grabbing additional plates and cutlery. She looked Beenie's skinny figure over, then continued, "You don't actually... um... look like you're expecting a baby." Robin finished her sentence despite Roami's slight pinch to her side. She glared at him and mouthed "What?!" Beenie looked puzzled by her comment. "Yes. I am sure I don't look as if I am having a baby because I am not. I am, however, expecting one because Boonie is expecting one and we are a couple..." She looked confused by the questions but still smiled good-naturedly at her guests. "Sorry. I'm confused... I understand that both of you are expecting a baby but you are having the baby, right Beenie?" Robin asked with an obvious look of bewilderment. "No..." Beenie said and stared at Robin with a look of even greater confusion. "Okay... so who exactly is having the baby?" Robin asked slowly while staring at Roami with a look of exasperation on her face. "Well I am, of course." Boonie spoke up. "What the-" Robin began. Roami rushed to keep Robin from saying anything she might later regret. "I guess the men have the children here Robin. You must remember this is another world. I told you things can be a little tricky..." Roami sent her a pointed look and she quietly nodded to show she would try to be a bit more open minded. "And I thought families in New York were complicated. Now this... I have to see." Robin said with a slight chuckle. "Do you think we could possibly be there for the birth?" She asked the couple. "Why yes, of course. Everyone must be present during a birthing..." Boonie continued to look uncomfortable about the topic. However, he answered the questions so as not to be considered rude. "Everyone?" Robin asked. She eyed the couple then gave Roami a secretive glance to see how he was reacting to all of this.

Beenie was moving around busily dishing out each plate and setting them before everyone at the table. Roami picked up his large blue glass cup, drank quietly and stared blank faced back at Robin. She knew him well enough now to know that meant they would discuss this matter later in private. "Yes, everyone. The whole city must attend." Beenie answered the question as she had noticed Boonie's growing discomfort. She stopped a moment to stand behind him and rubbed his back softly. It was at that moment that Robin took a good look at Boonie and saw his stomach did look a bit bigger than one might on such a tall and slender man. She had noticed it before but had assumed he just liked good food and plenty of it. The couple appeared nervous and it became obvious to Robin that they did not want to speak about the birthing event. She decided to let the topic drop. Beenie had placed two additional settings on the table and Robin and Roami watched mesmerized as their meal came alive before their eyes. All the utensils, plates and bowls were made of wood or glass. While they looked worn they were very clean and of the brightest hues the two had ever seen. It felt as if they were eating on a rainbow.

Dinner was soon served and Robin and Roami found that the common food was not so common after all. After they had finished eating the bulk of their meal Robin broke the silence. "I think that was better than anything we've eaten here so far, right Roami?" Robin smiled with gratitude and sipped on her blue colored Bonleekin Tea. Beenie had served the delicious beverage in a small green and purple teacup. "I must agree. You are great cooks and even greater hosts." Roami said to the couple who bowed profusely in response. They each looked uncomfortable by the Sky-Ones praise. When the group had finished their dinner, Robin and Roami thanked the couple and walked out of their quaint home. The day was coming to an end and the orange sky was quickly turning a deep red. Robin and Roami smiled and waved to the few villagers they passed as they walked side by side down the darkening streets. Their sandals made a loud crunching sound as they moved down the pebble ridden, gray cobbled streets. The two made their way back to the main entrance of the village in complete silence. Both were overcome with their individual thoughts about the day's events. Since the village was very small, before they knew it, they were standing back near the spot where Thister had dropped them off. As promised, he was there waiting patiently in his water buggy. When he saw them he jumped out with a broad smile and motioned for them to ascend the stairs into the carriage. "Enough of the slums for ya, huh?" He asked with a knowing smile. Without responding, Robin and Roami entered the buggy. Both remained deep in thought during the entire ride back to Thister's house. The common theme of each of their ruminations was, in a word, "Escape".

CHAPTER 7

Robin drifted within darkness. It was not cold or painful like the feeling she had experienced her final night in Central Park. That night felt so far away it was almost as if it had never even happened. The only proof that it actually had occurred was the fact that she was spending her days underwater in a city of green people and water buggies. She let these thoughts drift away as she continued to snuggle within the welcoming darkness of sleep. Nothing had ever felt so good and fulfilling. "Rise and shine Sky-Ones!" Thister's loud voice boomed throughout his large home and reverberated in Robin's sleep dazed head. Robin jerked awake with a start. For a split moment she had no idea where she was or even who she was. When it all started to come back to her she was left with nothing but exasperation. "You've got to be kidding me!" She groaned. Robin peeked out from under her plush sea of pink and green jewel embroidered pillows and purple covers with their decorative perpetual patterns playing across them. With one eye still closed she glared in the general direction his voice had come from. Her nose scrunched up and her brow furrowed. Taking a deep breath and pulling from her diaphragm she screamed, "The Sky-Ones are still sleeping for god sakes!" She waited for a moment to see if there was any response. When only silence greeted her she smiled triumphantly. Moments later Robin snuggled deeper into her warm bed and proceeded to fall back to sleep. "No female Sky-One. You are mistaken for your friend is here standing before me ready and eager to tackle the new day!" Thister said this so giddily, Robin was sure she would 'accidentally' strangle the small green man before the day was through.

"Oh my God, Roami! What are you doing up this early? Why must you mess everything up for me!" She cried out and began to whimper under her covers. Her whimpers died down as sleep began to do its work and pulled her back within its warm embrace. Outside of this cocoon of happiness she heard something rhythmic pull her back towards the real world. The annoying sound of footsteps grew louder as someone approached her door. Seconds later she heard the sound of a hand slowly pushing it open.

"Come now... Get up Robin; we have business to attend to. We will never figure out the riddle if we sleep all day, now will we? Get dressed and I will have all of your favorite breakfast foods ordered. Deal?" Roami stood there and waited for Robin to move as if she were getting up. When he saw her sleek brown leg drop from under the covers and plop to the ground, he chuckled victoriously then left the room. As soon as he left the room, Robin slowly pulled her leg back up beneath the covers. With a smile she proceeded to return to dreamland. After a few minutes without hearing a peep from Robin's quarters, Roami realized he had been duped. "I believe extreme measures will have to be taken." He said to Thister as they sat at the dining table. With a grimace he marched from the dining hall and back to Robin's bedroom. Slipping into the room he stood beside her bed with a smile on his face. Only her head could be seen amidst the mountain of covers and he could not help but notice how peaceful she looked when she was asleep. Her soft braids covered her eyes so that all that was visible was her pert nose and parted mouth. He also noted she was snoring slightly. Drawing closer he whispered softly into her ear, "Robin... Get up..." She wrinkled her nose, turned in the opposite direction and continued her soft snoring. Smiling Roami walked around her large bed and approached her once again. "Now, now Robin..." He whispered softly then continued ever more gently, "You know you must get up so..." He placed his mouth next to her ear and screamed, "Get up!" Roami screamed at the top of his lungs; like a madman on the prowl. Robin flew from under her covers, with fear and confusion swimming across her face all at once. Her fists were up and ready to fend off an attack if necessary. After all, you could take the girl out of Brooklyn but you cannot take the Brooklyn out of the girl, or so she had heard it said. Robin looked around her room to find the source of the disturbance only to find to her amazement she was completely alone.

Snickering, Roami had fallen to the floor beside her bed immediately after yelling. As Robin stumbled from the bed disoriented he had crawled to the door and ran back to the main serving hall. He struggled to keep his laughter in until he made it back to the dining room table.

An hour later, Robin had dressed in an outfit similar to the ones she had seen members of the upper class wearing the day before. It was comprised of a silky thigh length tunic with cinched belt, velvet undershirt, sleek trousers and sandals. This particular outfit seemed extraordinarily extravagant given the amount of jewels on it. However, Robin did not focus on the intricate details of her outfit. She threw the yellow contraption on and hastily pulled her hair up into a bun. She was far too busy thinking of ways to make Roami pay for his little morning prank to worry about fashion. When she made it to the dining hall and sat to eat, she secretly vowed to get Roami back for what he had done.

Yes, she had wanted him to loosen up and have some fun but definitely not at her expense. He would certainly pay for this. At the moment, she was not sure how but she was creative and would eventually figure something out. With each upward faraway and glazed look Robin had; Roami nearly shook at the thought of what devilish retribution her mind was plotting against him. Thister had left the hall immediately after eating to ensure the servants prepared the buggy. They would bring it around to the front of the building for the sky-ones.

Robin and Roami had simply glared at one another during most of the morning meal. And even now walked beside one another like contenders towards the front door. Robin was slow to forgive and was overwhelmed with thoughts of possible pranks to play on Roami. Roami looked exceedingly nervous as he was sure Robin would come up with something diabolical he could never imagine or anticipate.

The two made their way back into Thister's waiting water buggy. They were dressed in matching bright yellow velvet and silk outfits. Sprinkles of tiny emeralds encrusted in her dress as well as his tunic and pants. At breakfast, Thister had gleefully explained that they had been presented these extraordinarily grand garments as today they would be honored guests at what was to be one of the biggest balls of the year. As the water buggy slowly made its way through the city, Robin and Roami sat glued to the windows watching as the city people passed by in a green blur. Robin found even the simplest daily activities, gestures or words held a great amount of interest for her. She now understood why New York City tourists looked so dumb all the time. Many times she had laughed at their "I love New York" clothes, bright sunny smiles and looks of awe as they took pictures of even the dirty sidewalks. To be a visitor in a strange place made one want to experience everything with an intense ardor.

When they made it to the royal ball, they were surprised to finally lay eyes on the majestic house that Thister had rambled on about all morning with such pride. "Here it is Sky-Ones, one of the grandest houses in the city of Fitz!" He jumped from the water buggy. With a simple hand gesture he had one of the light green servants standing before the house move forward to help Robin and Roami out of their carriage. Robin started laughing quietly. Her shoulders shook and her mouth was pursed shut to keep from crying out loud. Roami squeezed her arm slightly to remind her to keep quiet. However, he too fought against a smile. Their laughter stemmed from what stood right before them. The mansion appeared to be no bigger than between four and five feet in height. Robin could not imagine how any of the abnormally tall people standing in line outside would fit into the tiny but elaborately decorated contraption. It looked to Robin like a beautifully designed sardine can!   The exterior coral façade was painted a bright hot pink color. The outside walls were encrusted with large diamond shaped pieces of jade and the slightly slanted roof was made of glossy brown wood.   Robin did not move away from the carriage although a servant beckoned her to come towards the house. She stared in open confusion at Roami and whispered, "Really?"   Roami sighed in response as realized he would have to be the compromising and logical one this evening. He too thought the mansion's structure was a bit insane but he was also sure it was in their best interest to do as their hosts did. That was the best way to avoid any uncomfortable confrontations... or possibly even death. "Please Robin..." he mouthed at her while dramatically widening his eyes, hoping she got the message. Rolling her eyes and sighing in exasperation, Robin moved closer to Roami. She took his hand so that he could not get too far away from her. "If I have to go in that cramped death trap, you better be at my side..." she said through clenched teeth.   Roami could only chuckle softly in response. He held onto her hand tightly to ensure she knew he was there for her and would not leave her side; no matter what. "Line up everyone, please do line up in a civilized mannerrrr." A tall green man who appeared to be the butler moved throughout the crowd trying to keep everyone in an orderly procession. The butler was light green like the rest of the serving class. However, instead of the plain gray woven outfit most wore, he had gray silk pants and a matching tunic covered in silver glitter. His fuchsia hair was cut Cesar style and his face was very angular. Apparently, his status was above most of the serving class as evidenced by his huge, knobby nose swinging haughtily in the ear. The lean man spoke nasally and stressed all of his 'r's to the point of being outright hilarious. Robin could not help but stare at him as he dramatically attempted to keep the long line moving from the front of the home and circling around the block. There were very few homes in this part of town. The few that were nearby, were very short yet extremely expansive. Each seemed to take up the same lot of land that nearly 10 of the average homes would have. The streets running through this blatantly upscale neighborhood were made of glistening emerald cobblestone pieces. The sidewalks were made of equally sparkly green cement. Robin thought the whole effect beautiful but wholly unnecessary, as the ground was only meant to walk on. Just as she was about to share this thought with Roami, the snobbish butler marched towards them. His nose hung high and his eyes looked nearly shut. He wore a bored expression on his face. "Please follow me Sky-

Ones. You are of course V.I.P" The butler said this with such snobbery, Robin could not help but glance at Roami in comical astonishment. She struggled to smother the laugh at the tip of her tongue and her eyes were alight with merriment. The butler ushered Robin and Roami to the front of the line since they would be the honored guests. When his task had been completed the butler stood before the waiting procession. With a dutiful smile he leaned down to dial a few numbers into a small keypad. Robin watched as he lifted a metal lid constructed into the front of the home then tapped each number of a secret code. "Roami...there's no front door... Do you see one anywhere?" She whispered softly. "No... I'm sure there's another way in though..." Roami whispered back. A loud beeping sound rang out. The brown wooden roof of the huge but short pink coral home began to open slowly. Robin drew closer to get a good look as the inside of the strange house became visible. Everything inside was made of the finest quality fabrics. Everywhere she looked she saw the sparkle of emeralds, jades and other jewels embedded in anything that did not have a pulse.

"Wow!" was all Robin could say with her mouth gaping open. "Well now, don't be afraid. Please do come in and take advantage of our home's comforts, Sky-Ones." A tall man and woman with dark colored skin, blue eyes and bright fluffy hair stood up from their seated position in the house.

Their clothes were all made of silk, velvet and glitter. Atop this they wore mounds of precious jewels. The royal couple walked up a small flight of stairs then stepped out of their home and down a small flight of wooden steps situated beside the butler. Robin and Roami had not noticed these stairs when they first glanced at the home. As they had not then understood their purpose they had probably overlooked it. The couple smiled broadly showing all their pearly whites once they stood before all of their guests. With a small gesture of their hands they motioned for Robin and Roami to climb the steps and enter their home.   Robin was too busy staring at the couples elaborate garments to realize they were being beckoned. She noticed that even their sandals were encrusted with emeralds. As the couple were now standing just feet away, Robin could better see the women's outfit. She marveled at her long bright green skirt and matching shirt with a sleek silver, jade encrusted belt cinched at her narrow waist.

The man wore dark hunter green silk pants and a similarly colored shirt covered in silver glitter and emerald stars. Altogether, their garments were so shiny, Robin had to look away to avoid the glare. She quickly forgot about their clothing and began to wonder how they had sat comfortably in such a short home while wearing such stiff jewel laden outfits. "How in the world... Roami how can we all possibly fit in there? It's like a luxurious sardine can!" She whispered to him. "I know Robin." Was all Roami could think to say at the moment as he too was wondering what they had gotten themselves into. Stepping in front of Robin in a protective stance, Roami moved towards the house. He stopped short once he stood before the small block of steps that ran up into the front of the box-like construction. Their hosts smiled at them then went back up the stairs and motioned for Robin and Roami to follow their lead.

Roami walked up the steps and then stepped down into the house where he continued to follow the immaculately dressed couple. Roami held on tightly to Robin's hand to ensure she was right behind him and did not run away. He was pretty certain that was exactly what she wanted to do at the moment. They walked through rooms that while wide, did not reach past the average Fitzian's chest. It was hard to take the jewel studded lamps and finely made rugs seriously when they could easily turn around and look at the waiting line of guests or look up and see the red watery sky above them. "Now, here we have the dining room. Of course, to my left is the study and over here is the ballroom. Please position yourselves comfortably and we will see to the rest of the guests. The servants will come around with serving lists and you may order as you wish." Their male host smiled at them then added. "I am Byrum, by the way. And this is my lovely wife, Myrum." Smiling the two walked out of the room and left Robin and Roami to stand knee deep in confusion.   "Uh, Roami?" Robin said with a sly smirk. Roami stared at her and within moments they both started laughing at the same time.   "I really have no clue as to how this is supposed to work..." Roami said as he sat down on the ballroom floor cross legged. The carpet was made of purple velvet and there was not a single piece of furniture to be found. Along the gold painted walls were a few jade-framed mirrors and wall sconces that gave off a soft glow.   "I guess we just sit like this because lying would be even more awkward once this room fills up with all the guests." He said this as he took Robin's hand and pulled her down to sit beside him.   The two stared at each other daring one another to laugh. Their laughter died down as the other guests slowly came pouring in to sit in a similar fashion. Soon the house was full and the roof was lowered shut. Just as Robin had said, the house quickly began to resemble a packed sardine can.   "You know what makes it even funnier is that they are so prim and proper. How can you act all snooty while sitting here uncomfortably in this ridiculous thing." She said while trying to hide her amusement behind her hand. Roami smirked in agreement. The crowd began to mingle although moving from person to person proved to be very difficult while sitting cross legged or squatting down. Robin watched with laughter in her eyes, as people tried to wiggle and crawl from one person to another in a dignified manner. Thankfully, as they were the main attraction, Robin and Roami did not have to move about as much as everyone else. They remained where they were and watched as most of the royals found their way to their side at one point or another. After their latest group of fans had stopped by to introduce themselves, Robin leaned towards Roami and whispered, "So why do you think they are so crazy about having such short houses?" She said this with a serious expression on her face. While it had seemed highly comical earlier in the day she had slowly lost all sense of humor at how uncomfortable the home truly was. She was now sporting a crick in her leg from having to sit for so long. Once the automated roof had closed and the last guest had entered, she started to feel immediately claustrophobic. Why would such an expensive home be so unlivable? She could not help but wonder about the mental health of the royal class. "Good question Robin. I do not know. Perhaps that mystery is where this worlds' riddle can be found." He was cut off by their hosts who stood up in the center of the seated guests. The royal couple's outfits seemed to shimmer and sparkle amidst the many lamps and wall sconces littering the walls of the dining room. Robin could see how and why the serving class would look at such people with awe.

Between their aloof attitudes and sparkling clothing, they seemed like super beings. Calling their attention to him, their male host Byrum began his speech, "Today as you all well know, we have two distinguished guests. They are of course the Sky-Ones that everyone has been abuzz about. Robin and Roami have been sent from the spirits above. No doubt to inspect our world and our worthiness as a civilization. What better place to show off our advanced ways and superior society than a great ball where only the best of the best; the royal families of Fitz, are in attendance. As you can see for the benefit of our honored guests I have even gone so far as to use only the finest servants to see to everyone's needs. There is not a mutt amongst them; all pedigrees I daresay." He cleared his throat and continued. "Well enough of all that. I do hope you are all enjoying yourselves. Now, today we do have some special entertainments picked out especially for our sky guests so that they may witness our civilized ways more acutely. Today we shall have a..." He paused dramatically trying to rev up anticipation. Licking his lips he completed his announcement, "Viewing!" The crowd gasped with delight and their eyes glistened with private merriment. Apparently they all knew what this was and were very excited to witness such an event. Robin and Roami just looked around in confusion. They both stared at one another then shrugged in shared ignorance. "Yes, a viewing has been set up for this special occasion and I do hope you all enjoy it!" When their host completed his speech he beamed at the crowd. After taking a quick bow he returned to his seat beside his wife. She did not say a word but smiled broadly for everyone to see. Somewhere past the 'ballroom' was what Robin and Roami could only guess was a theatre room with a very short stage elevated just a few inches from the floor. The doors that separated each room were very wide to accommodate people squatted or crawling through rather than walking upright. The guests made their way from the ballroom and into the theater room which was even more expansive than the ballroom with red velvet carpet covering the floor. Robin gasped at the beautiful emerald studded walls painted a deep bright red. The stage was painted black. Though it was no more than a few inches above the ground, this was enough to make standing or even sitting on it very uncomfortable. The roof slanted upward dramatically above the theater to accommodate anyone standing on the stage. It was therefore the only place in the entire mansion that would allow average sized people to stand upright. As the guests sidled over on all knees, or squatting like ducks, Robin once again felt tears of laughter fall from her eyes. No matter how hard she tried they refused to remain hidden. She shook with the power of her laughter and Roami had to squeeze her hand to keep her even passably collected in front of the other guests. "This is just so silly... I think I'm going to scream... I need air." Robin said between short gasps as she tried to get herself together. A few guests looked her way with question but dared not question the actions of a sky-one. They simply smiled at her and continued to enter the theater room. When everyone was seated and staring at the empty wooden stage with a single spot light shining on it; the wall lights within the large room began to dim. Robin wiped away her tears and took a deep breath. She was eager to see what could possibly be more entertaining than what they had already witnessed this night. At a snap of the female host's fingers two servants dressed in drab gray outfits crawled into the room from a rear door just to the right of the stage. Their outfits were woven, frayed at the edges and nearly identical as both wore loose pants and shapeless sleeveless tunics. With their heads hung down submissively they quietly made their way towards the stage. They were greeted by complete silence. Both stepped up onto the black wood boards and made their way towards the stage center. There they squinted under the brutal glare of the white spotlight. Robin now saw to her surprise their faces were painted an even paler green with some form of cosmetics. From this closer vantage point, Robin could now see that they were a light green male and female both with vibrant heads of straight chin-length fuchsia hair. The moment both servants reached the center of the stage a bell sounded. Robin jumped back at the abrupt sound then watched in shock as the two began insulting one another and themselves. Their speech seemed a bit forced. It was obvious to Robin that they were following a script. She looked around to gather everyone else's thoughts on the weird play being orchestrated for their entertainment. All she saw were smiles and eyes alight with merriment. Robin officially felt as if she was in the twilight zone. She wanted to tell Roami this but realized he might not get the reference. Robin decided to keep her thoughts to herself for the moment and shakily returned her gaze to the stage. The man was busy yelling now. "Women! You work all day and come home dirty and smelly. And when was the last time you saw to my needs? Huh? I want a divorce! Rather be alone than deal with the stench of ya!" He shoved her shoulder and she fell back slightly. While his words were angry his eyes were blank and his speech monotone. The woman stumbled back slightly her eyes looked pained for a flash then returned to a similarly blank expression. "Man, if I smell then you are pure sewage! If I had the guts to cut off my own nose I would. This ten year marriage has been nine years too long. I want out!" She ducked down and swung her leg to sweep his legs out from underneath him. He shrieked and jumped high in the air before her leg could connect. The skinny man then did a backflip. Robin cringed. She was almost sure he would hit his head on the roof and knock himself out in the process.

 They were apparently professionals and had done this particular routine countless times. The man ran up to the woman and pulled at her bone straight hair. It fell into his hands while she escaped. It was a wig! Her actual hair was cut in a short fuchsia fade. "Ah so the real you is uncovered to the light of day!" He screamed. Tucking the wig onto his own head he cackled and laughed hysterically. "How could you?!" She screeched. While he laughed she snatched at his shirt ripping it in the process. Underneath he had painted his chest dark green with make-up.

"Ah! So looks like someone else's secret is found out! Secretly trying to be one of the higher class eh?" She cackled with laughter. He raced over to her and choked her neck with a crazed look on his face. Robin sat with her mouth gaping open. She was completely entranced by what was happening before her. Once again she tore her eyes from the stage to glance at either side of her. She wanted to discern the royal's response to this absolute insanity. She got her answer within seconds. Thunderous applause resounded throughout the room. A few royals even struggled to stand up in the small space to show their appreciation. "You've got to be kidding me..." Robin whispered then stared at Roami with eyes wide with disbelief. He looked sad but thoughtful as he too looked at the royals then back at the two actors who bowed politely. When they realized the guests expected an encore, the two servants continued to denigrate themselves and throw some additional jabs at their counterparts. The man did a few flips and hit himself in the head while acting dimwitted. The crowd of royals laughed with gusto. Robin and Roami were even elbowed a few times with winks from the royals seated beside them. They ignored these attempts to make them part of seemingly good natured camaraderie which covered something so repulsive. The crowd applauded louder as the couple bowed profusely. The looks in the actor's eyes were pained. Robin and Roami had trouble looking at them without feeling sickened by the entire display. When silence finally fell, all that could be heard was the actors' heavy breathing from their bowed positions. The male and female hosts stood up and made their way towards the stage. They stopped when they were at the base of it. "Stand up!" Byrum thundered with an obvious air of authority. The two servants stood up and meekly stared at their feet. "Now, ladies and gentlemen... this is really no act as we all know. These people are like this all the time. They are barbaric savages and know nothing but what they are told and can do nothing without being properly instructed." Staring directly at the Sky-ones he continued, "I'm sure you two Sky-ones have seen them during your time here already. They are the lower beings we call Mubbins. And we are the Royals of Fitz of course. We keep them around solely for manual labor and entertainment purposes. Other than that we try to keep them at arm's length to ensure their base ways do not spread among our class." Robin wanted nothing more than to stand up and slap Byrum directly in his face. Her fist balled up at her side in preparation. Roami saw this and grabbed Robin's hand. He looked at her with a look that said, "Please don't." Swallowing hard, Robin worked to calm herself down and put on a false yet neutral expression. Continuing without a hitch Byrum said, "Now. Watch here as I try to teach them just a small morsel of true civility." With that said he faced the two actors and asked them, as if they were just small children, several questions for which he expected an immediate and obviously scripted response. "Now is it nice to treat your wife like that?" Byrum asked haughtily. "No." Came the simple emotionless response. "And should you not have dinner ready and yourself all tidied up when your husband comes home each day?" Byrum asked the woman. "Yes, sir." Came her soft response. The two servants stood with their heads down dutifully as the host

169

whispered to them. Moments later the host patted them on their backs and ushered them towards the watching crowd. Smiling openly, although it never truly touched their eyes, they hugged one another. It was as if their previous orchestrated grievances were now settled thanks to the diplomatic efforts of their benevolent host. The crowd responded with a resounding applause. Byrum's wife stepped forward with tears glistening in her eyes as she too applauded. "I've seen this time and time again and it never ceases to move me. Thank you all for attending this evening's viewing. Please do not forget that without our guidance these poor folk would be little or nothing. We must teach them and they must be controlled for their own benefit. Now, back to the festivities!" She dabbed at her tears and continued to smile at her guests. Byrum turned and glared dismissingly at the two actors. They scurried away into the shadows quickly and the party resumed with even more fervor. Having seen more than they could stomach, Robin and Roami slowly inched towards the main door of the theater. They made a run for it as soon as it was possible to leave unseen. When they reached the entry hall they saw the butler sitting there cross-legged. He looked even more bored than usual and was distractedly pulling at invisible lint on his gray shirt. When he noticed them he looked up eager to be of service. "Ah, dearrr Sky-ones.

How can I help you?" He asked demurely. "How can we get out? We have...uh...other engagements we have to get to." Roami said hoping the butler would buy this story. "Ah, yes. Well we do not open the roof while the festivities are still underway, of course. You two may use the side door. It is just through here." He motioned to his left where a dark green door stood. The butler opened the door and instructed Robin and Roami to crawl out.

When they were finally outside, the teens stood up and worked to get the kinks out of their legs and necks. "Freedom!" Robin breathed a quick sigh of relief. She then grabbed Roami by the hand and nearly screamed, "We seriously have to get out of this place! They're completely insane!" Roami nodded gravely, "Yes, it is definitely not the place for us. They treat us like royalty now because they think we are heaven sent beings. If they found out we really are nothing more than just stranded travelers they may treat us just like the Mubbins... or perhaps even worse." "Ah there you are! I was wondering where you two disappeared to. How did you like the party and the entertainment?" Thister crawled out of the same side door they had just exited. As he was hefty, it was not the most eloquent exit and Roami had to stop himself from helping the man to his feet. He was sure given Thisters' prideful personality he would be offended by the gesture. "We uh... it was a very... interesting party. We actually just needed some fresh air and thought it was time to get back home." Robin lied. "Okay, no problem at all. I'll have the servant bring the water buggy around and you two can-" Thister began but was cut off by Robin. "Well actually... We were hoping to walk back home ourselves. We're not too far. Besides, we can easily see your home from here so we won't get lost." Robin said with a false smile. Roami looked at her and was sure to keep his confusion from showing as he nodded in agreement. "Yes, we would like to see the great city of Fitz at night. No need to take us. We feel much more comfortable getting around ourselves now. Thank you for all your help Thister." Roami added. "Oh okay. Well then I'll get back to the party then and see you all back at home later. Goodnight Sky-ones!" He said with a big smile. Squatting down with some measure of difficulty he struggled to get back through the mansion door. When he was completely gone from sight, Robin sighed in relief. "Right, so what is your plan Robin? It seems as if you have one..." Roami said as she turned and started walking down the bright green cobbled street. He followed behind her. "We need to talk...alone...without any outside ears. I figured a walk through the city without Thister would be the best thing to do right now. I dunno... I was happy feeling like a rock star for once in my life... The attention felt great... But this place... It's just not fair treating people different just based on their looks or how they were born. I can't stand around and see this every day and not try and start a revolution or something..." Robin walked faster as her thoughts spurred her on. The red light of day was completely gone and in its place the City of Fitz's sky took on a charcoal gray hue.

Robin stopped abruptly when she noticed what kept the pathways throughout the city illuminated. All along the streets were the tall metal poles she had seen littered across the city. They each had long ropes hung between them. She had assumed these were power lines of some sort but now realized they were in fact meant to light the streets. Robin watched as light green servants hovered on compact circular footholds that hovered in the air. They moved along the lines of string, hanging small glass lanterns. Each lantern was filled with a light greenish gel in which tons of small white glowing nuggets floated. Altogether they emitted a bright green light into the darkness. "Wow..." was all Robin could think to say as she watched one such process occur on the street they were currently standing on. Without realizing it she began walking towards the sea of shining lights and the busy looking lantern laden servants. When she stood below a man hovering a few feet in the sky with a lantern in hand, she spoke up, "Excuse me, what is that?" She asked. The servant jumped a bit and was apparently startled by the

173

unexpected attention. Apparently he did not receive much consideration while doing his daily task. "Uh... it is.. I mean... they are street lights. We fill the lanterns with emerald gel and add flob nuggets to help light the way for city dwellers." The servant said while looking around nervously. It seemed he did not want to be caught speaking while on duty. Nodding Robin could not help but ask just one more question. "Where do you get those Flob nuggets? They are beautiful." She asked and could feel Roami stand very close behind her in a protective stance. "We Mubbins pick them on the outskirts of town near the Tower. That is where the Flobbins Forest can be found. They fall year round and they're all over the grounds there. Their light lasts only for so long so we must continually pick them to replenish the lanterns." The servant looked as if he was sweating with fear so Robin decided to end her inquisition. However, Roami piped in where she left off. "How can we get to this place you speak of?" Roami asked. The servant pointed towards the opposite side of town. Past a sea of lights, dark shadows of homes and trees, Robin and Roami now noticed another tall edifice jutting above the city. Whatever it was, it nearly touched the water's surface. "Why didn't we notice that before?" Robin whispered. "Sometimes you only see what you expect to see..." Roami whispered back. "Thank you sir."

Robin said with a genuine smile for the servant who nodded and quickly returned to his work.

Robin and Roami began walking towards the large Tower. As they made their way out of the Royals district they noticed there were less lanterns hung in the average districts of Fitz. It soon became increasingly difficult to see where they were going. Thankfully the Tower shined like a beacon against the glow of some planet high above; in the sky above the water. "It looks like the tower has a green glow around it, how weird..." Robin said as she looked towards their destination. "I am not sure how smart it is for us to go exploring in a strange world late at night. Perhaps we should go back Robin." Roami thought aloud. He was not afraid for himself but more concerned for her safety. Roami wondered if he could protect Robin when even he did not know what dangers they might face. "No, we can't sleep in every night and act like we're not stuck in the wrong world. The riddle won't find us. We have to find the riddle. Maybe it's hidden in this tower thingee." Robin tried her best to explain her reasoning although even she shivered when passing some of the more shadowy streets of the city. Everything basically looked the same. They passed the same red cobbled streets and they walked on similar red concrete sidewalks beside colorful coral houses with prim gardens and green windows and wooden roofs. However, as they moved farther from the city Robin and Roami began to see more and more of the gray paths they had noticed during their last adventure in the city. "Did they run out of red paint or something?" Robin asked as they looked the gray paths over from a closer vantage point. When they were close enough Robin stuck her right foot onto the gray cobbled stone to see if anything magical would happen. Nothing. She was still the same old Robin. Not a frog, monkey, pig or wolf. "So, what do you think they're for?" She looked up at Roami who was busy glaring at her for stepping on something without knowing what the consequences would have been. "Someone's coming!" Roami whispered as they heard the shuffling of feet. A few shadows were making their way towards them from the direction of the city. "Mubbin servants." Robin whispered once the shadows grew close enough and could be seen against the darkness. Everything about the group of servants was drab but their blue, gray and green eyes shone brightly in the darkness. Robin had never seen such a sad and ghostly procession. "Look where they are walking." Roami said. "On the gray path.... Only on the gray path..." Robin responded while staring at the group as they grew closer. Bowing, the group of five servants dressed in gray, showed proper reverence to the Sky-ones. Without a word uttered they then continued on their way down the gray path and back towards Hartan

Village. "Oh my god..." was all Robin could say as they watched them disappear into the darkness. The true purpose of the gray paths was now apparent and Robin felt sick upon gleaning the newly acquired knowledge. "How could I have thought for a minute I wanted to stay here forever..." She said more to herself than to Roami. "Come on let's go. The tower is not much farther." Roami said while taking her hand and gently leading her forward. They made their way to the tower and found the closer they got the easier it was to see where they were going. The small forest of trees surrounding the base of the tower had silver colored trunks, deep purple leaves and was littered with tons of Flob nuggets which glowed brightly all over the ground. Robin and Roami were surprised to find that while the nuggets hung in the trees they did not emit any light. Those hanging on the tree twigs and branches looked like small clear glass acorns. It was once they were 'ripe' and fell to the ground that they shone with a bright white glow. There were still a few servants leaving the forest and taking the gray paths towards the direction of Hartan Village. The closer Robin and Roami got to the tower the more desolate their surroundings became. When the two stood directly at the base of the tower they realized they were completely alone. "Look at this Roami. It is made completely of emerald. The tower's bricks are emerald... that's why it looked like it was glowing green..." She said as she smoothed her hand against the cool surface.   The ground beneath them was the same red sand as all uncultivated areas of the water world of Fitz. Robin noticed that a few of the fallen Flobbin nuggets were reddened by the sandy ground they lay on.   Deciding the glowing nuggets were much more interesting to behold, Robin ditched the tower and walked over to a small young Flobbin tree standing just a few feet away. She had to step over countless lit Flob nuggets to get to it.   Getting on her tip-toes she took a good look at the purple leaves fluttering in the wind and the small clear glass Flob nuggets nestled in clusters amidst the leaves.   "They look sort of like acorns...like diamond acorns... I can't believe they don't use this as jewelry or money. It's absolutely beautiful. I'm sure back on earth each one of these would go for a pretty penny..." She whispered. She pulled one of the Flob nuggets off the tree and watched as it instantaneously began to glow white in her hand.   "Oh my..." She gasped in wonder with a smile lighting her face as she looked over at Roami. He was still standing near the tower. "I have to take some of these home with me. I mean... if I ever go back to Earth I could be rich!"   Screeching with joy she began to round up at least two handfuls of Flob nuggets from the tree. When she had her fill, Robin deftly put them in the small pockets of her trousers. Roami could not help but laugh at her antics and the fact that her pockets now shone with light. "Yes, very inconspicuous Robin!' He laughed. Moments later he grew very serious as he realized they had been wrong to assume they were not alone. "Do you hear that Robin?" He asked as he quirked up his ear. Robin stopped her picking spree for a moment and grew still and quiet. "Singing..." She whispered in response. "Yes..." He said. "I think it's coming from the tower. At the very top." Robin said as she placed a few more nuggets in her pocket then tossed one in her bra since she had run out of pocket space. Roami started circling the front of the tower which was quite wide. His guess was that it probably ran about forty feet around the base. Backing up he stared up and noticed a small green glass window at the very top.

"There are no doors or steps here. Let's try the other side." Robin said as she began to walk in one direction and Roami walked in the other. They met back at the front of the base and concluded the same thing. "There's no way in." Robin and Roami said simultaneously. Roami backed away from the tower with his head held back. The surface water above them rippled making the charcoal colored sky sway and move rhythmically. The tower's green glass, double windows high above them were slightly ajar. If he squinted Roami could just make out a shadow hiding inside. He could sense the eerie feeling of someone staring back at him. "What do you see Roami?" Robin asked as she watched his expression go from curiosity to fear. "Let's go." Was all Roami said as he grabbed Robin's arm and pulled her towards him. Without another word he marched back towards the red cobbled path that would lead them back towards the city. "What the... what happened? Did you see something?" Robin asked while trying to pull her arm from his tight grasp. He did not let her go until they were several feet away from the tower and walking down well lit paved streets.

He did not speak again until they stood before the front door of Thister's building. Turning towards her he said, "Someone was up there watching us. This place is not safe... Robin we must spend our every waking hour looking for the riddle to get out of here. Can I count on you to help me do this?" "Of course, Roami. I'm your...your friend. And I think you're mine right?" She looked down a bit sheepishly. She had never felt as insecure at she felt at that particular moment. "Yes, of course." Roami said with a reassuring smile. Robin smiled back and her soft brown eyes shone in the green light of the two lanterns hanging beside Thister's front door. "So, we're a team. And our mission is.. to get out of here as soon as we can." Roami said with a grim look of determination. "Yep! We'll be like batman and robin." She said with a laugh. Robin could tell from his look he had no idea who or what she was referring to. With a silly 'I'm tired' giggle she added slyly, "And no I will not be playing the less-popular part of my namesake 'robin'..." She laughed. Pushing open the door Roami looked at her in confusion, "Huh? You won't be 'robin'... I don't get it." The rare and melodious sound of Robin's laughter resounded in the cool night air. Thister's mystical looking metal door, with its crescent moon window and tiny jade stars, shut behind them.

CHAPTER 8

Robin and Roami spent the next few days wandering throughout Fitz City trying to piece together the world's riddle.   Time and time again, they came up with nothing. The streets were impeccably clean; the people they came across were all well-mannered and helpful. Everything about the world was orderly and well-constructed. The only ugly stain on an otherwise perfect society was the issue with the Mobbins. However, no matter how many Robin and Roami probed, not one of the serving class openly admitted having any desire for change. Furthermore, Robin and Roami were not sure the riddle lie within that particular issue. More importantly, even if it did; how would they know when the riddle was unearthed and solved? Would a yellow light bulb appear over their heads or would a bell ring? As they began their search in earnest, they both began to realize just how many questions remained unanswered. In truth; they were completely lost.   Roami said as

182

much to Robin early one morning as they ate breakfast. They sat side by side and alone in Thister's dining hall as their host was away on business. Both were well rested and wore the basic Fitzian outfits they had worn since their arrival. Today they wore red and blue. Robin's pants and tunic were royal blue, with a red short skirt sewn over the pants. The tunic was littered in shiny triangular jade gemstones. Her braids were pulled back in two ponytail buns. Roami sported a red tunic with the same gemstones and a blue pair of loose fitting trousers. Without looking up from her meal Robin said, "Yes. And it doesn't help that none of the Mobbins will tell us how they feel about being treated like garbage day in and day out. They say they are happy and even honored to serve the Royals and yet... I honestly don't believe it's true. Have you looked into the Mobbins' eyes? Look at them closely next time. There is a deep...I don't know...I guess it's like a sadness there that screams out to me that things are just not right here..." Roami reflected on Robin's words for a moment and nodded his head slowly in agreement. "Yes, I believe you may have a valid point, Robin." He said. Finishing the last spoonfuls of her hearty breakfast of Hoaty Eggs and Swirled Finny Cream, Robin looked at Roami and sighed heavily. "So, we have checked nearly every inch of this world. The City, the village; visited every home and spoke to every person we've come across. There are... only two places we haven't searched yet." She gave him a pointed look. Roami smiled mischievously. "Yes, I know exactly what you are thinking. The tower and...we must finally search upstairs today. Thister seems very secretive about the upper floors of this mansion. He must be hiding something important. It's time that we get to the bottom of this." Roami pushed his green glass bowl away and checked to see that they were not being watched by the servants. "Looks like it's all clear so let's go now." He took Robin by the hand and led the way towards the elevators.

They pressed the up button and the green doors opened automatically. "Well here we go..." Robin began to look like she might be having second thoughts. "Come on." Roami pulled her into the elevator and pressed the number thirty-two as that was the top floor. The doors shut them in and they waited. Both teens took a look at the luxurious interior while the elevator climbed higher and higher. The walls were covered in velvet green wallpaper, a golden frame separated the top part of the walls from the gray metal bottom. The same green marble on the floors of the main hallway covered the elevator floor. The buttons were all green against a rectangular silver backing. Their fear increased as they passed each floor on their way to the top. "I honestly can't take the suspense, Roami. I think I'm going to be sick..." Robin

184

leaned against the soft velvet walls of the immaculate elevator. "Whatever happened to elevator music anyway? I'd do anything for some soothing jazz right now." She mumbled as her eyes remained glued to each number lighting up above the doors, steadily showing their progress towards the top. The elevator came to a halt and the doors opened on the top floor. Robin and Roami both gasped in astonishment. Their eyes grew large and their mouths drooped open dramatically at what they saw before them. "There's nothing here. Nothing at all..." Roami whispered as he stepped out onto the shiny black marble floor that seemed to go on forever. His voice echoed loudly around them.

"No. It's not completely empty. Check this out..." Robin said as she walked towards the large glass windows which surrounded the huge room at all sides. She stood before a large telescope and began looking through it curiously. "What do you think these are for?" She asked in amazement. Roami walked up behind Robin and bumped her hip playfully to get at the telescope. "Who knows? Let me see." He pleaded. She moved aside and he placed his eye to the opening.. "All I see is the city. Nothing more." He sighed dejectedly. "It's not the only one. Look around. There are a bunch of them situated near the windows. Probably about five in total. They are all overlooking the city. Maybe Thister is a guard or watchmen for the city of

Fitz. Or just a really nosy dude!" Robin laughed at her own joke. Roami just stared at her with a sad expression. Robin sobered a bit upon seeing her friends sorrow, "What's wrong Roami?" "What is wrong is that I feel, at this moment more than ever, that we will never return home." He said as he listlessly walked back towards the waiting elevators. Robin followed him, "And where is home for me exactly? I've never had one so I guess I am not taking this whole situation to heart as much as you are. I'm sorry if I seem like I don't care Roami. Part of me is so used to getting the short end of the stick... I kind of don't let anything really get to me. I've stopped trying to believe that things will turn out right, because they never seem to; at least not for me. But that was back when I was on my own...but now...I'm with you..." Clearing her throat she walked into the open elevator. She turned to ensure Roami was making his way towards her. When he stood by her side she pressed the down button before saying, "Believe me, I think between the two of us we'll get back to Source One... Eventually." They slowly made their descent back to the ground floor. "Believe me. In time everything will be fine." Robin reiterated and squeezed Roami's arm softly.

*** Robin and Roami found themselves walking on the outskirts of town. Here the red streets were not as polished and the trees not as well groomed. While it was not as dilapidated as

Harkin Village it was evident that the lower class dark green Fitzian's lived here. They had decided this was a good place as any to find out more information about the Tower and try to uncover the riddle that was eluding them.

"We'll pass through here and ask some of the locals questions. Then when we're done we'll make our way to the final mystery of Fitz; The Tower." Roami said as he held Robin's hand in a protective gesture. A group of rough looking Fitzian men stood on a corner in front of a grocery store looking like they were just itching for trouble. Robin knew full well she could handle herself but did not push away Roami's hand. She liked the idea of Roami being her personal savior and protector. "Excuse me? Can we ask you a few questions?" Robin asked a passing woman holding a child in her arms. The woman smiled politely since they were the Sky-Ones, but blithely ignored their request and kept walking. "Sir, can we bother you for a moment of your time?" Roami asked a man walking quickly in their direction. The man turned completely around upon realizing he was about to be questioned. He stumbled twice as he raced away from them with a look of fear contorting his face. "Is it just me or have the citizens become shyer since we started our question campaign? It's like they all know what we're after and are trying to keep something from us... Or am I just being paranoid?" Robin asked

Roami. After just a few minutes of this she finally understood how those annoying activists and flyer handlers felt in Manhattan. She had outmaneuvered and ran from enough of them to know just how hard it was to get people to stop, connect and help. Perhaps if she ever made it back to earth and new york city she would stop for them. Well, not all of them... maybe she would talk to at least one of the poor nuisances now that she could see it from their perspective.

Focusing on the here and now, Robin awaited Roami's verdict. "Am I or am I not paranoid? Survey says..." she snickered at her private joke. "Nope. I feel the same way... But there has to be at least one person willing to answer us." Roami said with a sigh while looking around him imploringly. They stood on a corner now and wondered which one of four possible paths they should take. "Look over there; on the corner of that street. That man...he looks like he's talking to himself." Robin said while inching forward slightly to get a better look. Roami held fast to her hand to keep her from crossing the street and walking straight into harms' way. "You're right. But he does not seem like he is right in his mind. He could be dangerous... See how everyone else is staying far away from him..." Roami said. The man in question had very dark green skin however his face, arms and hands had been smeared with light green paint. His gray clothes were in the same style of the Mubbins people but were so dirty they were very near to being red in color. He had obviously spent some nights sleeping on the loose red sand on the outskirts of town. He smiled broadly at everyone who passed by and kept rambling on and on to himself. Robin was instantly saddened by the sight as she had seen very similar people on the streets of New York City, time and time again. The homeless were sometimes riddled with serious psychological problems in addition to poverty. "Yeah, you may be right about that... Can't say I've never been attacked by a few crazed homeless people back in New York City... But still part of me can't help but think that maybe...just maybe he may let loose something that the rest of the more 'civilized' city people wouldn't..." Robin let this idea sink into Roami's head. "Hmm..." He looked thoughtful. "You may just be on to something there..." He said as he held her hand firmly. With an indrawn breath, to prepare himself for what might transpire, Roami led the way across the street. They stopped just a few feet away from the man squatting in front of a beautiful florist shop. He looked up at them then smiled brightly before waving his hand excitedly in greeting. Robin and Roami did not wave back but slowed their gait and moved more cautiously towards him. "Greeting sky-ones! I knew we would eventually meet. I know a lot of things, yes that I do! Being the towns Desposer makes me privy to many

189

things others don't know." He chuckled and slapped his knees as if he had cracked an incredibly funny joke. "Desposer? But isn't that Thister's job..." Robin could not help but blurt this out. "Ah Thister! Poor fool... He has no idea what that job will do to his soul...what that job can do to anyone's soul... Yes, dear brown one, he is the current Desposer... I was the past..." His happiness seemed to change in a blink of an eye. He looked reminiscent and deeply depressed by the memories flowing through his head. It soon became apparent to Robin and Roami that he had forgotten all about their presence. The poor man began to speak his thoughts aloud. "It was all so wrong...what we did to those poor people...for that's exactly what they were... people... ah, what man will do to another when money and power corrupt. The worst gifts in the world are money and power! Like tainted food they poison all who consume them...I did not truly mean what I did... I was so blind...so blind... now they all laugh at me...poor Mantu...poor Mantu! they scream and throw rocks. If only they knew I am free! It is they who are poor, they who are caged, they who are slaves!" As his anger grew the man named Mantu stood up on his bare red soled feet and began to scream hysterically. "You know what they hide... I have heard that you ask everyone about it. Yes, the tower has eyes and knows the sins of men. It has seen the rebirth of all those wrongfully killed... Haha! What you don't know may kill you... Want to know the secret dear Sky-ones... well then here you go: To go up you must first go down... To go up you must first go down!!!"   Roami had seen and heard enough. The man named Mantu, grew increasingly angry and within moments began to scream and wave his arms blindly. Roami grabbed hold of Robin and quickly led her away before things became violent.   "Oh my god..." was all Robin could say as they quickly moved away from the crazed man and walked down the street at a near run.

"Did you hear what he said... What could he have done that was so horrible...what are they still doing?" Robin said as she tried to get her heart rate back to a normal rhythm.   They did not slow down until they were three blocks away and the man was no more than a small green blur.   "I told you he might be dangerous... but you were right... I think there is some truth to what he had to say... We'll discuss it later at Thister's. For now we need to check into the last mysterious place in Fitz." Roami said while biting down on his blue lower lip nervously.

"The tower..." Robin said a bit breathlessly. It had been the subject of her dreams since the night they had first laid eyes on it. Who lived in the tower? Who had been spying down at them that night? Why were they in the tower, secluded from society? There were still so many questions and little if any answers to be found.

"You heard what he kept repeating: To go up, you must first go down... Maybe there is something to that..." Robin said while still deep in thought. "Yes, maybe." Roami said as he led the way towards the tower and Flobbin Forest. It took them a few minutes to make it to their destination. Both remained silent as their minds were overrun with thoughts and questions. Robin was slowly realizing that it was one thing to read a good mystery thriller then return to the real world when the book was done. It was another thing entirely when your actual life was riddled with mysteries. She could not help but feel a bit overwhelmed by the challenge she and Roami had to tackle in order to return to Source One. When they stood back at the base of the forest they were happy to see that they had come at just the right time. Whereas there were usually scores of Mubbin Laborers gathering Flob Nuggets from the grounds, the place was now deserted. "It is midday so perhaps they are all on break." Roami said aloud. "Yes that's great but we still don't know how to get in..." Robin stated the obvious. Roami did not respond immediately but studied the glossy green bricks of the tower wall. "Maybe there is some sort of secret door..." He kept walking along it while running his fingers over the smooth brick. Robin was still lost in her thoughts about crazy Mantu. She whispered to herself, "The tower has eyes... To go up, you

192

must go down...Down?" She looked down at her feet and saw only red sand and rock. Sighing she began to walk around the base of the tower while kicking at the ground with her foot. "My god!" She whispered softly. "Roami, come here! I found something!" Robin knelt down and sifted the sand away from what looked like a silver handle. "What is it?" He asked as he ran to her side. "To go up you must go down... There is a door here in the ground. It was barely covered by sand today but the other day it must have been completely covered. Maybe this will take us down then up to the top of the tower?" She was excited to have potentially solved a major problem. "I think you're right, Robin!" Roami beamed at her then got to work brushing off the rest of the sand and opening the metal door slowly. There were about eight emerald brick steps leading down into complete darkness. Looking down into the black pit, Roami said, "Maybe I should go first...who knows what we will find in there..." Robin shook her head forcefully. "No. We're a team. Remember R&R, R squared, batman and robin, the dynamic duo...we go together." She grabbed hold of his hand to ensure he could not leave her behind. Smiling Roami began to step down when Robin stopped him. "Wait, we'll need light. One sec!" She raced over towards a cluster of fallen, Flob nuggets and took two handfuls of the small glowing spheres. Running back towards Roami she handed him the ones in her right hand. "Okay, let's go!" She said while taking a steadying breath. "Thanks Robin." Roami said. He took a step down into the opening and pulled her behind him. They moved slowly and with caution. Once at the bottom of all eight steps they saw that the passageway was a few inches higher than their heads but wide enough to ensure they did not feel closed in. The ground was made of dusty decrepit emerald bricks while the walls and ceiling were constructed from red cement. They held their hands; filled with the glowing nuggets, out before them to light the way. Roami surmised the length of the passageway was the exact length from the trapdoor and into the center of the tower. When they stood in what must have been the basement of the tower they found more brick stairs but these made their way upwards. "So this is it. This is how we'll enter the tower...Are you ready?" Roami whispered. "Yes. Let's just do it..." Robin whispered back. She squeezed his hand so tightly she was amazed he had not yet complained. Yet another reason why she was slowly falling under Roami's spell. Without waiting another moment, they made their way up the spiraling flight of stairs. Up and up they walked into the dark stairwell for what seemed like ages. Though they tried their best to be quiet and cautious they could not help but breathe a bit loudly as they made their way up the final steps. "We're here. We're at the top." Roami whispered as they came to the last three steps and saw an alcove entryway leading into a large room. Robin struggled to see past Roami in her excitement to know what was hidden in the tower. "Step back! Who are you? What do you want?" A soft voice belted out from somewhere on the other side of the room. As they still stood in the entryway they could not be sure who had uttered these words. The two moved forward slowly to stand fully in the large studio. Robin took a quick look at the room. There were two large windows on either side of the tower. Each had double windows made with green tinted grass. The floorboards were wooden but painted gray. There were a few basket weave gray rugs thrown across the floor as well. Each was bland and did not have any exotic patterns or decorations. A single metal cot and a wooden chair were situated at the far left. The cot had a large red comforter lying on it. Just across from them was another entryway with a single metal door. It was shut and had a matching silver lock dangling from it. A little to the left of this the wall jutted forward again and held another entry way. It had a doorframe but no door attached to it. They could clearly see that it led to what looked like a tiny bathroom. Robin and Roami still searched to see who had spoken. The speaker finally stepped out from their hiding place behind the wall in the

195

bathroom. She nearly took Robin and Roami's breathe away. They had seen all sorts of people during their stay in Fitz but none so beautiful as the woman who now stood before them. She wore a gray skin-tight long-sleeved dress. It shimmered with silver dust and fell to the floor in graceful waves. Her body was similar to that of a super heroine; all sleek muscle tone and soft curves where necessary. They noticed her skin was the palest green they had ever seen; she was almost as white as the inside of a cucumber. Her face was a beautiful oval with a pointed chin, faery like nose, green eyes beautifully large and slanted and arched eyebrows. Her vibrant fuchsia colored hair fell down to her navel in a sea of silky waves. She held a sharp metal pick in front of her and pointed it threateningly at Robin and Roami. "I asked a question." She reminded them while they stared at her with dumbfounded expressions. "I...we... we are the sky-ones." Roami said a bit stupidly. Rolling her eyes and feeling slightly jealous at Roami's reaction to the stranger, Robin stepped forward and spoke up, "We are visitors to the city of Fitz. We saw this tower and were curious to know what it was for and who lived here. Sorry if we barged in on you..." Robin said as she looked around and doubted there was much anyone could be busy doing in such a barren and lonely space. "I see..." Was all the pale woman would say as she lowered her weapon. She apparently did not take them as a threat so put it away altogether in a small wooden jewelry box hidden under the cot. "I actually have heard about you sky-ones... I just didn't think I'd have the privilege to ever meet you face to face." She replaced the red blanket over the bed then sat on it. With a sigh she turned to face them. "I'm sorry I don't have much here. There is only one chair but you are welcome to it." She motioned towards the chair besides the cot. Roami led Robin towards the chair, pulled it back from the bed; a safe distance from the beautiful stranger then offered it to Robin. When Robin sat down, he stood right beside her, just in case things went awry. Smiling softly at them the woman turned to stare out the window nearest to the cot. She had a sad and wistful air about her. Upon closer scrutiny they could tell she was not as young as they had initially thought. "Who are you?" Robin asked without preamble. "No one." The woman answered while still staring off into the distance. Robin scrunched up her face in question then stared up at Roami. Roami looked down at Robin, raised his brows then looked back at the woman. "Do you have a name?" He asked softly. "I am called Mirub... But there are not many who are here to call me anything so does it really matter?" She said with a sad smile. Trying to pull her out of the doldrums enough to give them some concrete answers Robin spoke up this time, "So Mirub... Why are you in this tower? We have never seen you in the city... do you ever go there?" Mirub chuckled softly. She moved forward slightly and it soon became apparent to Robin and Roami that Mirub could not go very far. A thick metal chain snaked out from beneath her dress and was clasped around her slim white ankle. It had bruised her where it rubbed against her soft skin. They had not noticed it dragging against the floor before but now everything seemed to come together in their heads. "Someone is keeping you prisoner here..." Robin said as anger built within her. "Yes." Was Mirub's simple reply. "Well we'll just help you escape. I'll take a look at the clasp and lock. I'm actually an expert pick-lock..." Robin stood up and moved towards her to do just that. "No." Mirub inched away in fear. Seeing her odd reaction Robin slowly returned to her seat. "You see... even if you free me from the tower... He'll still find me and just put me back here. There is no place in this world I can hide... not from him..." Mirub said with a dark cloud covering her expression. She sighed sadly. "Who?" Roami asked with concern etched on his face. "It doesn't matter who. I don't want to get you two in trouble. Staying in the Fitzian's good graces is... a very timorous feat...believe me... They are very fickle people. One moment they will revere you and the next they will cut you to pieces without a thought... I should know this better than most." She laughed as she got caught up in her own private thoughts. "Yes, I don't want to end up like poor Mantu...poor guy." She said with a sad shake of her head. "Mantu? We just met him. You know him?" Robin asked with excitement. It appeared they were finally getting somewhere with respect to secrets being uncovered. "Yes, of course. Everyone knows the 'madman of Fitz'. He wasn't always a wandering lunatic you know. He and I share an intimate connection... this Tower. This was his old home. As city deposer he was granted this tower to live and... work from." Mirub bit her plump red bottom lip. She realized she may be giving away too much information. To keep the children safe she grew quiet then stood up to walk around them.   When she stood at the window she stopped and sighed heavily from the weight of all the secrets she was burdened with. Mirub leaned on the green brick window sill and looked out at the beautiful city landscape. "What exactly does a Deposer do anyway?" Robin asked slyly hoping Mirub was still in a talkative mood. "You children are putting yourselves at risk with these questions. I will not help you dig your own graves... you seem like good people... I could not live with myself if my information brought you harm. Just live your days like the celebrities the city's people have made you into. Be happy you are not the Mubbins, poor Mantu or myself..." She swallowed hard and wiped away a few errant tears.   "You are very beautiful... why would you be hidden away like this?" Robin asked softly. Mirub laughed softly then spoke through her tear choked throat, "Beauty... it's one of the worse curses ever made... My beauty made me stand out amongst my people... my beauty made me a rich man's pet... my beauty stole away every chance I had to be a normal young girl who finds her partner, gets married, has little babies and dotes on them as they grow up... My beauty made me a possession to be had; a rich man's trophy...a broken doll sitting in a tower hidden away from.... life..." She finally broke down and began to cry openly. Robin motioned for Roami to do something. He walked towards Mirub and patted her back soothingly. "It's okay. We consider you a friend Mirub. Robin and I won't let you remain a prisoner here. We are looking for a way out of Fitz and when we do we will get you out of here too. This is a promise." Roami said with determination. Mirub's crying died down into small hiccups. "I've had so many dreams destroyed and killed... I can't dare to believe this promise will come true but whether it happens or not... Thank you for your kind words and intentions sky-ones..." She whispered. "Don't worry... We will save you Mirub." Robin added with conviction. "You two are not bad people so you can't imagine the darkness that lies beneath the city of Fitz. Beneath the class system and obvious injustices...there is an even darker evil... I see the evil of men easily from my bird's eye view...believe me..." She said cryptically. It became apparent she knew quite a bit but was still trying to protect them from the truth. "What evil? How can we help you without knowing everything?" Robin asked in exasperation. While Mirub wiped her tears away and Robin spoke to her, Roami moved towards the locked door at the other end of the room. "Where does this lead to?" He asked as he tested the lock only to find that it was only for show. Someone had already broke open the padlock. Removing it altogether, he opened the door and walked inside before Mirub could stop him. "Stop! No, don't go in there!" She yelled but was so weighed down by the chain around her ankle, she could not reach him in time. Not wanting Roami to get hurt Robin grabbed the jewelry box from under the bed. In seconds she pulled out the metal pick and raced after him. By the time she caught up with Roami she found that the room behind the door was just as bare as the rest of the tower. It had the same wooden floorboards but these were painted black. On the far side of the room was another window. The only object in the entire room stood before that window; an old rusty metal telescope. "What the..." was all Robin could say as she and Roami stared at the telescope then at each other. Moving towards it, Roami looked through the foggy lens afraid of what he might see. He was

201

shocked to find he saw exactly what he had seen at Thister's penthouse; nothing. All that could be seen was the city and the water's surface just above the tower. Nothing more. "Looks like another dead end..." Robin said with a sigh. "I'm not too sure about that... we'll talk about this all later." Roami said as he saw Mirub finally enter the room with a sigh. "I did not want you two to see this... It is the old Deposer's workroom... Please... Please just leave. You will only bring trouble on yourselves..." she said as she motioned for them to leave the room. They did as she bid. Mirub closed the door behind them before placing the broken lock back on it. "He does not know that I broke the lock and have seen what hides behind that door." She said more to herself than to the children. "Who?" Roami asked hoping she would let loose her biggest secret. Looking up Mirub realized she had spoken her thoughts aloud. "Please...just go..." She repeated the words pleadingly. "Who knows when he will come back to visit... you cannot be here or... he will make you pay. No one must know he visits me... it would destroy him." She said a bit frantically. "Okay, okay, we will go." Robin promised to appease her. She did not want to be the cause of the beautiful woman's pain. It was apparent she had already lived through more pain than she let on. Robin knew, better than anyone, that just because someone did not appear wounded did not mean they had not been through a lifetime of emotional warfare. Before they turned to leave a thought stopped Robin in her tracks. "Wait. We'll go now but first let us open your chain; the same way you broke the doors lock. It will still look like you're chained but you will be able to leave once we give you a signal that we have found a way out of the city. Is that okay?" Robin looked Mirub straight in the eye praying she would agree to the plan. "Okay... I guess that could work." Mirub said. Smiling Robin took the pick she still held and walked Mirub over to the chair. Robin motioned for her to place her foot on the chair then leaned down to pick the lock. When the metal fell from her ankle Mirub sighed with release. "Oh wow... that feels so much better..." She looked overjoyed as she rubbed at her tender ankle. "Right so when 'he' comes back just clasp it back on like this but without locking it and he'll never know the difference. When we find a way out of here we will come back to get you, okay?" Robin showed her how to clasp the chain back on then handed her back the metal pick. "Robin we should be heading back to Thister's now or he'll begin to wonder." Roami said. Nodding Robin smiled back at Mirub. They said their goodbyes and made their way out of the tower the same way they had entered it. Once back outside Roami closed the trap door and Robin quickly worked to cover it with sand. They took note as to where the trapdoor was located so they could easily find it again if necessary. Luck was once more on their side as they saw the Mubbin workers were just beginning to return to the forest to pick the Flobbin nuggets. As they walked past the forest in an effort to seem inconspicuous Robin stopped a pair of the light green workers and said, "Hi, we just noticed this tower and was wondering what it was for. There is no way to get in." She said with a lost look on her face. "Ah, sky-ones!" The two Mobbins bowed quickly then one responded, "The tower is nothing more than an old relic. Some people even believe it is....well... haunted. It is best you two stay far away from it. Everyone else in the city does." With that said they bowed to Robin and Roami once more then continued walking towards their work in the forest. Robin and Roami made their way back towards Thister's home. While thinking over what they had just been told Robin rolled her eyes and muttered, "Haunted my behind..." Roami just chuckled, happy to see that despite their potentially dangerous circumstances and depressing realizations Robin had still managed to hold on to her Robin-like sense of humor. He could only hope the events of the near future would not kill her spirit altogether... *** A short time later the two found themselves sitting across from Thister at his dinner table enjoying a superb meal of Rainbow Dust pie and Briggle-Brag Soup.

When the meal had been brought in by a handful of servants, Robin had gaped in amazement. She had never seen such colorful food or mouth watering smells. Her stomach had growled in agreement and she nearly gushed with joy upon placing the first few spoonfuls to her lips. Apparently there was at least one reason to stay in Fitz if the riddle never presented itself. Robin wished she could take some spoonfuls of the Fitzian food in her pocket for keepsakes once they returned back to Source One. She chuckled slightly at her own incredibly silly thoughts. For the greater part of the meal Robin continually kicked at Roami under the table. He knew why she was being annoying but decided to ignore her nudging. During a private conversation the two had had earlier that day, Robin had asked him to ask Thister what the glass windows and telescopes on the top floor were used for. When her kicks became uncomfortably painful, Roami glared and grunted at Robin but she only smiled back in response. Thister was speaking enthusiastically about the next day's birthing process when Robin finally got the gall to ask him. "So, Thister. I must tell you. We accidently pushed the "up" button in the elevator yesterday and found ourselves on the very top floor of your home. I know you asked that we not leave the main floor but it truly was an accident and for that we are sorry. While we were up there we noticed a few telescopes.. What are they for exactly?" She asked innocently. Thister appeared flustered by both the question and the topic. "I-I-I... That is... I thought I told you two not to go up there! Oh my, oh my... this could be a problem..." He looked as if he were thinking something over in his head before continuing, "But, well... I guess at this point you two are one of us now so it wouldn't do to keep this from you. Especially not with a major birthing only hours away. Yes, I suppose it is time!" He said this all aloud and yet more to himself than his two visitors. When he had worked it all out in his head, Thister finally looked at his guests and continued, "I use the telescopes for Birthings. It is my job as city Disposer to conduct the Birthings and discard the garbage if necessary." He said and began to fidget uncomfortably in his seat. "Um... garbage?" Robin prodded. "Yes, I must ensure garbage is discarded of properly and need a high vantage point to do so. I help discard the villager's garbage, you see." He smiled at her once more. "Oh... okay." Robin said with a confused look on her face. "You discard the villager's garbage. Right but... but what about the royals' garbage. Who discards that?" Robin asked. Thister looked absolutely shocked by her question. "No one, of course! There is no need. The royals' do not make garbage." Thister replied with some level of agitation. "Yes, well I must bid you two goodnight as I have a busy day ahead of me."

Smiling at the two he bid them good evening and went to bed for the night.   Robin and Roami just stared at one another in disbelief, "That is what he calls an answer? That is as much a riddle as this world is. Oh no Roami...we're never going to get out of here!" Robin said and let her head fall against the table in exasperation.   "Well, I guess we will just have to wait for tomorrow. This birthing event seems to be the answer to everything. I can just feel it. Look at how excited the people are about it. And don't forget how vague they all are when we ask for details about the actual process." Roami took Robin by the hand and led her out of the dining room.   "I think we need to get our rest tonight and pay close attention to this event. It may hold some important clues." Roami said as they made their way towards their rooms.   The two found later that night that they could hardly sleep. When they did finally enter dreamland they each had strange visions of garbage cans, telescopes and crazy Mantu racing towards them while screaming at the top of his lungs.   Robin woke up with the most disturbing image of all; a scary dump trunk with gnashing teeth chasing them across the city. Across the large green trunk written in angry black lettering was the word, "Disposer". *****   Robin was awakened by the sound of a shrill bell resounding throughout the city. It was so loud she hat woken with a jump and wondered if perhaps it was the signal for the apocalypse. "Get up Robin! Get up! They are beginning the birthing process for Boonie!" Roami rushed into Robin's room while pulling on a dark green velvet shirt in haste. Seeing his bare muscular blue chest; Robin jumped out of bed, tripped over her slippers and crashed into a nearby wooden dresser. "Oh my goodness! Roami, please... for the love of all that is holy! Please don't wake me up like that ever again!" She screeched as she picked herself up from the floor and ushered Roami back out of her room. "Let me get dressed and I'll be out in a sec." She said while still rubbing at her eyes. Once he was gone and the door was shut she took a look at the silk outfit laid out on her bed. Today's colors were green and purple. Her velvet shirt and woven pants were royal purple and her miniskirt was light green. She wore the same green sandals she had worn since their first day in Fitz. While she was rushed she could not help but fill her trouser pockets with a few Flob Nuggets and other important souvenirs. Robin could not fight the odd feeling that something epic would occur today. When Robin finished dressing moments later, Roami was waiting for her just outside her door with a frown on his face. He wore a green top and dark purple trousers. All of their garments were sprinkled with emerald crescents as today's birthing was considered a huge event. "Did you say Boonie? It's Boonies' birthing? Oh my god how exciting! Oh no, it's probably over by now. Come on quick, let's go!" Grabbing his hand Robin raced out the door. She had a way of making it seem as if it were him and not her who had made them late. They did not take the waiting buggy but ran towards the city center as they were just a few blocks away. When they reached the spot where they could see a large crowd growing, they stopped. They were delighted to spot their good friend Boonie among the mob of strangers. He stood in the center of the semi-circle of Mubbins, Royals and average Fitzians and looked visibly nervous. The event was being held in a small park amidst a mini-mall. Several streets lined with shops ran in four separate directions from their current spot. The roads were all paved in red concrete. The small park was the only exception and was littered with young trees, as with all the trees in Fitz they had green trunks and purple leaves. Wooden benches for the casual shopper, ran around the border of the small park area. In the very center was a circle of red sand which was piled up into a small hill. This pinnacle was where Boonie stood for all to see. Boonie's tall lithe light green figure could easily be seen from some distance. When it seemed everyone of importance had arrived he sat cross-legged atop the small circular mound of deep red sand. While everyone wore their usual Fitzian garments Boonie wore an odd pitch black gown. It looked very much like a judge's robes or a

Muumuu to Robin. It had long, flaring sleeves and hung with no shape at all. He had it bunched up at his sides and the dark fabric fanned out around his seated figure. Boonie's eyes closed. It appeared he was meditating or deep in thought.

Robin and Roami pushed their way towards the front of the crowd and stood in front of their friend. They both beamed with happiness. "So, uh... how do we know when it's going to begin?" Robin whispered impatiently after a few moments of silence. "I mean, his stomach isn't even all that big. There can't be anything in there bigger than a baseball." "Shh..." Roami shushed her. Before Robin could hit Roami in response a murmur spread throughout the crowd. "It's coming soon I know it! He has that look about him!" Someone in the crowd said aloud. Robin and Roami strained to see if they could see any signs of a baby. "He must have dropped the egg inside the sand already! It'll show itself soon enough!" Someone else yelled. "There! It's there! I see a finger I think!" Robin said as she pointed to the sand surrounding Boonie. Within seconds a small hand lifted from the red sand beneath Boonie. Boonie jumped up when he felt the baby's hand. He got up instantly then stood nervously beside the circle of sand. "Ah!" a scream ripped from the crowd and was mimicked by several others. As they each saw the hand that stuck out of the sand; gasps of horror filled the air. The tiny hand was a deep purple color as opposed to the various shades of green prevalent among the rest of the city dwellers. The hand was followed by an arm and a head as the baby steadily pushed itself out from the ground.   The child's hair was a shocking red color and curled nicely against its face. It was stark naked but unlike any infant Robin had ever seen, it began walking within just mere seconds of its birth.   "Garbage! He's produced common garbage! I knew it!" Someone yelled from behind Robin. She turned to see who would say such a disgusting thing about such a cute baby. Before she could open her mouth to respond to the thoughtless remarks she realized that almost everyone there was screaming out similar comments.   "He's leaving! Boonies going!" Roami cried in astonishment.   "What?" Robin asked as she looked to see Boonie was indeed rushing past the crowd in the general direction of his home. They saw too, that Beenie who had been standing among the crowd was now at his side racing away from the city while crying hysterically.   "What about your baby? Boonie! Beenie, where are you two going?" Robin screamed as she began to run after them. Roami grabbed at Robin's wrist and pulled her back towards him. "Don't. He knows what he is doing. I don't think either he nor Beenie want anyone bringing them back here." He said sadly as the truth hit him.   "But... Roami what about their baby?" Robin asked in astonishment.   "We

211

will take it. We can't let this crowd get to it. Everyone here is glaring at it like it's some sort of monster." Roami said with equal amounts of shock. "I think it may be a little too late for that. They are leading him away!" Robin screamed as she ran after the tiny purple youngster. The small infant's large luminescent gray eyes shown with fright as it was dragged from its birthing spot. The poor child was being pulled towards the base of the large Nommo tree by two large dark green soldiers dressed in their traditional emerald armor. "What are you planning to do to him? He is just a baby!" Roami yelled as he raced past the crowd then quickly grabbed the child from the soldiers. Before the soldiers could react, Roami had the baby safe in his arms. Robin rushed to stand by Roami's side then faced the soldiers and the crowd of Fitzians with an angry glare on her face. She looked at her feet searching frantically for something to use as a weapon. While she had been premature in looking for weapons in the past, she was pretty sure this time she would definitely need to kick some serious butt. Just then a loud bell sounded across the city. Moments later, Thister appeared from within the crowd. "It appears we have yet another piece of garbage to dispose of. I am so sorry you all had to witness this, my dear people. But do not worry. I am ready and willing to do my job as Desposer. Please my dear guests; our beloved Sky-Ones be so kind as to hand it over so that we may discard of this filth appropriately." Thister moved towards his two guests who now held the naked child in a protective stance. "No! Back up! I am sorry Thister. We thank you for your hospitality but we cannot sit here quietly while you destroy this innocent child. Why exactly are you ready to kill this little baby anyway?" Roami asked although he was almost sure he already knew the answer. "That should be plain enough. Do you not see its purple skin? It is not one of us. It is common refuse and must be discarded of at once!" Thister looked annoyed at having his job delayed by none other than his own house guests. Roami stared at Thister in disbelief but had his suspicions confirmed. "This is unbelievable! This child should not be killed just because it is not the same color as the rest of you. Believe me it is wrong to judge something by its color. Just because this baby is purple it is still Boonie and Beenie's child. He should be allowed to live his life." Roami said loudly for the entire crowd to hear. King Hurtz, who had heretofore quietly stood among the crowd now stepped forward in his emerald encrusted robes. He glared at the kids and bellowed, "Please hand that thing over now Sky-Ones or you will share its fate! We would hate to see you go for we think you may have been a sign from the heavens. However, we will do what we must to keep order in our world. Make your decision

213

now!" The king said as he stepped before the entire crowd with his tiny chest puffed up. "We have already made our decision. We will not allow you to destroy this innocent baby. There is no other logical choice to make." Roami said and Robin nodded her head in confirmation. "Okay, so be it. Guards! Take the Sky-Ones and this... garbage and send them all up the great tree now! When they reach the surface they will be obliterated into tiny pieces just like all the rest of the trash!" The King yelled. The Guards who were each well over six feet tall and quite large in girth, moved forward menacingly. Grabbing hold of the Robin and Roami's arms, the kings' men began to push them towards the base of the large purple trunk of the Nommo tree. Before the guards could push them towards the series of wooden steps constructed into the side of the tree trunk a voice within the crowd piped up, "Stop it at once! Leave the sky-ones alone!" Everyone turned to see who would dare speak out against the king's edict. Robin and Roami also turned to get a good look at their champion. There in the center of the crowd of tall and lithe green faces of varying shades stood one even taller. She nearly towered over even some of the kings guards. "Mirub!" Robin said happily. "You made it!" Roami looked at Mirub, happy that she was there as well. He had been afraid they would be forced away before he could explain to Mirub why they could not keep their

214

promise to save her. "Who is this?" The King sputtered, his face turning nearly purple with emotion. Roami looked at him and noticed there was some level of guilt just lurking beneath the surface. Mirub spoke up, "You know full well who I am! Don't dare lie to these people, don't dare lie to your wife, and don't dare lie to yourself!" Her fiery mane of hair swirled about her making her look like an avenging warrior princess. She wore the same gray dress they had seen her in while in the tower. The bottom, however, was now reddened from dragging against the ground. "I am the one without a name. The one taken from her home as a babe; the one too beautiful for her own good; the one her own people shunned out of jealousy; the one whom they called the Tower Ghost... the one you made your unwilling slave all these many years King Hurtz!" She said this with such anger Robin was sure she would attack the king. However, Mirub kept her cool and did nothing more than glare. "How dare you, you common piece of Mobbin trash!" The King's wife stepped forward. She was just as short and squat as he was and looked as if she could have easily been his cousin. They looked almost identical. The Queen wore a dress and robes of green velvet weighted down by hundreds of green gemstones. Her straight fuchsia hair was pulled up in a severe bun atop her head. Her dark green skin sagged with wrinkles. Robin and Roami

215

had seen her in passing from time to time. However, the quiet women seemed to stand demurely in her husbands' shadow so well they could not even recall her name. "I dare because I can. I am no longer anyone's slave; no longer anyone's possession! I will go with the sky-ones and away from this ugly society. I want nothing more to do with this city and the evil that occurs here. I have seen all of your deepest darkest secrets from my tower window and I am sick...so very sick and tired of it all..." She said sadly. Her anger seemed to die out as she made her way to stand at Robin and Roami's side. "Yes, well go! Go with your lies and silly accusations! Anyone who would think I would stoop so low as to be with a Mubbin must truly be out of their mind. You and that crazed old disposer Mantu can rot for all I care. You're both delusional traitors! Guards, send them up the tree and to their deaths!" King Hurtz bellowed loudly waking everyone from their shock. The guards moved to stand between the King and the outsiders; blocking their way and making the tree their only choice. The three large soldiers then began to prod Robin, Roami and Mirub's shoulders forward. The young baby who was already bewildered by everything that had occurred since its birth, finally seemed to react to the insanity. He began crying as his little shoulders were also prodded by the guards' large hands. Roami turned to see Thister running back to his home while yelling something about confirming 'the removal' from his watch tower. When they reached the base of the trunk Roami placed the child between himself and Robin so that they both could hold each of his purple hands securely. Mirub took up the rear. From this vantage point, they could now see the small wooden steps running along the tree trunk to the top of the water. Apparently, they were meant to go up those steps as the guards were brusquely pushing them towards just that. Robin and Roami obliged and began walking up the steps as they knew fighting the large hulking mammoth sized men would be useless. "Don't worry little one, we will find a way out of this somehow. Don't be afraid of those meanies." Robin said soothingly. She smiled reassuringly for the benefit of the baby then glared at one of the guards as he shoved at her shoulder. "Do you have any ideas Robin?" Roami whispered worriedly. "Nope, none whatsoever." Robin said sadly. "Well, unless we can figure out the riddle to this world in the next few seconds... I guess we're dead." Roami stated the obvious. "What are you two whispering about? What riddle?" Mirub asked in confusion. They ignored her as they were too busy looking for an escape plan and just moments away from their imminent deaths. "Yes, well... I don't think that would work either. If we solved the riddle we'd be free but what about Mirub and Boonie's baby?" She said sadly. "Oh, yes. I wasn't thinking. Who knows if they would be able to come with us back to Source One?" Roami said.

"Move it or lose it!" One of the guards yelled at them as they continued walking up the steps. "Walk quickly! We all have places to go and things to do. You have to die and we have warm meals waiting for us at home." One of the guards said and ended with a few huge guffaws. "Oh, Roami! I am so sorry. I don't have a clever plan to share with you. I can't think of anything but walking up this tree to our deaths." Robin said as tears formed in her large brown eyes. "Don't be sorry. We are doing the right thing. We could not stand by and let this poor innocent baby see such a horrible fate. If we had we would be just as bad as the rest of those people down there." Roami said as he quickened his steps up the tree and tried desperately to think of an ingenious plan for all of their survival. "Okay, Sky-Ones. This is as far as we go, keep walking and don't you dare look back. You made your decision and now you must die for it." The largest guard with the hairy fuchsia colored uni-brow said as he shoved the group forward to the edge of the watery sky. Fear shone in all three of their eyes and before another moment passed Roami stepped forward, "I will go first. Robin, while I am broken to bits and they all watch, push the guards down the stairs and race down the tree as quick as possible. You may be able to outrun

218

them and get away from the city. I know it's not a great plan but it's worth a try." Roami whispered into Robins ears. Robin began to cry bitterly. "No. No, you stupid, stupid boy! I won't do it! I won't let you die!" Roami stared into Robin's eyes silently pleading with her to be sensible. Turning abruptly he began to walk through the surface of the water above them. His face was stoic and his steps were sure. "Please help us get out of this alive." He whispered under his breath softly. Just as Roami's head surfaced he tensed up waiting for his body to break into a million pieces. He guessed the sensation would feel like being sliced and diced by a meat grinder. His legs kept moving him higher and yet the slicing pain never came. In fact, nothing happened at all. Roami's brow furrowed in confusion. He continued to ascend the stairs only to feel Robin's hand grab his as she too ascended the stairs and broke the surface of the water with the young baby in her hands. "No!" Roami shouted as he realized that by following him she was on the verge of killing herself. He was just about to give her a piece of his mind and turned around to confront her. Suddenly he was struck by something. Staring at her beautiful brown face dripping with droplets of water, he realized she had not been chopped to bits but was staring at him in amazement. "We're alive. We're all still alive Roami!" She screeched and hugged him to her. The baby giggled joyously and the three pushed themselves to continue up the steps of the Nommo tree to give Mirub room to fully surface as well. "Yes, of course we're all alive. What were you two going on about?" Mirub looked at them as if they had lost their minds. "Well...just like the people below we thought we would be killed once we hit the surface." Robin explained while wiping the water from her face. "Yes, well. I've been in the tower long enough to know that that's just a myth. Once I finally got access to the locked disposer's room in the tower I was able to see through the telescope. The babies they banished did not die at the surface but continued on. To what? I don't know but I know they all kept on moving onward..." She said as she too wiped the water from her beautiful face and arched her head back to look up at the top of the tree. She quieted as her private thoughts consumed her. Robin and Roami took in what Mirub had shared then focused back on one another. "But what does this mean?" Roami said to Robin as he led the way higher to the heights of yet another sky. He tried his best not to look down at the endless body of water surrounding them. "These steps in the tree were not here when we first came into this world, I'm almost sure of it. Isn't that odd? What do you suppose is up there at the very top?" Robin asked. Before Roami could respond Robin heard a loud splash in the water below them. Jerking in surprise she turned around to see if Mirub was okay. She was not. She had fallen several feet and into the sea water. "Oh no!" Robin screamed out. "Roami we have to go back down and get her!" She turned around and started back down the steps towards the water's surface. Roami pulled the baby in his arms securely and turned to follow Robin when Mirub yelled, "No!" They both froze at her scream. She was leaning over a broken purple branch of the Nommo Tree and using it to keep herself buoyant. As Roami's feet slowed to a halt he realized something was not as it seemed. "How did that branch get down there..." He wondered aloud. "I broke it off... I did not fall...by mistake." Mirub looked up at them; her wet hair plastered against her minty white face. Her large green eyes stared into the distance sadly. "Can you explain why you'd purposely do something like that? Now we have to go down there and-" Robin was about to go into a full out tirade when Mirub interrupted her again. "Dear Robin, there is no place for me... The City of Fitz was no home for me and I could not return there even if I wanted to. But this place you are going now... I know...deep in my heart...I would not belong..." She said as she pushed her legs behind her and began to drift away from the tree; away from Robin and Roami. "Believe me when I say this; There are not many places a beautiful woman with a good heart can call home..." She added in explanation when she realized Robin

221

and Roami still appeared shocked by her decision. "What are you talking about? What place are we are going to? We don't even know where we are headed...Let's just follow the steps up past the clouds and we'll figure something out...eventually." Robin knew even to her own ears this sounded like a weak argument. "No, dear Robin and honorable Roami... I know what you do not... For me there was never a place I could call home... at least none that I know of. This is the curse of all that is beautiful in the world of man...any...world of man... I must go elsewhere...either I'll find a place that is safe for me or... I'll die alone. Either way I'll finally be at peace. Do not argue and do not try to stop me... It is what it must be..." With that said she maneuvered herself around, facing away from them and looking towards a horizon of only reddish sky and murky gray water. Holding onto her small branch Mirub pushed her long sleek legs out behind her and dove towards the unknown. "Mirub! No Mirub please come back! We can fix this! We can help!" Robin cried with tears spilling from her eyes and wetting her already water drenched cheeks. "Robin... Robin! It's okay..." Roami came down a step and grabbed her to his chest to calm her down. The small baby wiggled between them and hugged Robin as well. His soft chubby purple hands wiped at her eyes and somehow seemed to make some of the pain go away. "We cannot fight her.

This is her choice and who knows... maybe it actually is the best choice for her..." He said while still hugging Robin to him tightly. Robin hiccupped and ceased her cries. "Oh Roami... I hope she'll be okay... I really can't think about... I mean... what if..." She did not know how to finish her fearful thoughts. "Don't worry about 'what if'... We have to believe she will find what she is looking for... Come now... We have to keep going. We have the baby to think of now..." Roami pulled the toddler securely against him and started walking up the steps. He turning slightly to ensure Robin was following him. "Keep going where... what is up there anyway?" Robin asked while dutifully following Roami's lead. Every now and then she could not help but look out at the gray water as Mirub's figure drifted farther and farther away, getting smaller with each moment that passed. "I don't know... Guess we will find out in a few moments. But please Robin, let me go up first to test it out and make sure it is safe for you and the baby. Okay?" Roami asked. "Oh... okay. But don't be too long or I will follow to make sure you are alright." She said this as they reached the large green leaves of the Nommo. They immediately found it almost impossible to ascend further as the leaves and thick swirls of gray clouds made a sort of barrier. Roami stopped and looked down at Robin and the baby one last time. "Okay, you two wait here please." He said then turned to continue climbing until he disappeared into the cluster of huge succulent green leaves and clouds of gray mist. "Right... Okay, please don't panic Robin..." Robin whispered to herself. The little baby grabbed her face with its pudgy hands and planted a kiss on Robin's nose. Robin giggled and held the baby even tighter. "How could anyone get rid of something so precious?" She said to the baby as she lightly tapped its purple nose with her finger then kissed its cheek.

"Alright, I will give him ten more seconds then we're following, okay baby?" Robin began counting. "One, one thousand-" Roami yelled out to her, "Hey, Robin! You won't believe what's up here!" She saw Roami's lean blue hand appear from within the green leaves. He beckoned her with a twist of his hand. Robin rushed up the remaining stairs and fought her way through the huge leaves of the tree. When she and the baby finally surfaced at the top, she opened her eyes to the oddest sight imaginable. It was undoubtedly, the very last thing she had expected to see...

CHAPTER 9

All Robin could see were green leaves and dense white mists as she climbed higher. The intensity of the clouds grew with each step heavenward and she could not help but cough as her throat filled with the alien substance. Robin surged forward and quickened her steps to get the poor baby out of the uncomfortable smokiness. When she finally reached the end of the stairs and stood on a hard platform of leaves and yellow dirt, she nearly stumbled back down the tree in amazement. "You've got to be kidding me..." Robin's mouth was agape with surprise. She could barely walk straight and proved as much with her next step. She nearly tripped into Roami's side. Roami steadied Robin and took the small baby from her arms to ensure its safety. He gave Robin time to get her bearings. "What the heck is this..." Robin said while looking about her in wonder. The sky was still red but as she looked up higher she saw it gradually turned a deep purplish hue. A rainbow of multicolor lights splayed across the sky. They looked like stars but each was a different color, Robin had never seen the sky look more beautiful than at that very moment.   A whole new world had been hidden away at the top of the tree. They stood at the end of the stairwell, with leaves and mounds of wispy white clouds gathering at their feet.   While the sky was clear from their current vantage point it was all but hidden several feet ahead of them where something even more spectacular stood.   A large city of mammoth sized buildings shot out of the ground and seemed to nearly conquer the skies. The magnificent sky-scrapers made of every imaginable color of stone, were littered all over the place. Each was taller than any Robin had ever seen; even in New York City!   In her mind she envisioned how this world must look from a bird's eye view. It was essentially, a large flat expanse of dark forests with black leaved trees, miles of barren gold colored plateaus then in the center of it all a rainbow city with monstrous sized buildings which blocked out the sky's light.

Robin surmised that the land they now stood on, must be drifting somehow in the sky. She imagined it looked like a large land mass, suspended in the air and hidden by flurries of white clouds. Since they had not seen it from the water's surface she guessed it was only clearly visible to those who walked upon it. Blue street lamps; glowing brightly, were sprinkled throughout the city. Although it was very far away Robin could also just make out a dark forest surrounding the city at every side. At the moment, Robin and Roami had little time to peruse their new environment in more detail. Someone cleared their throat to warn them their immediate attention was needed elsewhere.

The two quickly realized they were the object of intense curiosity. They looked to see a growing crowd of people leaving the city and making their way towards them. When the natives stood just a few feet away they stared at the newcomers intently. Robin and Roami looked back with just as much inquisitiveness. Robin looked at the people more closely and noticed to her surprise that they looked exactly like the green people of Fitz except instead of green their skin was a beautiful plum color and their hair... thankfully was not fuchsia. It was at that moment, Robin realized just how tired she had become of seeing fuchsia hair. Before her were heads covered in hair of every color of the rainbow. The styles were just as diverse as some sported curly, straight, kinky and frazzled hair.

Their eyes were also a myriad of colors; gray, brown, blue, orange, violent, green and black. Just like most of the people of Fitz they were all very tall, lanky and were definitely an awesome sight to behold. Each adult stood well over six feet tall but unlike the people of Fitz they did not slump or slouch while walking to appear smaller than they actually were. They stood up straight, proud and tall.   While both sides continued to stare at one another, one male stepped out from amongst the group and spoke directly to the trio standing before them with looks of amazement.

"Welcome strange ones! We will take the child as he belongs here with his own kind. There is a family among us without children who have waited for quite some time for one to call their own. Mika and Tika please come forward and welcome your new son. What will you name him?" Before Robin or Roami could protest the small purple child was taken from their grasp by a pair of large but gentle hands.   "Oh..." Robin breathed in sharply, feeling as if a part of her was being snatched away with the abrupt parting.

"Can you believe this?" Roami said with an incredulous look on his face. He shook his head back and forth, which tussled his curly wet hair. "The Fitzians must have sent all their purple babies up the Nommo Tree thinking that they would be disintegrated when they touched the sky. To them the choppy currents at the waters' surface made it look like they were being broken to bits. Thankfully, they were completely wrong about it. It appears all those poor discarded children started their own society up here. They did not die but were... reborn here in a sense."

"Wow..." Robin stood beside him listlessly with her mouth agape. She really could not find the right words to express the overwhelming thoughts and feelings racing through her head at that very moment. Just then an errant thought came to her, "Do you think Mirub knew about this? She said something cryptic once...about rebirth... I think she must have seen the babies past the surface time and time again. That's why she was not afraid of dying when we..." Robin spoke more to herself than to Roami as she tried to put all the pieces together. "Yes... and maybe that's why she decided not to come here...she knew...what we might find here..." Roami too looked as if he were being swamped with thoughts. However, now was definitely not the time for inner reflection; the two realized as they looked at the multitude of rainbow eyes staring directly at them. "We will name this beautiful one... Brifton." A pretty purple woman with long straight blue hair said as she held Boonie's baby gently in her arms. Her golden colored eyes alighted on her husband who had a shock of curly silver hair and sparkling blue eyes. He stood beside her and tousled Brifton's bright red hair playfully. "Have you any objections to this, strange ones?" The short purple man who had spoken initially piped up again. His words brought the growing crowd's attention back towards the brown and blue colored beings standing before them. The boisterous man was nearly as short as their old host, Thister. He wore a brown silk business suit with a pink silk shirt beneath the suit jacket. His shoes were black and shiny and his wavy hair looked like freshly spun gold. Although he did not wear a single jewel or adornment, his attitude along with the piercing look in his large green eyes made it obvious he was someone with considerable power in this society. The air nearly crackled with tension as the two groups sized one another up. Neither could be sure the other was not or would not soon become a serious threat of some sort. Robin took a moment to take in their style of dress. Everyone seemed ridiculously overdressed. All the men wore identical silk business suits of various colors and the shiny black shoes seemed to be uniform among everyone in attendance. The women wore short-sleeved shirts, silk vests and either long or short, silk business skirts. Their black shoes looked nearly identical to the mens' except theirs had a very short square high heel.

Robin could not help but hope she and Roami would not have to do as the 'romans' in this particular world. She had never been one to don a suit. At least not comfortably; she cringed inwardly at the thought of having to wear one. That was not the only thing that worried her. Roami knew something was bothering Robin when he saw her lips slowly make their way into a pout. That was her signal that she was peeved at something or someone. At the moment he did not care to ask her what was so upsetting but she was keen to inform him anyway. Robin pulled Roami closer to her and whispered, "You know, I actually kinda liked being called 'the sky-ones'. This 'strange ones' business, though, is really not working for me..." Roami sighed and pinched Robin, "Can you just focus on the life changing situation we are currently faced with right now, Robin? Please? Who cares what they call us?" Turning back towards the crowd Roami replied, "If they will take care of him and cherish him, then no, we have no complaints. He was abandoned by his blood parents and needs a loving family to take him in." The leader of the group spoke up again, "Yes, believe me, he will have all that and more here in our home; the town of Wongswited. We heard the bell of the water world resound and knew another of ours would be sent up. However, we did not expect such strange guests to accompany the newcomer." He looked at them pointedly then smiling a bit stiffly added, "Do not worry, unlike the nasty people of Fitz, we are good to outsiders. You two will find your stay here a pleasant one." He smiled again but suddenly a thought dawned on him. "Oh my! I'm sorry. I have yet to properly introduce myself." He chuckled then added, "I am the king of Wongswited; King Philtu. We welcome you, oh strange ones. You may live here with Mika, Tika and their new son Brifton until you find your place here among us or elsewhere." With that said the king smiled at the group at large, nodded his head toward their two new guests then turned to leave. Robin and Roami watched him make his way back towards the city. He was surrounded by four massive men who were apparently his guards. Each wore matching blue suits with black undershirts. They flanked him to ensure his security. Everyone watched King Philtu leave. The crowd was silent in a show of respect. Amazingly, it did not take long for the king to reach his destination. The royal entourage stopped right in front of one of the first buildings at the edge of the city. It was a grand structure with elaborate geometrical designs cut within the hot pink marble facade. There were too many windows to count, all of which were made of clear glass and were encased in golden frames. Apparently the actual front of the palace faced inside the town and could not be seen from their current vantage. What they did see was a dark green emergency exit door strategically facing the town's entrance and the treetop portal. Robin guessed the King liked to be one of the first responders when newcomers arrived via the Nommo Tree. However, it was not the intricate designs that made his home truly spectacular. "Woa! Is that their City Hall?" Robin asked aloud as she took it all in. "No, of course not. That is the King's Palace." Someone in the crowd said with pride. "You've got to be kidding me..." Robin said and blinked to ensure she was seeing correctly. The building seemed to stand well over four hundred stories high! "Wait..." Robin looked deeply confused about something. "What is it Robin?" Roami whispered. "The king called this a town not a city. I know a city when I see one and with buildings that tall... this is definitely a city..." Robin muttered aside to Roami. "It is absolutely amazing how high the buildings are constructed. I have never seen anything like this in Source One. I thought maybe you would be used to this; being from the large city you come from back on earth..." Roami whispered in awe. "Nope, not even close. These things nearly block out the sky..." Robin's head was held back as she looked in awe at the massive constructions littered throughout the city they mistakenly called a 'town'. The male called 'Mika' overheard Roami and smiling said, "We Wongswiteds love tall buildings. Wait until you see our home. It is not as grand as the king's home but stands one hundred and fifteen feet tall. We hope you will like it dear Strange Ones." "I'm sure we will be happy with it. Thank you so much for taking in little Brifton. Oh, and us too." Robin said gratefully. Robin took Roami's hand and squeezed it, and glared at him a bit, "Hello? Thank them." She mouthed. Roami had been deep in thought and blinking he quickly muttered aloud, "Thank You." for the couple to hear then lowered his voice to speak to Robin in private. "I do not think we should trust and thank these people too soon. I have a feeling that something is wrong here. Something just does not feel right to me..." Roami whispered. Many of the people had had their fill of the newcomers. Most of the crowd members had started to disperse back towards the town. They made their way to the bright golden stone pathway that led directly to the main entrance of Wongswited. "Come now, we will take you to our humble home. Do not worry, it is not too far a walk from here, Strange Ones." Mika's wife, Tika said as she held little Brifton in her arms. She and her husband began to walk amidst their fellow people as they all made their way from the tree top entrance and into the very heart of Wongswited. Robin and Roami followed slowly pondering what novel wonders they would discover in yet another new world. Robin gawked at her surroundings as they walked. She also stared at the backs of their hosts in an effort to determine if they were 'good' people and would not end up being quacks like Thister the evil Disposer.   The tall, lean couple held Brifton as if he had always been a part of their family. Robin was happy to see there was a place here for the awesome little purple baby with the sweet disposition. To think the Fitzians had wanted to kill something so precious; seemed more and more outrageous each time she set eyes on him. "Thank you again for making Brifton your own... You don't know how much this means to me and Roami." Robin said with true feeling. Robin and Roami jumped slightly when Mika glanced back and yelled out for them to hear, "It is no problem at all! We Wongswited do sometimes have children of our own but from time to time find that a young one is sent from the water world below and... We just feel it is our duty to care for them. Tika and I were not blessed with a child so-" Before Mika could finish his thought, Tika made a choked sound and stumbled a bit.   "Are you okay?" Robin asked with concern. She took Tika's elbow to ensure she and Brifton did not fall. Once Tika was sure on her feet, Robin ensured she had a tight grip of the small baby in her arms then back away to give Tika room to breathe.   Whereas the ground near the tree had been littered with the large green Nommo Tree leaves, the path towards Wongswited was just several feet of flat, carefully laid, golden stones. Alongside the main road on either side were acres of barren gold dirt. There were no plants, no trees, just a few scattered rocks and flat ground. Robin checked to see if maybe Tika had stumbled over a rock but found nothing to explain her near fall. "Yes, oh yes... I'm okay. I am sorry. I don't know what came over me." Tika said shakily. As they made their way through the Town entryway, the path gradually became golden cement. Up above them hung a Purple sign with gold lettering which read, "Welcome to Wongswited". Robin smiled with excitement. She could not wait to see what kinds of delights this world had to offer. Once again she felt like a little baby exploring, testing out and experiencing the world for the very first time. As they walked under the sign and into the town she immediately noticed two things. The first, was that the atmosphere within the town was very dark as the buildings blocked out the sky. Second, was the lack of transportation. "Too bad they don't have water buggies or cars here. We wouldn't have to walk... Seems odd to have such a large city and no means of quick transport..." Robin looked around to see if anyone was doing anything other than walking. "Wait.. Look there; see that stream of water... looks like a narrow water channel running through the streets. I bet it goes throughout the entire city. What do you think it's for?" Robin asked Roami. She hoped against hope it was nothing as diabolical as the gray "Mobbin Only" paths back in Fitz. Looking around she noted there were no light-skinned purple or lavender people walking about so it was safe to say there was no ugly cast system here in Wongswited. Everyone seemed to look similar so there could be no obvious division of classes. Robin sighed happily. Thankfully the banished children of Fitz had not repeated the sins of their fathers. They both eyed the tiny water channel as they passed it from a closer vantage point. Roami was about to say he did not know what it was for but before he could utter the words its purpose became apparent to them. Right before their eyes, a man in a red business suit dropped a blue wooden skateboard onto the stream of water and glided smoothly down the small canal. When the man made it to his destination he hopped off the stream of water and lifted the board in his hands. Roami noticed there were chips of purple gemstone embedded on the underside of the flat piece of wood. "Well, guess that mystery is solved." Roami looked over at Robin and winked. "Seems like many things here are unlike the city of Fitz..." Roami mused. "Roami look... There are tunnels all over the city. What do you think they're for?" She whispered as she stared at the dark purple brick tunnels now surrounding them in three separate directions. "I don't know but I guess we're about to find out. There are only three ways to go from here and each is covered by a tunnel." Roami said while taking Robin's hand. She enjoyed the feel of his warm skin against hers in this protective gesture. Whereas the 'old' Robin would never have allowed him to hold her hand or show her any measure of care; the new Robin was not as standoffish. She enjoyed the feeling of being part of something more than just herself. Mika and Tika noticed their guest's hesitation as they stood at the crossroad. Laughing Mika spoke up, "Do not be afraid Strange Ones. These tunnels are a common and necessary part of life in the town of Wongswited. As you've noticed it is very dark in the city and we don't get much light from the red Planet Yur during the day. We have therefore devised a way to harness this light from Yur into special stones which line the ceilings of these tunnels. These crystals are called Akwo stones." Smiling he motioned for Robin and Roami to follow him into the tunnel at the far left. Roami walked ahead of Robin to ensure it was indeed safe to enter. As they followed behind the couple and walked through the tunnel's alcove they noticed that while the exterior was made of purple stone the inside glowed with sky blue light. At first it was so bright it seemed to burn their eyes after having walked in the darkness outside for some time. Here again, they saw the same water channels running through both the right and left sides of the tunnel's path. The center of the walkway was paved with the same gold cement as the rest of the streets they had already walked on. To their right people were gliding over the four side by side water channels that moved in one direction. Their shoes somehow allowed them to hover just above the water as it pushed them forward. There were also four identical streams located on the left side of the tunnel which ran in the opposite direction. Robin could tell by the looks on everyone's face that this incredible sight was nothing new to them at all. They spoke to one another, laughed, coughed, yawned or hovered by with their arms across their chests waiting impatiently to get off. Mika and Tika chose to take the middle path of cement and explained their actions, "Like our fellow townspeople we usually take the waterway however, you two do not yet have Wongswited shoes. The bottoms are covered with the precious Hapblo stone which allows us to hover over water. For now we will take the middle path until we get you two a pair. It will take a little longer but we will eventually make it home." Tika smiled reassuringly. Nodding in response, Robin walked while looking all about her in amazement. Up above them the ceiling was encrusted with the large blue Akwo stones which shone with an intense light blue akin to earth's day sky. "Robin, take a look at the walls a little further up." Roami pulled at her hand to bring her attention from the ceiling for a moment. He was sure she would be delighted to see this.

"Wow! It's like Time Square to the tenth power! Where are those images coming from and how are they changing so quickly?" Robin asked aloud. "It seems like it's very similar to the technology the Fitz used to perpetuate the patterns in their curtains and rugs." Roami said this aloud without thinking. Tika and Mika stopped so short that Robin and Roami nearly stumbled into them. Mika looked slightly enraged before covering this extreme emotion with a blank look. "No... that is not it at all Strange One. We here at Wongswited are nothing at all like those barbaric heathens in Fitz!" Mika looked so overwhelmed with his anger he could not easily complete his thought. Seeing this, his wife tried her best to clear the air by adding, "Yes, well Mika is right about that. We are nothing like the Fitzians. Our technology was based on decades of study and development. You will find nothing like this in that backwards city. In fact, we can't even tell you how the technology works; it is so advanced only our top scientists could properly explain it. What we can tell you is that the pictures shown in the Akwo Tunnels; that's what these tunnels are called by the way... Um, well the pictures are of different new fashions, products, events, shows and important news around the town." Tika stared at their guests to gauge their reaction to her words. Robin and Roami just smiled and nodded at her and motioned for them to continue to lead the way. Taking Mika by the arm Tika turned and continued to lead the group out of the Tunnel and back into the darkness of the town's main streets. Robin just gave Roami a pointed look which said, we should be careful what we say around them. He nodded his head in agreement. As they walked on the streets outside of the tunnels they saw that the pathway had now turned into golden cobbled stone streets and wide golden cement sidewalks. On either side of them quaint store fronts, offices and the like were lined up side by side. Street poles and hanging lines, similar to those in Fitz ran some feet above them. Each one was laden with clear glass lanterns holding the same glowing blue gems which lit the Akwo Tunnels.

While Robin noticed a keen similarity between the street lamps here and in Fitz she was sure to keep her mouth shut about it. She feared their hosts would spontaneously burst at even the thought. Robin simply poked Roami, pointedly eyed the lanterns then quirked her eyebrow at him. He rolled his eyes but laughed a little at her silly antics. They continued to walk on dark, dimly lit streets then through a maze of bright blue tunnels. While the walk seemed long it was giving Robin and Roami a great opportunity to see the city and determine what they had gotten themselves into here in Wongswited. "Have you noticed there aren't many trees..." Robin whispered to Roami. "Yes... Oh but wait, I did see a few on that last street. There was a small park near a mall. I think they were tree sculptures..." Roami said as he thought back to what he had seen. "Tree sculptures?" Robin looked at Roami as if he had lost it. "Yes, really Robin I'm serious. Wait... look over there...right in front of that flower shop there are two of them!" He pointed towards the opposite side of the street and Robin noticed two small trees planted in the cement before a pink and purple painted flower shop. "Wow! They're beautiful!" Robin said as she looked at the clear crystal trunks and branches and the leaves which were made of rainbow colored gemstones. When the wind blew they tinkled softly against one another making a sweet melody. "I see what you mean. As beautiful as those are, I doubt they are real..." Robin said as she arched her head backward to look up at the mounds of rough marble buildings stacked so high the sky itself had been blocked out. "Why would anyone want to block out the sky like this... I bet that's why we don't see too many plants or trees..." She whispered near Roami's ear. "Yes, exactly." Roami muttered. He was listening to Robin but was also somewhat entranced by the wisps of white mist that continually found their way across the streets and over their feet. Robin noticed what Roami was staring at a bit fearfully. "Don't worry Roami. I doubt it's like the blue mists of Source One... and even if it was, we've already fallen into a world already...maybe a blue mist right now is just what we need to bring us back to Source One." She had been trying to make him laugh but he looked even more distraught. "Actually..." She thought for a moment, "This mist is probably just the clouds...I mean... we are high in the sky right now. We've been in the city for a while now so you probably forgot where we truly are..." She said with a forced smile. Robin did not like to see Roami sad or disillusioned; it made her angry. She was trying her best to get his spirits back up. "No, I have not forgotten where we are... We are lost." Roami said then clinched his teeth together angrily. "Yes... but we're together." Was all Robin could think to say as she took his hand in the same gesture he always used to soothe her. When his hand was in hers, she squeezed softly. Roami looked down at her then smiled in response. Neither Mika nor Tika spoke for the rest of the walk through the city center towards their home. Robin's eyes were slowly getting adjusted to the darkness above them and the unnatural sky blue glow from the street lamps followed by the intense blue experience of the Akwo Tunnels. The cobbled stone streets also glittered and shimmered so brightly under the false light they made everything shine and glitter. Robin felt as if she were in some sort of fairy land. The obsessively wide streets which could have held eight people side by side; zigzagged in a maze throughout the city that was oddly enough called a 'town'. All the building exteriors were made of rough marble in every shade of the color spectrum. The windows were clear and shiny. However most details of the immaculate construction were lost on her. All Robin could clearly see was the first few floors bathed in blue light, then as she looked higher the buildings seemed to disappear into intense blackness then reappear at the very top. The building tops stood hundreds of feet above them, where the Planet Yur still shone against the rooftops. The stores had large window displays with items Robin had never seen in all her life. She found herself stopping a dozen times to look at an odd flying toy or buzzing food item as they walked towards Mika and Tika's home. For the most part Robin tethered in her curiosity to keep up with their hosts. However, they eventually came across a particular store front display that nearly took her breath away. She just had to stop. It was as if she had no say in the matter.

"Robin!" Roami chided when he realized she was not at his side but a few feet behind him with her nose held up against a storefront window. Her eyes were huge with excitement and her breath was fogging up the glass. On the other side of Robin's upraised nose, sitting on a red velvet display was a large beautiful doll house. Actually it was a doll building to be precise. Unlike the buildings surrounding them it was not drawn to scale but had only three floors. Each room was created in beautiful detail with tiny lamps, carpets, beds, dressers, bathrooms, dining halls, living rooms and kitchens. A family of dolls sat in a room filled with games, couches, comfortable chairs and a fireplace. Instead of golden flames, inside the alcove brightly lit Akwo stones glowed well enough to light the entire miniature room.

Robin noticed a large golden remote control with purple gemstone buttons lying besides the doll house. She then realized to her delight that the small purple dolls were in fact mechanical. With the remote their actions could be programmed. There were four dolls in total. Parents, a young boy and a young girl.... "A family." Robin whispered against the glass, fogging it up even more so. Robin stood entranced as the tiny figurines sat down in a family room drinking from small cups by the blue fire. Roami came up to stand behind Robin and see what had grabbed her attention. Mika and Tika stood impatiently in the middle of the street. They waited for him to collect her so they could continue on. He knew they should rush but he could not push himself to break the spell Robin seemed to be in. Roami looked at her face first, etched with a strong desire for the toy before her. But even more acute was her passionate desire to have what the toy portrayed; a loving family and a place to call home for once in her life. "Robin...come now. They are waiting. We must go." He said softly so as not to pull her too quickly from her fantasy. He took her hand from the glass and slowly pulled it towards his chest. When she felt his heartbeat she finally broke away from the glass and her eyes found his. He wanted to scream when he saw the emptiness shining there. Gulping, he took her hand and led her back towards their waiting hosts. "Sorry about that." Was all Roami would say to them as they turned and continued walking down a few more streets before stopping before their final destination. All along the way Roami noticed how listless Robin's hand felt in his. It was as if her body was there but her mind was thousands of miles away. "Well... Here we are. Home sweet home!" Mika lifted his arm dramatically and pointed towards the dark blue front door. The group stood before a massive fuchsia colored marble building which towered over them.

"Wow... It must have taken decades to build something so large." Robin let her head fall back in amazement. Then she added, "And...it's Fuchsia...God how I missed that color..." Roami snickered at her sarcasm but covered it up with a slight cough so as not to anger their hosts. "Well, no. Not really. We have tons of laborers so it-" Tika was rudely shushed by her husband Mika. Roami watched the couple closely and grabbed Robin's hand to pull her closer to him. After a private stare the couple simply smiled back at their guests to shrug off the odd moment. "Well let's show you the inside then." Mika said with a smile as he motioned for Robin and Roami to enter their home. Roami stepped forward first and kept Robin close by his side. What they saw inside was even more grand than the exterior. The entryway was circular with a pair of elevator doors to the far left and a number of doorways and hallways leading in various directions. Everywhere they turned they saw furnishings of every kind. Both the entryway, hallways and connecting rooms were filled with all types of furniture made of the most colorful and beautiful jewels either had ever seen. There were couches made of bright orange velvet and trimmed with countless rubies and diamonds. Chairs made entirely of what looked like gold were littered throughout. Small decorative sculpture trees were planted in crystal vases and sprouted leaves made of purple and green gemstones. The entire effect was warm, airy and magical. Both Robin and Roami were surprised to find so many jewels in the interior furnishings as there were few if any jewels worn by the actual people of Wongswited. They were finding a lot of things did not quite add up in this new world. Roami stared at the blue jewel encrusted golden elevator doors at the center of the entryway and asked, "With so many floors, there must be others who live here right?" "No. It was just Mika and I. But now we have our little Brifton to share this all with us." Tika beamed joyously.

"What a waste." Roami said under his breath to Robin. "Really." Robin had to agree. She could think of thousands of people on earth who could use the vacant shelter this single home could offer. Leave it to Robin and Roami to be housed with what seemed to be the most eccentric couple in the entire town. They really needed to take a look into why they kept attracting only the oddest hosts in each world they fell into. "Well, do we get to pick which floor we want to live on?" Robin skipped towards one of the elevator doors which automatically opened before her. Her mouth gaped open as she stared at the amazing amount of buttons. "I love the number twenty-four so maybe I'll just stay on that floor!" She mused happily as she prepared to push that very button. "No! No!" Tika rushed forward and pulled Robin out of the elevator. "We do not live past two. No one goes past two here!" Robin stared at Tika as if she had gone crazy and backed up towards Roami fearfully. Roami stood in front of her preparing himself for a possible confrontation. Tika however calmed herself and said sweetly. "I am sorry, but the top floors are... um... under construction for the time being. Please...just... we have rooms set aside for guests on the second floor. You will find the pillows plush and the carpeted floors soft enough to sink into. Okay, so just forget about the top floors. There really is no need to go so high anyway. The uh...air quality gets thin the higher you go..." With this said Tika smiled again then excused herself saying she had to feed and settle Brifton into his room for the night. Running her hand nervously through her long blue hair, Tika nodded at their guests, held Brifton closer to her bosom and walked through one of the three hallways on the main floor. She was apparently going to the kitchen. Mika stepped forward and guided Robin and Roami into the elevators quietly. The two followed their remaining guide with some level of anxiety. Mika pressed the button for the second floor. Once the elevator made its way to their floor he stepped out and began walking down a long corridor filled with doors. The wall sconces and recessed hallway lights above glowed blue from the Akwo stones set into the fixtures. There were a few potted sculpture plants and small wooden tables along the walls. The carpet beneath them was made of a green velvet-like fabric that had what looked like silver dust sprinkled throughout it. The doors each looked completely identical. They were all painted dark green. "Out of the frying pan and into..." Robin whispered to Roami who looked at her in confusion. "I do not understand this saying." Roami said with confusion. "Oh, yes.

249

Sorry. I just meant to say that-" Robin began to explain but was interrupted by Mika. They had walked to the end of the corridor where there were only two doors left. One to the left and the other to their right. "Here is your room." Mika pointed to the green door to his right then at Robin. "Robin. My name is Robin." She told him. "Yes. Robin." Mika said quickly then turned to walk to the door across the hall. "And here is your room." "Thank you. And my name is Roami." Roami said as he ignored Mika's gesture for him to walk into his own room.

They had only just then realized that they had never been asked their names. Everyone had jumped straight into calling them the "Strange Ones". Again Robin grew upset with the annoying nickname. "I think I will see Robin to her room first, Mika. We thank you for your hospitality." Roami said to him politely. "No problem at all." Their host said. "Oh and there is no need for you to come down to eat tonight. Your meals will be left at your door by the servants. Please ring a bell and speak aloud anything you need and the servants will ensure you have it. Now, I will bid you two goodnight." Mika bowed slightly then walked back down the hall to the waiting elevator. Robin and Roami watched him until he walked in and the doors shut behind him. "Wow, unbelievable! Everything gets crazier and crazier with each second." Robin said as she walked into her room and dove straight onto the huge king sized bed. It had a wooden frame and mounds of purple and blue pillows and covers. The rest of the room to her surprise had many of the same furnishings as her old room at Thisters' home in the city of Fitz. "It's like they copied some things about Fitz and with others they went to the opposite extreme." Robin said as she eyed jeweled vases, crystal side tables and small velvet sofas. The room was very large and filled to the brim with unnecessary furniture, decorations and odd looking gadgets. Instead of perpetual patterns, the curtains and rugs shone the same advertisements that had been on the walls in the Akwo Tunnels. When she noticed this Robin grimaced, "I hope there is an off button for these... I don't want to have my dreams filled with the latest shoes and hair products..." She rolled her eyes dramatically at Roami who just laughed in response. "Oh, oh, ohhhhh!" She exclaimed as she felt how soft the bed was. "I think I will sink into it and never come out again!" she said in awe. Running her hands over the covers from her sprawled position, she noticed a pair of silk pajamas laying on the bed. It was just a simple silk tunic and pair of trousers. "Thank Goodness. I thought maybe they wore business suits for pajamas too." She laughed at her own joke. The pajamas were actually very similar to the ones she had wore in Fitz except they were nearly every color of the rainbow and shimmered in the blue light of the metallic lamps in the room.   "Whatever. It cannot be all that comforta-" Roami sat at the foot of the bed and nearly fainted from the pleasure of its softness. "See…" Robin said and threw a pillow at her friend's head. Roami laughed and hopped off the bed to get far away from her silly attacks.   "Before we get comfortable we really must talk about all that has happened so far. Remember our goal is still the same. We need to try to figure out how to get out of this world once and for all. I am just confused now though. Has the riddle changed now that we are in another world within this world?" Roami thought aloud as he paced the gold colored carpet.   "Okay, look… I'm hungry. You can try and figure out the riddle while I order some food." Was all Robin said as she got up from the bed and made her way to the golden bell near the wall beside her bed. She pulled it twice then remembering Mika's odd directive she yelled out, "Chicken sandwich, Strawberry ice-cream sundae with rainbow sprinkles and a big cup of hot cocoa!"   Looking at Roami she nodded for him to follow suit. Rolling his eyes Roami said loudly, "I guess I'll have the same." Robin's eyes alighted as she saw she was having an effect on her dear friend.   Roami stood up and was about to continue his thoughts on riddles and worlds when a slight tap came at Robin's door.   "Who is it?" Robin called out cautiously. There was no response and so Roami walked towards the door to check it out. When he opened the door no one stood outside but a large golden tray of food sat on the ground before his and Robin's doors. "Wow, it's everything we ordered! That was fast!" Robin said with delight. Roami brought both trays into Robin's room and placed them on one of her many wooden tables. They sat down in matching wooden chairs and the two dug in after ensuring themselves that it was edible and not poisonous. When they finished their food their bellies were full and they were quite tired.   With a yawn Robin said, "Roami I know it's important we start figuring this whole riddle business out and everything but... I'm sooooo tired..." Roami nodded, "Yes, you're right... I guess we can work on discovering this world's riddle tomorrow." Roami stood at Robin's door prepared to bid her goodnight. Before leaving he smiled sleepily at her then said, "Tomorrow we will figure a way out of all this and back to Source One." "I hope so..." Robin stifled a huge yawn. When Roami closed the door she quickly slipped on her rainbow colored silk pajamas then dove into her bed and under the covers.   With another stifled yawn, she clicked off the crystal lamp on her bedside dresser which had been giving off a soothing sky-blue glow. Robin then turned into her soft mountain of covers and dove into a fantastic dreamland that while exciting could not compare to her adventures since leaving the House of Intrigues. *** Robin opened her eyes... The first thing that came to her mind was why on earth would she have opened her eyes in the middle of the night? Especially given how tired she had been when she finally drifted off to sleep. She remained quiet waiting to see if some errant sound had disturbed her rest. For a moment there was nothing but silence. Then she heard it; the sound that had awakened her. Robin looked towards the door to her bedroom. The blue light from the hallway lanterns beamed below the closed door. She stared at it to see if any shadows passed by, signaling someone was at or passing her door. Nothing. And yet she heard it; the sound of small feet shuffling nearby followed by the sad whistling of an incredibly melancholy tune. The hairs on Robin's neck stood up as she realized she would either have to cower in fear beneath her covers until daybreak or tackle her fear face to face. As always Robin chose the latter. Pulling the covers off, she dropped out of the comfortable bed, slipped on her slippers and made her way to the door slowly so as not to make a sound. When she stood there, her ear against the wood, Robin noticed the sound had grown louder as if the perpetrator was just about to pass by. She swung open the door to come face to face with... absolutely nothing. "What the fudge..." Robin whispered as she looked at either side of her in the hallway and even checked out the ceilings to see where someone could have quickly hidden. "Hello?" She asked aloud. Her eyes went wide when she realized that was always the famous utterance in horror movies before some poor hapless blonde got slaughtered by a deranged killer. Robin had never been and would never be a blonde, hapless or not, if she could help it.

Running she made her way to Roami's quarters. She threw open the door and flew inside. His room was bathed in darkness but she quickly got readjusted to the blackness and walked towards his bedside. When she was just inches away she stopped and stared down at her friend. His beautiful blue skin shimmered where the street lights from outside his window shone in. His sculpted face which was usually set with grim determination or mounds of seriousness seemed for once to be completely at peace. Robin could not help but softly smile at the endearing picture he made sleeping. "Who is that?" Roami's voice seemed to come out of nowhere. Robin had fallen into a daydream without realizing she was just standing there staring at Roami. He was now wide awake and wondering why she stood at the foot of his bed watching him so intently.

Feeling uncomfortable and like a grade-A creep, Robin fumbled to explain why she had invaded his privacy. "I uh... It's me Robin." She said as she put on a small crystalline lamp made of frosted blue and gray glass. The room lit with a light blue glow and Robin watched as Roami sat up and stared at her in confusion. "Is everything okay Robin?" He asked as he wiped his face with his hand and blinked his eyes to force himself awake. "I umm.... No. I woke up because I heard footsteps in the hallway and someone whistling. When I went out to see who it was there was no one there..." She sat at the edge of his bed. "Well... maybe it was just the servants. Haven't you noticed they are sort of hard to pin down here?" He said with a yawn. "Yes... I guess but... Believe me Roami, there is no way anyone could have just vanished into thin air like that. They were right outside my door then gone the next second... You know what I think? Oh my god, it's so clear now..." Robin's eyes grew large and Roami prepared to hear one of her great conspiracy theories. "What?" Roami asked. "I think this place is...haunted..." Robin said this and stared at Roami to gauge his response. He just stared at her blank faced for a very long moment. "Okay Robin... Um... I need to get back to sleep. Actually, so do you for that matter... we won't be able to explore and figure out the riddle if we're exhausted." He said while yawning once again. "Roami... did you hear what I just said? I think this place is..." Before she could finish her thought they heard an odd sound come from outside his window. "Oh no... what now?" Robin breathed heavily in exasperation as she stood back up and stared at the window in fear.

As she spoke Roami made his way out of his bed and towards the window. "Stay there. Let me check it out first." He said knowing Robin would undoubtedly, not listen. Almost immediately he was proven correct when he felt her arm bump into his back while he stared out the window. They both stood there near the pane and quickly saw what the commotion was. The sound of tiny hard rocks falling outside was soft at first then grew faster and louder as each moment passed. "Is it hail?" Robin asked as she squinted to see what was falling from the sky. As the fury grew they could clearly see the gold streets below them fill with what looked like tiny blue crystals.

"It's raining...gemstones?" Robin looked incredulous as she looked towards Roami. Roami shrugged in response and was about to respond when they heard an explosive sound. It was a loud collective moaning that nearly shook the very foundations of the city. The intense moaning continued and was accompanied by shrill emergency alarms blaring across the streets. "What is going-" Robin spoke just as Roami's door flew open. There stood Mika in his black pajamas made in the same style as their own. He looked like he had just woke up as well since his silver hair was in complete disarray. His blue eyes appeared frantic but his speech was slow and measured. "Uh, strange ones... I am glad to see you are both awake. I am sorry for the inconvenience but there is a...uh... slight emergency in town that is being taken care of as we speak." He gulped noticeably then walked in. Robin noticed he was barefoot as he had probably forgotten his slippers in his haste to get to them. "A slight emergency? It's raining gemstones out there. Anyone caught in that will get sliced up pretty badly... I think that's more than a small emergency..." Robin eyed Mika as if he had lost his mind. "No, no! There is absolutely nothing to worry about. This does not happen often but it does happen from time to time. It is simply raining... uh...gems. It is a rare Blue Storm... Believe me, it will be taken care of quickly. By the time we all leave this building for the day every trace of it will be cleared away." He said a bit breathlessly. Roami looked at Robin's expression and knew she was not buying any of it. "So, what do we do now?" Roami asked. Happy to be able to change the discussion to something he actually had answers to, Mika piped up, "For the time being, to ensure our own safety we must all go to the dining hall in the center of the house. It is the room farthest away from the windows. That way we are safe from being hit by these stones as they fall and potentially break through the glass." Robin and Roami nodded. "We will just get dressed and..." Robin said. "No, there is no time! Please follow me now Strange Ones." Mika said as he stepped back into the hallway gesturing for them to follow. When they stood beside him he explained, "Tika and Brifton are already waiting for us there. Let us go." They followed him down the hall, which Robin noticed was now silent and void of any whistled tunes. They took the elevator down to the main floor and entered the dining hall. Tika and Brifton were already seated at one end of the table. Both were still dressed in their pajamas as well. Tika in white and Brifton in blue. Robin smiled when she saw the little baby. She gave him a quick peck on the cheek while Tika held the bubbling little boy in her arms protectively. All along the table were mounds of every food imaginable. "We ordered beforehand to ensure there was food waiting for you two. I hope you don't mind." Tika said with a warm smile. "Of course not. Thank you." Roami said. Robin echoed her thanks as well as they looked over the mouth watering bounty of food and drinks. From the dining hall they could barely hear the sound of the raging stone storm outside. Mika sat beside Tika. Robin and Roami found their own seats, beside one another. They all ate quietly. Tika was the first to break the silence, "I don't know if you two have already made plans for the day... but I was wondering if I could take Robin away from you for a bit. Just for a little girl-time." Tika looked at the two with a cautious smile. "Um... what exactly would that girl-time include?" Robin asked in her usual no-nonsense fashion. "Well uh... I actually am an author. A somewhat

259

famous author here in Wongswited." Tika said with a bashful smile then looked over at Mika. He beamed with pride and nodded his head. Tika continued. "I will be at a local Bobble Shop for the book signing today. I figured we could go there, grab a nice cup of hot Bobble then maybe do some clothes shopping together. Just us gals." She said with yet another toothy grin. Roami looked at Tika then at Robin. He did not seem too happy about letting Robin out of his sight for even a moment let alone a few hours. "I actually think that wouldn't-" He began to share his thoughts on the subject when Robin interjected. "Wouldn't be such a bad idea. I'm sure there is a lot of information I could gather about Wongswited and the people here during our girl-time." Robin looked pointedly at Roami, and then smiled at Tika. "Perfect! Well if that's all set, I guess it only makes sense for me to take dear Roami here out for some male bonding while you girls are out on the town." Mika said with a smile and a nod before diving into his bowl of mint green Manna Pudding. "Great... but what about Brifton? Who will watch him while we are all away?" Robin asked with concern. "Ah... well I have already designated a nanny for him. Do not worry; he will be well cared for in our absence Strange Ones." Tika said then planted a sweet kiss on Brifton's purple cheek. He smiled back and said, "Muh muh!" Everyone smiled and laughed at Brifton's contribution to the conversation. Tika smiled in delight and held Brifton even tighter in her arms.   In that short moment of revelry, Robin wondered if this was the sort of connectedness people with family's felt every day. Looking at Roami she smiled again. *** "How does it feel to be living with Tika; famous author of "Purple is Beautiful"?" A tall and hefty woman with short pink curled hair and red eyes, was completely invading Robin's idea of personal space. The space invader wore a garish orange business dress suit and yellow shirt beneath it. The combination of colors made Robin want to rip her eyes out.   They were in one of the most popular Bobble Shop's in town. For the special occasion, Tika had worn the traditional dress suit made in a sky-blue color with a red undershirt beneath it. She was seated while signing copies of her best seller. Robin waited impatiently on the sidelines. One of Tika's biggest fans had found her way over to Robin and was now shamelessly quizzing her. "I uh... well; we just got here but so far so good..." Robin looked at the women with her eyebrow quirked in an effort to show her she was not welcome this close to Robin's face.   Robin was not sure if it was the women's closeness or Robin's stiff and uncomfortable wardrobe which made her want to scream at the top of her lungs. The Wongswited dress shoes she had been given were tight and pinched her feet. If that was not bad enough, she had been forced to don the

261

Wongswited business suit as their Fitz garb was looked down on among the citizens. Her new short purple skirt and vest were nice but bound to get dirty given Robin's penchant for making a mess. The gray undershirt was bland and really not worth mentioning. The only plus to the clothing change was that she was now able to float on the water channels in the Akwo Tunnels. She had giggled with glee the first time she stepped on the moving water path and hovered towards their destination. Turning around Robin made her way to Tika's side and whispered, "How much longer?" Tika laughed in response while signing a book then said, "Just a few more autographs and we'll sit down to chat over some hot Bobble juice." Robin had learned that Bobble Juice was akin to Hot Chocolate on Earth. The one major difference being that the liquid was hot pink and looked like a ton of pink rose petals had been liquefied into a hot gooey cup of sweet nectar. From the wonderful smells filling the café she could not wait to taste a cup of it herself. She looked at Tika's now familiar book cover which read "Purple is Beautiful". It had a cover with a Blue haired, purple skinned, pink eyed model on the front. "Ah, well that's it for today! Please no more autographs as I must attend to our strange guest. This will after all be her first taste of Bobble Juice!" Tika announced to the small crowd who applauded her then dispersed. Some left the café and others went and ordered some food and drinks.   Tika and Robin made their way over to the counter as well and Tika bought two cups of Bobble. They found a small circular wooden table near the glass window and sat down to watch the passersby's.

Robin took a sip of the pink liquid in her mint green ceramic cup. "Mmmm....." was all she could say as her senses were overtaken by the most delicious taste she had ever experienced. Tika laughed good heartedly. "Haha! Now you see why this is such a famous drink here in Wongswited." "Oh my.... I could live on this!" Robin dove in for another sip of the magical liquid. "I definitely have to get one for Roami before we go back home." She said giddily. "Yes we can order one to go for your friend." Tika promised with a delighted smile. "So... what do you think about my new book?" Tika asked while running her black manicured fingers through her hip-long blue hair. "I um... well I haven't read it yet." Robin stated the obvious. Tika laughed, "Oh yes, there is that. Well to give you a quick summary. It is just about how beautiful...the purple-skinned people of Wongswited truly are. It goes into the psychology of what was done to us by the people of Fitz... and how we have overcome all of this by becoming such a strong and industrious people. We are so much more advanced than them now... we have actually gone from the student to the master in such a short time... Overall I wrote this so that we here in Wongswited could revel in the beauty that...we are." She said with a tear in her eye and a small smile on her lips. Robin being...well... Robin... could not help but speak her mind. "I guess overall that's an interesting topic. The only thing about it is...well... I mean... I always thought of beauty as being something that societies measure based on relative examples...So... how could you say that Purple is beautiful without having other options... I mean... you're all purple..." Robin realized just a few seconds after she had spoken the words that maybe; just maybe, they would have been better left kept in her head. If Tika's glare was any indication; she may have landed in a heap of trouble. Robin hoped wherever Roami was, he was faring better with their male host. Otherwise by the end of the night they might find themselves not only lost in a strange world...but also...homeless.   ***

Roami was in fact having a better time than Robin. He and Mika spent most of the next day exploring the town of Wongswited. True to Mika's word, when they stepped outside the building later that day all traces of green stones had been removed although there were a few broken windows and street signs here and there. Roami was dressed in the official outfit of the Wongswited. He wore a silk business suit in white and had a red shirt beneath it. Mika wore a red suit and a brown under-shirt. They had stopped at a few stores as Mika needed to buy some things for Tika and Brifton. Roami too had run an errand which he needed to see to in one particular store. At the moment he stood with a large dark blue shopping bag in hand waiting outside a toy shop while Mika searched for a few toys for Brifton. Roami was quickly becoming used to the look, feel, sounds and smells of the town. He was no longer as anxious as he had been the day before. The people who passed by looked at him openly as he was obviously different from everyone else. Some smiled and waved and others just stared and continued walking. A bit annoyed by all the attention, Roami sighed and stared at up at the building above him. It was then that he noticed something that he had not seen the day before.

At the top of the buildings where the sky's light hit them, he noticed tiny planked bridges crisscrossing across the building tops. He was mesmerized by the sight; trying his best to understand what they could be for. He made a note to ask Mika once he finally left the store and returned to him. Once again someone was staring at Roami's every move intently. A little purple boy licking a green creamy sweet treat in a purple cup of some sort watched Roami's confused sky-ward gaze. Skipping over to him the child asked, "Why are you looking up sir? There's nothing up there to see...nothing at all." The kid said this nonchalantly while looking up as well. At no point did the child stop greedily licking his candy treat. Roami glanced down to see the kid's straight frock of silver hair and smiling green eyes. Chuckling Roami said, "Ah but there is something, there's always something somewhere...if you look close enough. There are wooden bridges up above, can't you see them?" Roami pointed up with his blue index finger.

"No, my Mom tells me not to so I don't look up too much." The kid dropped his gaze from the sky then focused on Roami. "Everything we need is down here anyway. The sky is just a place for... ghosts..." The kid smiled and then skipped back over to his mother who just walked out of a nearby shop. Her hands were full of shopping bags so she nodded for her son to follow her and they both disappeared into the bustling crowd. Roami stared at the child for a moment as he walked away then with a look of confusion stared back up at the bridges high above. "What are you looking at?" Mika stood behind him and nearly made Roami jump in fear.

Before Roami could respond and ask Mika about the bridges Mika said, "Don't look too closely at the sky. The light can play funny tricks on your eyes that far away. There is nothing there but building tops..." With a pointed look Mika looked at Roami then began to walk down the street. Roami ran to catch up with him. He could not wait to see Robin at home later so he could tell her what he was sure he had just seen.

He had that and another surprise to share with her. Roami could not wait to see her face light up again. It was at that moment he realized just how much she was coming to mean to him. To him, she meant...well...everything.

CHAPTER 10

"Mmm... It is delicious!" Roami said after taking a sip of the Bobble juice Robin had brought home in a large blue paper cup. "See, I told ya!" Robin said. She was overjoyed to have brought Roami some level of pleasure. They sat cross-legged in his room, resting after their respective day trips with their hosts. Each had washed and was dressed in silk pajama pant suits. Robin in white and Roami in Red. Their feet were bare so that they could feel the comfort of the plush, fluffy sky-blue rug. Robin had never felt so at ease and happy than at that moment just sitting there and relaxing on the floor beside Roami. Both, however, knew that beneath the soothing normalcy of the moment, they had a dire task at hand. It was high time they started to work on figuring out the riddle. While the flashing Akwo Tunnels and delicious Bobble juice were fantastic, it did not take away the sneaking suspicion that things were not as they should be. Earlier that day Robin had experienced an exceptionally odd moment which made her wonder about the new world they were in.

Now that Roami had received his present, Robin felt compelled to tell him about her little adventure. Without preamble she spoke just as he opened his mouth to say something, "Well, here's what happened today. It was the oddest thing…" Robin pulled her knees up to her chest then hugged her legs as she recalled the incident. "I was walking with Tika back to the house when all of a sudden…we're going down this pretty empty street and I… well… I bumped into thin air." Robin watched as Roami's eyebrow slowly quirked up.   Before he could ask her if she had lost her mind she quickly continued, "I know what you're thinking but that's the only way to describe what happened to me. I swear, one second I was walking with no one in front of me and the next I was flat on the ground. But I wasn't the only thing that fell... right there near my hand was this-" Robin pulled a fist-sized blue Akwo stone from the pocket of her white pajama pants. "See? It is the same Akwo crystal they use in the tunnels to shine the light of the Sun... I mean not the sun, the Planet Yur." Robin handed the brightly glowing stone over to Roami. He took it and looked back at Robin.   "Are you sure you just didn't see it lying there? This stuff is all over the city. Maybe someone dropped it and-" He was interrupted by Robin.   "No, no and no. Believe me, I know what happened. I bumped into nothing and this fell out of thin air. Plain and simple." Robin looked back at Roami obstinately and he was sure arguing with her would do no good. Besides he had much better things planned for Robin at the moment. Handing her back the blue stone, Roami stood up excitedly.   "Okay, I have no idea how to explain that but let's pause for just a second. You gave me a present... now it is your turn." Was all he said as he ran towards his large walk-in closet on the far side of the room.   "My turn for what?" Robin looked a bit nervous as she had never seen her friend act so nervous or excited for that matter. "I um..." Whatever else Roami was saying was muffled as he stepped into the large closet that could have doubled as another bedroom. "Huh?" Robin said as she stood up and flounced on Roami's bed. She gingerly sat indian-style while impatiently awaiting his return. Roami left the closet with a huge dark blue bag in hand and a timid smile on his face. His golden eyes seemed to sparkle as he drew closer to her. Robin had hardly, if ever, been given gifts so she was still not completely sure what Roami was doing until he handed the bag directly to her. "A gift...for you." Was all he said before blushing slightly. He quickly sat across from her in the large bed covered in blue and silver covers that glittered like the night sky. Robin did not open the bag, did not move and could barely remember to breathe. She simply stared at Roami as if he were some odd thing that had just fallen from the sky above. "What? Don't you want to see what it is?" He asked, looking increasingly nervous. She was not responding the way he had envisioned in his many elaborate but perhaps not so realistic daydreams about this exact moment. In answer, a single tear fell down Robin's cheeks. Swallowing hard she simply said, "I...I...." Laughing at the look of complete bewilderment on her face, Roami rolled his eyes the way he had seen her do hundreds of times and said, "Just open it." With a smile, Robin wiped the tears from her face and did as he instructed. She gasped when she saw what the bag held. "Oh my..." Was all she could think to say when she pulled out her gift. It was the doll house from their first day in Wongswited! The one she had been mesmerized by at the store window. She looked up at Roami and nearly screamed in excitement. "I can't believe you did this... for me..." Robin breathed a sigh of true happiness. "Of course. Why not? You are my friend after all..." Roami said with a smile. Robin smiled back a bit shyly. "Come on. Let's try it out!" He said as he took it from her and placed it on a nearby wooden table. Robin pulled the remote from the bag and raced after him. They sat side by side on wooden chairs and together figured out how to program the family of purple dolls. They played out different daily scenarios. Some were dramatic but thanks to Robin most were hysterically funny. Through the role playing, Robin secretly tested out how a family might work together.   For the first time in her life, with her friend Roami at her side, she truly dreamed of perhaps having a family of her own...someday. *** They did not figure out the riddle to the world the next day, nor the day after that. It was harder than usual to determine the difference between night and day in the town of Wongswited. Without a clear view of the sky or the illuminating planets above, days seemed to mesh together in a sky-blue haze.   The two friends spent their mornings eating elaborate breakfasts left by what seemed to be invisible servants. While they thought their absence strange, neither brought the issue up to their hosts; afraid they might think the question rude. When they had the chance they spent time playing with little Brifton. The beautiful boy grew rapidly before their very eyes. Each night Robin and Roami would hear sad melodies whistled or hummed in the corridors. This occurred around the same time each night, like clockwork. While Roami was sure there was a reasonable explanation, Robin assured him the truth was simple enough; there were ghosts roaming around. Her latest elaborate conspiracy theory was that Tika and Mika had somehow found a way to make the undead serve their household. Their afternoons mainly consisted of roaming the streets trying to determine the riddle. They walked across nearly every inch of the town talking to the people and asking questions of everyone they met. On one such afternoon, Robin and Roami walked out into the town dressed in matching blue suits with red undershirts and black shoes. Robin straightened her short blueberry blue skirt and pushed back her black braids which she had stylishly curled earlier that morning. Roami stared at her at odd moments. His intense look made her feel shy for some unknown reason. Given his extra attentiveness, Robin continuously found herself fidgeting with her hair and clothes to ensure nothing was amiss. They began walking down the shining gold streets basking in the unnatural blue glow of the street lamps. The streets were slowly becoming crowded as the day grew long. No matter how many times they went to town Robin and Roami never got bored with the sights and sounds they experienced during their explorations. "Roami look at this? You'll never believe what they're selling in here!" Robin had raced ahead to a store shop. She stared inside with eyes alight with excitement. Laughing, Roami ran up to her to see what had snatched her attention so acutely. "Rainbows! They have captured actual rainbows in these jars! How is that even possible?" She stared at the display of glass jars with golden lids sitting on a spread of purple velvet fabric. Roami looked down at the jars and tried his best to determine how they had worked this particular magic. "The Akwo stones... and water. The underside of the lids are covered in blue stones. So the light shines down to the bottom and they have water perpetually cycling through the jar. It makes little rainbows inside." Roami smiled as he figured it out. "Wow..." Robin was mesmerized. Roami stared at her beautiful face and could not help but smile at the thought that not too long ago those exotic brown eyes used to carry a world of sadness. Now as he looked at her, he felt as if it might be possible to help her forget her past... forever. She was slowly realizing she could move forward and towards a brighter future with infinite possibilities. Roami chuckled at Robin's infectious excitement. Turning away from the store front; he paused to consider their next steps. It was then he noticed a couple walking on the opposite side of the street moving in their direction. They looked like any other Wongswited couple; vibrant purple skin, matching pair of sky-blue suits with yellow undershirts, black shoes and brightly colored hair. The man sported red locks in a cropped fashion while the woman had her shoulder length brown tresses in a ponytail. Roami could not determine the colors of their eyes from so far away. But that was not his main concern at the moment. What had drawn his attention was not how they looked but what they were doing. Their baby was in a black stroller rolling in front of them. However, neither the mother nor father were pushing it along. They were, in fact, sipping on brown cups of Bobble Juice and laughing heartily at some private joke. Robin noticed Roami's sudden silence and turned to see what had caught his attention. "Robin do you see what I see?" He asked without taking his eyes off the couple in question. "Yes... I think I do. Who is pushing that stroller?" Robin asked. Roami had no answer. "Do you think maybe they have a new technology that no one else knows about? I mean we know the purple Hapblo stones help them hover but they can't navigate or push anything forward...right?" Robin looked confused. "Exactly." Roami began to walk towards the couple as they grew nearer. He made his way across the cobbled street and Robin was right at his side.   Just when they were about to step up onto the other sidewalk, a few feet away from the couple and their stroller; the pair of Wongswited parents finally realized they were under intense scrutiny.   Gasping aloud, the woman quickly raced towards the stroller. She looked flustered as she wrapped her hands around its handles and began to push it as it hovered above ground.   Robin heard a little giggle erupt from inside the contraption. A piece of gray fabric covered the little one inside but the child apparently thought the scenario as funny as Robin did...   The husband simply stared at the two strange ones with a look of guilt and embarrassment.   Robin did not let their discomfort stop her from getting to the bottom of this mystery. She walked alongside the woman, "Hello! We just noticed your stroller pushes and navigates by itself. How cool... Can you please tell us how it works?"   The woman simply stared at Robin with her large gray eyes and did not open her mouth. She looked afraid and slightly in shock. "Is everything okay?" Robin asked with concern.   The woman's husband raced around Roami and took his wife by the hand protectively. In the process he dropped his cup of Bobble Juice on the street. It's pink contents splattered like blood across the immaculate gold stones. He ignored the mess as he was in a hurry to grab the stroller handle with his other hand. "I'm sorry we must go!" He muttered anxiously. Without another word the Wongswited family raced down the street in an effort to get far away from Robin and Roami. "How rude..." Roami said. "Yeah..." Robin muttered. Watching the couple knock into pedestrians and nearly trip twice; Robin shook her head. "Something is definitely going on here..." She sighed deeply. "Yes, you're absolutely right about that Robin. We have to figure out what it is so we can get out of here. Let's get busy and start asking some more questions. Someone is bound to give us an answer eventually." Roami rationalized. "Okay, I'm game. Let's go!" Robin said with an encouraging smile. They began walking down the many streets of the town. Expertly, they scanned the crowds for people who looked 'open' enough to speak to them openly. "How long have you lived in Wongswited?" Robin asked an old man with short pink hair, black rimmed glasses and a kindly face. The man just smiled and sped up. He shook his head before walking away from her, down the busy golden street. "So, what do you guys do for fun?" Roami ran up to stand amongst a small group of teenagers hovering on skateboards in front of a candy shop. They wore the same business outfits as everyone else but in neon pinks, greens and blues. One sported a fluffy pink frohawk hairstyle which seemed to contradict the stuffy business attire. Robin noticed the small nuances of their clothing that showed that even in Wongswited, teenagers always found a way to rebel from the status quo. Their undershirts hung outside of their pants and skirts. Roami noticed that instead of the standard issue black shoes, they all wore shiny lace-up black ankle boots. The group of young adults whispered to one another laughed aloud then raced away. Roami watched disheartened as they disappeared into a nearby Akwo tunnel during rush hour. Robin just sucked her teeth and rolled her eyes at the teenagers. She watched Roami return to her side, all the while shaking his head in defeat. Her heart went out to him. It was not easy work, putting yourself out there and getting rejected, but they really did not have a choice if they were going to reach their goal.

"How long have babies come here from the City of Fitz?" Robin and Roami had spotted a lawyer leaving his office. They raced across the street to confront him then quickly blurted out the question. By this time they had spent all day asking questions and were starting to feel a little desperate. The bald man with piercing blue eyes and a gray business suit looked at them in surprise. In an instant he jumped onto the back

of a passing strangers hover scooter. "Leave me alone you strange ones!" He yelled as he rode past them. "Do you know why you were born purple and not green?" This question had made the beautiful young woman dressed in lavender, sitting in a popular Bobble café look at Robin aghast. "How dare you?!" She yelled at them furiously. Everyone in the café stopped what they were doing and curiously looked at their table. Turning dark purple in embarrassment, the girl with the long silver hair falling in silky waves about her, glared at them with her pink eyes. She did not say another word but angrily huffed, grabbed her shopping bags and marched away. No matter how many questions they asked and how many cryptic answers they received, Robin and Roami could not seem to put the pieces of the world together. They could not help but think they would be stuck in Wongswited... forever. *** "Do you think the answer lies within the unused floors in all the buildings?" Roami asked Robin one morning.
He fidgeted with the collar of his sky-blue shirt and smoothed out his black suit jacket uncomfortably. "I have to admit I do miss the more breathable clothes of Fitz. Why must everyone wear these rigid suits?" "Yeah, I have to admit this dress suit is annoying too. It looks like silk but I seriously think it's really made of wires it's so itchy and stiff!" Robin rubbed her hand on the dark purple knee length dress and

vest over a black shirt. Her shoes were way too hard and pinched at her feet mercilessly. "Now, about the unused floors in the building... well... I'm pretty sure there are no answers there...well, at least not Mika and Tika's building." Robin said slyly. Roami had grown to know Robin's facial expressions well after spending so much time with her. He was sure her current face screamed 'guilty'. "But how can you be so sure? It is not like you have been to any of the upper floors in Mika and Tika's home." Roami's words began to gradually slow as he finished his sentence and came to an obvious conclusion. When he realized Robin had remained quiet and sported a guilty look on her face he stared at her with both shock and hurt. "You went up there alone and didn't tell me!" he said with a look of disappointment on his face. "Well you know how curious I am. I just couldn't live another second without checking it out and so...one night I couldn't sleep and I basically..." Robin grew quiet but Roami urged her on. "Well, I basically checked out each of the one hundred and fourteen unused floors. Long story short; I didn't find anything out of the ordinary." Robin finished. "Wait a minute. One hundred and fourteen? You mean One hundred and thirteen and the second story and main floor make a total of one hundred and fifteen." Roami reminded her. "No." Robin said simply. "There's a basement as well." She smiled proudly at her acquired knowledge. "Unbelievable!" Roami said but laughed a bit as Robin would always be...well... Robin. "Okay, so we know it is not that. What else could it be?" He said dejectedly while pacing back and forth. When he realized he was pacing, Roami sighed loudly then sat down beside Robin. The two were sitting on a wooden bench in a small park near the city center. There were little if any trees or grass in the city except at little sitting parks like this. Here there was fake brown colored grass and the same sculpture trees they had seen when they first arrived. Robin looked at the clear slender trunks and beautiful rainbow crystal leaves on each. Hopping from branch to branch were a few very odd little flying creatures called Hindrits. Robin thought they looked like hand-sized blue teddy bears with rainbow colored wings. She had been afraid of them at first sight but after seeing the Wongswiteds feeding the little creatures bits of popcorn, she realized they were really very harmless. Robin and Roami remained quiet. Both were close to drowning in their thoughts for some time. "You know. This is the quietest park I've been to in a long time. Back home we would have been hit in the head by at least two Frisbees and run over by countless crazy little kids by now." Robin said without truly thinking about her words. "Yes... You have a point. There aren't many kids in this park and hardly any in this world at all. Isn't that odd Robin?" Roami said. "Yes it is a little strange..." She admitted while throwing a handful of popcorn at a group of nearby Hindrits at her feet. They made odd little giggling noises that Robin could not help but think were utterly adorable. In her mind the cute sound made up for their completely ridiculous physiques. "I mean there are a few kids here and there but not as much as you would expect given how many married couples there are. I wonder how they give birth. Do you think it is similar to the people of Fitz?" Robin asked Roami. "I do not know but we definitely need to find out. Come on!" He grabbed her hand and brought her to her feet. The bag of popcorn fell to the ground and a flurry of little Hindrits fluttered towards the delicious bounty. Ignoring the mess Roami pulled Robin behind him as he raced towards the city center. "Where exactly are we going?" Robin asked breathlessly as she struggled to keep up with him. "Actually... I'm not sure, really." Roami said just before bumping into someone. They stopped and realized the stranger they had just smacked into was one of the people who they had seen from time to time on the streets of Wongswited. The skinny man fell to the floor and the two children helped bring him to his feet. He wore a brown suit similar to that of King Philtu, but his shirt beneath was pearl white with thin peach stripes. He wore white rimmed glasses in front of intense black eyes and his white hair stood out straight and spiky all over his head. "We're sorry." Robin said sincerely. "No problem. Just please watch where you are going. I am a very important part of this town and it would be hard to replace me if I was run over by the likes of you two!" He said as he brushed his clothes off. Before he could walk away Robin asked quickly, "So what is it you do, exactly Sir?" She smiled at him and gave her most interested face. "You don't know?" He laughed incredulously. "I am the town Reposer of course." He said this haughtily and with a hint of annoyance that the two had not already known who he was. Without another word he sniffed disapprovingly then turned to march away. "Reposer?" Roami looked at Robin hoping she knew what that meant. Robin shook her head and said, "Perhaps he's some sort of pro-wrestler or something... I don't know." "Well I am almost sure we must find out what he does. It seems like part of the puzzle." Roami said excitedly. They spent most of the day asking the city people what a Reposer did. They did not get a straight answer from anyone. "Oh, he sort of reposes... I guess." "He takes care of repositing..." "Reposterousreposity and all that jazz..." were just a few of the odd responses they received during their quest. By the end of the day, the two were tired and mightily confused. They figured they would have to try getting their answer in a less straightforward manner.

"Let's just get some sleep and take care of this tomorrow morning." Roami said as they returned to Mika and Tika's home. "Well I just hope we solve this riddle soon. I can't stand another moment at Mika and Tika's home. They are definitely hiding something. There is a room on the second floor which was locked..." Robin began and made that sly guilty look Roami knew too well. "Was?" He asked with a smirk. Laughing slightly Robin continued, "Well, yes. I of course found a way in only to find it filled with children's clothes and none of it appeared to be for Brifton. I think they once had a child but won't tell us about it. Isn't that strange?" Robin said through a yawn. They had made it to their temporary home and now spoke in hushed tones so as not to be overheard. It sometimes felt as if the walls had ears in Mika and Tika's home. "Yes, very strange. But we will decipher all of this tomorrow." Roami whispered as they stood in the elevator and made their way to the second floor then walked down the long corridor to their respective rooms. Roami yawned and could think of nothing more than jumping into his bed for the night. Neither he nor Robin had been getting much sleep. Each night, in the dead of night; they would hear loud moaning sounds and sad melodies that seemed to be coming from the heavens above. It was an eerie sound that haunted many of their dreams and had Robin running into Roami's room more

283

nights than not.   "Get some rest my dear friend." Roami said as he entered his room then stood in the doorway to ensure Robin made it into her own suite safely. "Yeah, hopefully. I don't think I can take one more night of that odd moaning..." Robin walked into her room. She turned to smile sleepily at Roami before shutting the door.   When the door shut her smile faded away. They were in no way closer to discovering the riddle to Wongswited and she was starting to feel frantic.   What if they never left this place? What kind of life could she and Roami make together here in a world where they were still considered 'the strange ones'?   Sighing sadly Robin dressed in her bright yellow pajamas, god knows who, had left at the foot of her bed. Mere seconds after she dove into her bed and snuggled within the beautiful purple covers, Robin was already drifting into dreamland. But had a very restless sleep. She could not fight the feeling that she had left one dream world only to step into another... ***   That night Roami was awakened by the sound of horrific screams. The sounds jerked him from his slumber and out of the bed in a flash. His orange pajama pants crumpled up his legs and his hair was plastered against his head. Roami's was erratic from the scare so he paused a moment to get his bearings. He listened closely.   The noise seemed to be coming from somewhere far away, in the general direction of the town center. Just when he thought of racing there to verify the source of the shrieks they ended abruptly.   This was a first. While their nights were plagued by the sad moaning every now and then, neither he nor Robin had yet heard such blood curdling screams as he had just heard.   Opening his door slightly Roami searched the hallway then checked in on Robin to ensure she was okay. She slept soundly so he returned to his room.   He however, found it difficult to fall back asleep. His mind kept racing with possible explanations for the gruesome sounds coming from outside during the dead of night. He and Robin had to figure a way out...before it was too late. *** "I can't believe this? Do you see this Roami?" Robin gasped in awe as they stood in front of what had to be one of the largest buildings in the entire town.   The outside was made of dark blue marble and each of the thousands of windows were framed in gold. They had come to realize golden window frames were the norm for the more expensive and important buildings in Wongswited.   A sign ran along the front of the building just above the glass entrance and read, "Makabee Mall". The two had decided to visit the popular Mall everyone had been mentioning to them since their arrival. They had quickly gotten dressed that morning with the intent of goring directly to the Mall. Robin wore an apple green suit with a hot pink undershirt while Roami sported a gray suit with a light pink undershirt.

Although, she had been a bit rushed, Robin had taken special care with her hair and appearance. The small braids were pulled back into a perfect bun and she let a few purple and black strands out on either side of her face to add effect. She was not sure when she had begun to care about her outward appearance so much. Back in the day, she had dressed down to avoid male attention as she was well aware how dangerous that could be. However, she felt safer now and for some odd reason, wanted Roami to feel proud to have her at his side... She fidgeted slightly and grew uncomfortable with her line of thought. Sighing, Robin decided to leave off any deep thought for the time being and just focus on enjoying the mall. "How many floors did they say there was?" Robin asked as she arched her head back in an effort to see how far it jutted into the heavens. "Five hundred and eight, I believe." Roami said as he ushered her into one of the ten pair of revolving glass doors which made up the entrance. Robin had never seen so many revolving doors side by side. The flashing glass panels and colorful crowds of people flowing in and out, made for an awesome sight. She was so blown away, she seemed to have lost her ability to think so was complacent as Roami softly urged her forward. Once inside they were awash in hundreds of sounds, colors, and sights. Robin forgot to keep walking yet again and nearly started a pile up. As people exited the revolving door behind her they each crashed into one another. "Hey move it!" Someone said angrily. Roami took her by the hand and they made their way further inside to stand before a large map of the mall. It was stenciled into a large slate of black marble with lettering and maps all etched in gold. The large rectangular sign, held between two gold metal poles, looked as if it were a beacon shining for all to see. Robin realized it actually was shining once they came close enough to inspect it. Flat pieces of Akwo stone were attached to it along the edges and helped to illuminate the important visual aid for visitors. On either side of them were large stores with various types of merchandise. All the stores were made with high ceilings to accommodate patrons as the Wongswited were all extraordinarily tall. Bright blue lights lit the interior of the mall. The main entrance was absolutely breathtaking. A row of elevators were located at the very rear. The center had a maze of hover stairs which ran through every one of the five hundred and eight floors. Hover stairs, Robin noted; were just steep inclines of black marble with water canals running through just like in the Akwo tunnels. There was one for up and another for down. These zig-zagged their way like escalators through the center of the mall all the way to the top. People rode on them with their shoes or other hover devices. Inside each store the lighting from the ceiling came from Akwo stones as well. Most if not all the stores had aisles of wooden shelving that looked similar to bookcases. On each of these lay thousands of consumer goods. "This is absolutely out of this world!" Robin said as she focused on the map of Makabee Mall. "I can't even begin to imagine how many stores and restaurants are in here!" She smiled up at Roami before squealing with glee. "Where do we start?" Roami said with a smirk. He knew without a doubt where she wanted to go first.

Robin and Roami both said it at the same time, "Bobble Juice!" They laughed when they realized they had spoken simultaneously. "There's a Bobble cafe on the twelfth floor. Let's go!" Robin pulled Roami towards the hover stairs and hopped on. When they arrived at the Bobble Café, they noticed the long line wrapping throughout the store. Robin sighed but said, "Maybe I should find a seat while you order?" Roami nodded in agreement. Robin smiled at all the Wongswited she saw as she made her way throughout the beautifully decorated shop.

The blue lights shone brightly, behind the counter where three staff members stood. All personnel were dressed in matching pink aprons and brown suits. A plethora of delicious pastries and other sweet concoctions were placed within the glass displays along the counter. The floor was covered with sparkling golden tiles, while the table and chairs were golden painted wood.

Robin finally saw an empty table near the store front window. It would be a perfect spot for her and Roami to drink, talk and stare at the people passing by. She could not help but step back and look at herself at that very moment. The old Robin from Brooklyn, New York would never have recognized this new version of herself. She felt, somehow, lighter and more 'in the moment'. Before she could really delve into this spectacular epiphany she realized she had to focus if they were going to get a good seat in the crowded café. With a smile she quickly made her way towards the table before anyone else got it. Robin, however, was not fast enough. A very tall and beautiful Wongswited woman dressed in an immaculate white suit, with a matching short miniskirt and gray undershirt made it to the table just as Robin was about to sit. The woman sat down and stared haughtily at her with a quirked eyebrow. Robin noticed the table thief's' numerous designer shopping bags were placed on a large circular metal hover device with a clear glass cover. Poor Robin slowed her steps and dejectedly stopped beside the table. She looked at the table usurper in exasperation. The woman had long flowing white hair, dark gray eyes and a holier than though, attitude. It permeated the very air around her. Robin looked down at her shoes and noticed that while they were black like everyone else's, this woman's shoes had ten-inch heels. No wonder she had looked like a giant walking into the café, Robin thought with a twinge of annoyance.

Irritated but knowing she had lost the table fair and square Robin was about to turn and look for another one when she took a second glance at the hover device near the woman's feet. It had purple stones along the bottom edges however the woman had not been pulling the long metal handle attached to it for navigation. "Just like the stroller..." Robin muttered to herself. "What?" The woman looked up at Robin in exasperation with a look that said, 'you're still here...' Glaring at her, Robin said, "How is that cart moving by itself? It looks like it's being pulled but there's no one..." Before Robin could finish the woman sniffed loudly, grimaced at Robin then turned away from her as if she did not exist. Robin grew quiet and could not help but feel as if she had been slapped in the face. Balling her fists at her side she was just about to open her mouth and show the woman that not only did she exist but she had a pretty good idea where the woman could go with her nasty attitude. "Excuse me..." Before Robin could get into it, Roami was at her side with his hand softly resting on the small of her back. He moved his hand in a soothing gesture and whispered in her ear, "She's not worth it, Robin. Come on, let's go..." He gently took her hand and led her away.

Robin could only glare at the woman as they exited the café and made their way back towards the hover stairs at the epicenter of the mall. "But we wanted Bobble Juice, Roami." Robin complained. "Yes, but that place was way too crowded. According to the map there should be another one on the twenty-second floor. Let's just go where we can enjoy ourselves. That woman was delusional and drowning in her own sense of self importance. Just knowing she was there would have destroyed the whole Bobble experience for both of us. Right?" Roami smiled hoping Robin would too. She did not. "She looked at me like I was... nothing." Robin muttered to herself. "You don't know how many times I had to deal with that back in..." She quieted and seemed to be drawn back into her thoughts of the past. Roami looked on, helpless to stop her. "Just forget about it Robin... It doesn't matter." Roami said feebly. He was not sure how to convince Robin not to let that particular incident get under her skin. They got their Bobble Juice from the next café they found then walked through a few more floors of the mall. The entire time, Robin did not utter a single word. In fact she walked, head down and ignored all the stores and entertainments that would usually have had her running amuck, giddily motioning for Roami to keep up. Roami sighed at the sight and struggled to think of something to cheer her up. Just then he got an idea. "Robin, I have a treat for you..." Roami's voice seemed to come from miles away. Robin was so deep in her thoughts she felt as if she were again walking through a murky water world. But this one was not below the sea, it was in her head. "Robin?" Roami repeated. "Huh?" She asked then blinked her eyes to fully return to the present. "I saw this store earlier and knew you'd love to check these out." Roami said. Robin looked up to see they were standing in front of a store with a sign in front that said, "Hover Fun". Robin saw tons of beautifully painted hover boards, hover skates and hover scooters. "Woa!" She said aloud and could not stop a smile from creeping across her lips. Roami smiled as well. He was overjoyed his tactic had successfully pulled her from her dark thoughts. "Come on. Let's check them out!" Roami grabbed her hand and pulled her inside. "Oh... my... goodness! Look at these Roami!" The store shone with hundreds of bright blue lights above and had countless rows of merchandise on wooden shelves. Before they had taken more than a handful of steps inside, Robin had already saw something that took her breath away. "Purple hover skates! Ahhh! Look at the stars and zigzags on the sides. These are hot!" Robin squealed as she grabbed them in her hands. They looked like inline skates on earth however instead of a line of wheels there were just five small blocks of sparkling purple stones where the wheels would have been. Roami looked confused and held one of the skates in his hand. "They are not hot at all. They don't even feel warm..." He looked at Robin with a confused expression. "No, that's just a little slang from earth. Sorry, I forget every now and then where I am... now..." Robin laughed to herself and with a sigh moved to replace the skates. Roami smirked then stopped her hands with his, "No. They're yours." He said as he pushed the skates back towards her. Before she could say another word he began walking further down the aisle, "Now let's get something for me to ride also. I want to have fun too." He said while his eyes roved across the merchandise on display. "But Roami, how will we buy them? I mean... Actually, how are you buying all the things you've gotten for me? The dollhouse, the-" Before she could finish he turned around and said, "Don't worry Robin. I've been doing some work for Mika these past few afternoons. He noticed how astute I am and asked me to help him get his personal finances together at home. He of course paid me for the service." Roami said with a beaming smile. Robin smiled back, proud of her friend. "Wow! That's great Roami! You're amazing!" Roami grew serious for a moment, "Although I did notice something odd as I was going over his papers..." Robin perked up her ear, "Yeah? And what was that?" Sighing Roami continued, "They have tons of profit and not as much expenses as you'd think. It just doesn't... add up." "Hmm...." Was all Robin could say. She had never been great at finances as she had never had any real money to manage.

"Well, anyway, let's focus on fun for now. We will figure this all out soon enough. What do you think about this black and silver hover board?" Roami picked up the item in question and Robin squealed in delight! "Is it Hot?" Roami asked with a smile. "Yes, it's Hot to death!" Robin laughed then poked Roami playfully. "Let's get them and have a little fun for once then." Roami said as they carried their merchandise to the cashier waiting with a smile at the back of the store. *** Moments later Robin grinned broadly and stuck her tongue out playfully as they raced towards the opening of one of the Akwo tunnels in town. "You ready?" Roami said as they swung their tied black shoes over their shoulders and jumped on their new hover devices. "Yes sir!" Robin said playfully. "Let's go then!" Roami said as they hopped onto adjacent water canals and raced through the bright blue tunnel filled with serious faced Wongswited commuters. "Woohooo!!!" Robin had never felt so full of life. Her heart beat hard against her chest and she felt replete with happiness. Perhaps she was feeling a little too uninhibited, as just seconds later she nearly tripped. Roami was there in a second; grabbing her hand and keeping her upright. Feeling a little shaken but still filled with delight Robin looked up at him and smiled sheepishly while mouthing, 'thank you'. Roami nodded shyly. Robin noticed he did not take his hand from hers but held on to it firmly much longer than necessary. Her heart began to tremble and she gulped. She had never felt so shy or experienced the feeling of being cared for, as if she were a delicate possession. She found it hard to look Roami in the eyes for the remainder of their time in town that evening. The few times her eyes did catch his; her heart began to feel like it had turned into a large butterfly ready to flutter away and seek refuge in his arms... *** The next morning Robin awoke with a start and realized someone had knocked at her door. Her eyes were puffy and her vision blurred so she rubbed at them to fully awaken. She simultaneously sat up and slipped the sea of warm covers off her body. It felt as if a weight were pushing her back towards the bed but she pushed past the desire to return to sleep and straightened her canary yellow pajama suit with its purple stars littered across it. Suddenly she heard the sound of footsteps quickly moving away from her door. Robin raced to the door and opened it quickly. She hoped she would catch a peak of the servant who left her breakfast at her door every morning seemingly without a trace. Apparently she was not the only one awakened by their early morning room service. Roami's door creaked open and his head popped out to see his tray sitting before his door as well.

He glanced at Robin with a small but tired smile. "No servant sighting today... just like every other day." She said with disappointment. Roami only chuckled as he opened his door to pick up his breakfast. Robin could tell that Roami had not had much sleep. "Your eyes are bloodshot. What happened?" She asked with concern. "I woke up in the middle of the night. I heard screams again. You did not hear them this time either?" He asked. "No. But I have noticed that your hearing is much better than mine so that's no surprise to me." Robin said as she motioned for Roami to have breakfast with her in her room. "I do not know for sure but I have a feeling that those screams and the Reposer are all clues to the puzzle. We must go to the town center at night and see what happens there." Roami said. "I'm not crazy about standing out there in the dark but if you really think our answer is out there somewhere..." She looked at Roami intently then continued. "Then I guess we can start tonight." *** That night they raced to the town center to investigate. The two hid behind a few rainbow colored sculpture bushes which had been planted at the small sitting park. The park was nothing more than a circular space filled with artificial foliage surrounded by golden paths. A single marble manhole marked the exact center of the town. Robin and Roami crouched there at the park, hidden from view. They waited for a few hours only to find that nothing at all would occur. At least not there...

*** While nothing had happened during their midnight escapade in the town center, Robin soon found her night was about to get much more interesting. In the bewitching hours of the early morning, a sad whimpering sounded in the hallway just outside of Robin's bedroom door. Her eyes shot open and she looked at the window to gauge if the street lamps had grown brighter to signal the start of a new day. No, they were off which meant it was still very early. She wore dark purple pajamas with a white belt around her middle. The slippers left by her bed were the same shade of purple and so comfortable her eyes rolled back in her head in pleasure each time she set foot in them. Throwing these on in a hurry, Robin raced towards the door on tiptoe. Slowly; ever so slowly, she opened the door and peeked out. She had finally gotten lucky! A few feet down the corridor she spotted a glimpse of something green...transparent and green. Bringing her hands to her eyes, Robin rubbed them to ensure her vision was clear. She was sure she must be seeing things. But no, walking down the hallway was in fact a semi-transparent green little boy wearing gray shorts and a gray sleeveless shirt. He was barefoot and kept flashing in and out of focus. It was as if he were a flickering flame. Robin had seen enough horror movies on earth to know she should definitely be freaking out,

right about now. She watched frozen in shock as the ghost stopped before a side table against the wall and grabbed the small yellow vase resting on it. He pulled the fake purple flowers out of it and turned the vase upside town. Out fell a small black wooden vial with a white cork in it. He opened the vial then took two sips. In less than an instant he completely disappeared. Robin was astounded. She continued to watch as invisible hands returned the vial then the flowers into the vase. She could see soft imprints in the green velvet carpet as the ghost walked away. Quickly making her way to the side table, Robin pulled the vial out and took a small sip herself hoping that her hypothesis was correct. If not it was very possible she could be dead or worse in the next few seconds.
Replacing the vial, Robin followed behind the ghosts footsteps. As she walked, she turned to look into one of the mirrors hanging against the wall. When she looked for her reflection, absolutely nothing stared back at her. Ah, so she had been right! That liquid vial held; of all things, an invisibility serum! Robin quietly tiptoed behind the invisible ghost. He made his way down the rest of the long hallway then went into a single red door at the end of the hall. She had seen it before during one of her daily explorations. It was nothing more than an emergency exit to the buildings' only stairwell. She looked on in amazement. Why a ghost

would take the steps and not the elevators was beyond her. Ignoring the logic behind his actions, she followed his lead and made her way into the concrete stairwell. Both the walls and stairs were all painted the same drab gray that made one feel like you did not know what was up or down. Robin stopped short for a moment wondering if maybe she was being a little too brash. She turned to look behind her at the closed red door and hesitated. Should she go run to Roami and give him the scoop on what she had seen? As she debated this, she heard footfalls quickly going up the steps and knew she would have to make a decision soon.

Swallowing hard and getting up her courage Robin began tiptoeing up the stairs in her now invisible purple slippers. It was time someone got to the bottom of all the strangeness happening in Wongswited. This might be her and Roami's only chance to find the riddle.

Robin was in pretty good shape and had used her extracurricular activities at school to avoid spending time at her various "homes". But even she was out of breath after the thirtieth flight of stairs. However, she refused to give up. Like anything else, that you have put so much time and energy into in order to meet a goal, she would have rather died than lay down and admit defeat. She continued just so long as her invisible companion did. He apparently was superhuman as he did not stop or pause for breath until they were at the very top of the one hundred and fifteen storied building. Robin was drenched in sweat. She had struggled to breathe quietly during the entire run and now felt as if she would pass out. After what seemed like ages, the bodiless footsteps stopped altogether. There before them, stood an identical red door at the final landing. Here instead of yet another twist and turn of gray steps there was only a concrete wall. The door flung open a moment later and Robin waited a minute to catch her breath and get her bearings. When she felt as if she could breathe normally again and was not seeing double, she cautiously opened the red door to see what was on the other side. Her heart beat frantically against her chest and her silk pajamas were sweaty and plastered against her skin after her ordeal. Opening it just enough to get a good look at what lay beyond it, Robin saw it was in fact the door to the rooftop. Just outside, the ground was completely covered in slabs of the blue Akwo stone the town used for energy and light. It almost seemed like a glowing sea of cool blue water until one looked closer and realized it was actually hard stone. Robin thought the effect was very beautiful. However, as mesmerizing as this was, it could not hold her attention for long as she quickly saw she was not alone. Not by a long shot. What seemed like a whole community of people were walking to and fro across the blue tiles doing various activities.

The first thing that caught her attention was the clotheslines hung everywhere. Whereas Robin had seen clothes lines hanging from windows, between buildings and even on roofs of buildings in New York City, she noticed the same sort of zigzag of poles and black rope littered across the entire expanse of the roof. Instead of clothes, however, sheets of Akwo stone hung across each one of these lines. Also scattered throughout were brightly colored woven fabrics of various colors. They too were draped over the black ropes crisscrossing the roof top from high poles. This fabric was then tied to the ground at its four ends making little tents. She had apparently come across some sort of shanty town. Robin had seen similar places on television when they showed poor communities in Africa, South America and other areas that made up the third world. She had even seen similar settlements for the homeless in New York City as well. Robin quickly noticed the outstanding difference between those outposts and what she saw before her eyes at that very moment. First off, some of the people were blinking or flickering in and out. That was the best way Robin could explain the effect. Like her ghost she had followed, they seemed to be low on the invisibility juice. Some appeared one second then were gone the next then back again, while others just looked slightly transparent. Apparently the juice ran out after a certain amount of time.   Fearfully, Robin looked down to see if she was still invisible. She was. With that confirmed she slipped out from behind the door and onto the roof. When she finally got a better look at the flickering people she had once thought were ghosts she was met with an even bigger surprise. "They're Fitzian..." She said aloud without thinking. Thankfully no one was close enough or able to see her to realize she was secretly walking among them.   True enough the people walking around her in a flurry of activity were the same tall, green skinned, colorful haired Fitzian's she and Roami had thought they had left behind in that world under the sea. Robin could not begin to understand how this was possible. Her brain began to work in overtime as she tried to piece everything together.   While some possessed the tell-tale fuchsia hair of the Fitz; many others had the Wongswited penchant for a varying hair colors. However, the shade of their hair was apparently a non issue. Robin quickly noticed every one of them, male and female, had their hair completely shorn off so that only a hint of the bright color could be seen. Furthermore, she could not label them as Royals or Mubbins as they seemed to come in varying shades of green from light to dark. "Trilly! Trilly! Have you delivered the Strange Ones their breakfast yet? Is that you boy?!" Someone yelled from just outside a bright red tent. Robin turned to see a tall grass green women without hair and amazingly vibrant blue eyes step out of the tent. She continued to call for someone named 'Trilly'. Like everyone else she wore worn gray short trousers and a matching tunic. She looked skinny and frail despite her tall stature. Robin watched as the boy she had seen only traces of in the corridor finally came into full view. He was no longer invisible but stood before the woman nodding his head demurely. He was about Robin's height. His skin was a lighter shade of green than the woman's and he had purple eyes that seemed almost magical in the way they sparkled. He too was gaunt and had shorn hair. "Yes mother..." Was all he said in response. She nodded then pulled him towards her to give him a quick warm hug. "You're a good boy, you are, Trilly. Come inside and get some breakfast. It is Bimmy Porridge like any other day but I found a few Gulpy Raisins in the town earlier this morning so added them in for you, my love." She smiled at his look of both surprise and wonder then ushered him into the tent. Robin watched with sadness at how poorly they lived but then smiled warmly at the amount of love she saw between the two. "Who are you?" Before Robin could turn around to confront who had spoken, they angrily added, "And what are you doing here?!" Robin turned to see a tall young man with dark green skin and yellow eyes, eyeing her in disbelief. Apparently she too was no longer invisible. As she opened her mouth to explain he yelled out. "One of the Strange Ones is here in Dunber Quarter! Come and see for yourself!" He screamed this out and within seconds everyone stopped what they had been doing. A crowd of people rushed over to surround Robin who just gaped back at them in open shock. "How did you get up here? What do you want?" Robin did not know who all the questions came from as she was too busy trying to think of a way to escape. Her legs grew weak and she felt as if the world were closing in on her. What had she gotten herself into now? The boy named Trilly moved towards the front of the mob. When he laid eyes on Robin, he quickly spoke up. "Don't hurt her! I know her... Well...kind of. I bring her and the other Strange One food every day and I have watched her around the house. She is a nice person... she is not like the Wongswited. Believe me... I think we can trust her." He said this then rushed to her side and took her hand. He smiled at her slightly to show her everything was okay. Cautiously, Robin smiled back at him in thanks. "What do you know? You're nothing but a half-breed!" An angry dark green man yelled out. His comment received a few nods among the group. Trilly's mother stepped up to defend her son. "How dare you Garath! You of all people. My son is no half-breed and any mixing that created him only made him better! At least he wasn't born in Fitz and corrupted by the evil mind-set they teach there. I will not let you or anyone else make him feel inferior!" She stopped to look around at her neighbors and friends, "How can we ever rise up against the Wongswited if we fight even among ourselves and still stick to the backwards class system of Fitz?!" Her blue eyes blazed as bright as the blue stone surrounding them. The man named Garath stepped back slightly upon seeing the wild look in her eyes.

"Everyone stand down!" A single female voice came from the back of the crowd and made its way forward. The woman was shorter than the rest with pitch black eyes and a round belly.

"Last I checked... I, Garabeth, was the leader of this Quarter! I will ask the Strange One what I wish and make any decisions necessary. Trilly and Marin... I will take the Strange One to your abode and we will all discuss this privately. Everyone else, get back to work! The Planet Yur will be rising to its zenith soon and we need these stones to get as much Yuric energy as possible. Those who have forest patrol drink the Bunk liquid as dictated by our masters so that you do not blink between your homes and the forest. You know what happened to the last Fitz who got caught blinking while in town..." She let her warning drift off and watched as everyone dutifully went back to doing their daily duties.

"Come Strange One." She motioned for Robin to follow her past a few lines of blue stone hanging on a line. The group then circled around a large pile of shining blue rock sitting in the center of the shanty town then marched straight into Marin and Trilly's waiting red tent. Once inside Robin found the place was very small. However, despite its diminutive size it was made cozy with tons of worn yet plush gray pillows and two soft gray mats. In the center of the abode was a metal cooking device which had a small black pot of green porridge resting on it. Marin, who was apparently Trilly's mother, rushed inside first and pulled two large gray pillows towards a short raised rectangular wooden board which passed as a table. Robin and Garabeth sat down on the offered pillows and watched as Marin and Trilly sat on their own mats across from them.

"Porridge?" Marin offered. Robin was in no mood to eat and wanted to get straight to talking. Before she could shake her head Garabeth said, "No food for now. As you know we don't have much time before our Masters expect us to begin the days' work. Let's get this over with." Robin nodded then looked back at Trilly knowing he was the only one truly on her side at the moment. He might just be the only one she could trust. She sat nervously not knowing exactly what was at stake here. Would they hurt her, tell her hosts about her snooping or make things really easy and just throw her off the roof to her certain death? "What is your actual name?" Trilly asked; pulling Robin away from her morbid thoughts. Marin and Garabeth eyed him for speaking out of turn. He looked down duly chastised. "My name is Robin." Robin said with a warm smile for Trilly once he looked back. She was glad he did not just assume her name was 'strange one' as most Wongswiteds did. "How did you know we were up here? Our Masters have gone through great lengths to keep our existence unknown... especially from outsiders." Garabeth asked. "I did not know..." Robin was cautious with her words. She did not want to get Trilly in trouble and something told her if the truth be known about her seeing and following him... the young boy would have hell to pay. "I uh... was just exploring and had wondered what the red door was for and what was on the rooftop...I had uh... I had seen the bridges going across the buildings and just couldn't help but get to the bottom of the mystery." Robin said hoping they would buy her white lie. "And you just happened to take the steps instead of the elevator which does not even go to the roof..." Garabeth eyed Robin suspiciously. "I needed the exercise. I woke up last night and couldn't get back to sleep. I've been hearing screams coming from the city center and moaning from the sky every night..." Robin added the last two hoping to get some insight behind the two odd occurrences. "Hmm..." Was Garabeth's only response. "The moaning you hear is not from the heavens... it is our traditional songs of sadness..." Marin piped in. Garabeth eyed her pointedly. "What Garabeth? I mean she already knows we exist. What harm could it do at this point to tell her about our traditions?" Marin rationalized. Sighing Garabeth was about to speak when a young man with orange eyes poked his head in. "Mistress? There's a uh... issue we need your help with." Rolling her eyes Garabeth stood up with a deep sigh and said, "Try not to tell her anything that could come back to bite us in the... you know what. I have business to attend to. You all eat up then I want you two back to work. As for her... send her to me in a few minutes. I need to talk to her before she returns downstairs." With that said Garabeth stepped out of the tent. With her went all of the tension Robin had felt slowly suffocating her. Marin laughed as she watched Robin breath out dramatically and her shoulders sag. "She is somewhat of an acquired taste, that Garabeth. But she leads us well and really does care about all of the people in her Quarter." Marin explained as she pulled out three wooden bowls and filled them with the green porridge. "Please eat with us. It is not much but..." She left off the rest of her comment as she dove into the pocket of her gray tunic and pulled out a few bright pink balls. "Yumm! Gulpy Raisins!" Trilly said as he licked his lips. Robin laughed at his reaction. He pulled three wooden spoons from a small basket near the table and dipped them into each bowl.

"Eat up! We don't have much time before our day of labor begins." Marin said with a hint of both sadness and exhaustion. As the three began to eat, Robin could not help but think the porridge tasted absolutely horrid. It was like cement paste. Even though she had never eaten cement she was completely sure that is exactly what the porridge was like. The Gulpy Raisins on the other hand were like morsels from heaven. She did not know where they were from or what they were but they had to be the sweetest taste she had ever experienced. "What is a Quarter?" Robin found if she spoke enough she would not be expected to eat the horrible porridge as quickly. "A group. When we leave the tent and the Planet Yur begins to shine you will clearly see the other Quarters on each roof of each building in Wongswited." Marin said in answer. "And each Quarter has a Commander. Just like Mistress Garabeth. She's our commander." Trilly said with his mouth full of porridge. Robin looked at the edges of the tent and saw a number of black ceramic pots with golden dirt and beautiful plants. Each had purple trunks with succulent green leaves. A few even had brightly colored exotic looking flowers sprouting from them. "Real plants..." Robin breathed aloud. She had not seen any living foliage or trees since she had left Fitz and climbed up the Nommo Tree. "Yes. That is the one plus to being forced to live on the rooftops. We have direct access to the life giving planet Yur. You will see tons of trees and plants growing in each Quarter. They are our one true pride." Marin smiled as she traced her dark green hand across an exquisite looking orange and blue flower sprouting from a nearby pot. "Sometimes we are lucky enough to find fruits in the forests and bring the seeds back to grow them. That doesn't happen often but when it does we have a celebration!" Trilly said happily. It was apparent from the smile on his face that he was thinking of one such festival in his head. "Yes... we Fitz love to Party. We had tons of parties back in Fitz. But here...the Wongswited are a serious and industrious people. They don't like music, the arts or parties. They are more focused on technology and business. We are very different; the Fitz and the Wongswited." Marin said sadly. "How is it the Fitz came to be here? And why are you all hidden away and treated like servants?" Robin asked the main questions which circled about in her head. "We...the Fitz you see here on the rooftops of Wongswited... have a number of different origins. Some you see... usually the older ones, were forced here... by the Fitz under the sea. Either having been convicted of crimes or being ostracized, they were forced up the Nommo Tree to their supposed deaths. Instead of dying, they just ended up in this land of the purple babies who had been forced away. Others... like my son Trilly... Are first generation

Fitz-Wongswiteds. He was born here. His father was Fitz but of the...um... serving class back in Fitz. Here, as we all live side by side... things are different. At least for some of us. I had no problem loving one of the fairer colored Fitzians... others like Garath; whom you saw earlier, stick to the old Fitzian way and wish to force the lighter Fitzians to separate Quarters. There is talk they have even started a movement to do just that. To me it is just plain crazy to be treated as we do by the Wongswited then even among ourselves hurt one another..." Marin grew quiet as her thoughts overtook her. "I totally agree with you Marin." Robin said and smiled at her reassuringly. "And as for your last question... We are not treated like servants at all. We are considered full out slaves for the Wongswited. That is why they force us to drink Bunk Juice. It keeps us invisible so they don't have to see the wrongs they have done to us." She looked down sadly as memories seemed to sweep through her head. Robin cleared her throat softly to bring Marin back to the present. With a sad smile she continued speaking, "Most of us Fitz here, work in the forests during the day. We drink the Bunk by law and travel invisibly beside Wongswiteds in the town then make our way to the surrounding Forests. It is there that we collect the blue Akwo stones." Marin explained. "No one dares go deeper than the edge of the forest though. There is a legend that horrible monsters live inside those forests... they eat people!" Trilly said with a shiver as he finished eating his porridge. When he was done he stared at Robin thoughtfully. "We have to make sure we drink enough Bunk or carry an extra vial with us during the day. If any of us are found blinking during the day they are sent... deep into the forest...to our deaths..." Marin said sadly. "I am just happy my little Trilly was made a house servant. He does not have to worry overmuch about the hardships of forest work. Right Trilly?" Marin smiled proudly at her son although her eyes still looked quite sad and empty. Trilly just nodded despondently. "Too bad it wasn't the same for dad... he was one of those who blinked..." Robin looked at Marin and watched her drop her head in a gesture of defeat. Her shoulders began to shake slightly as she struggled to hold back her tears. "They sent him into the forest..." Was all Trilly said as he collected their bowls and set them aside. His hand accidentally touched Robin's as he took her bowl. He paused and looked her directly in the eyes. "I wish I were your color... Then maybe my life would not be so hard..." He said with a small smile then continued cleaning up. Robin just stared at him dumbfounded. She did not know how to respond to such an odd statement. "Come now you two, the Planet Yur is rising." Marin said as she led the way out of the tent. Robin and Trilly followed behind her. Robin watched in awe as the Red and purple sky turned even more red as the large Ruby colored planet made its way from the horizon and high above the city.   The blue stones on the ground and hanging on the lines glowed brightly in response and Robin began to notice the tons of flower pots and potted trees littered across the large expanse of the roof. She had never seen any place that sparkled so magically.   A thought came to her as she tilted her head backwards and stared up at the red sky for what seemed like the first time in ages. "But what about the Blue Storms? I was here during one of them. How did you all survive that with just cloth tents to protect you from the sharp stones?" Robin looked around her at the flimsy tents flapping in the breeze. "What storm?" Trilly asked without thinking. Slowly something dawned on him and he was about to open his mouth once more. Marin, however, stopped him in his tracks. "There are no storms... there are only revolutions..." A single tear fell from Marin's eye and she sniffled. "I'm sorry, I honestly don't understand." Robin said softly. She did not like to see the sweet mannered mother look so bereft but felt helpless to make her life better in any way. What could Robin possibly do to help on such a grand scale, she wondered. "The stones did not come from the sky, we threw them down in protest. In protest of what the Wongswited do to-" Trilly's next words were lost as Marin placed her hand over his mouth softly. "That is enough Trilly. Let us find Garabeth and get Robin back where she belongs..." Marin looked at her son pointedly. With a sigh he nodded and let her lead the way. Robin wanted nothing more than to continue questioning them but also did not want to add to their burden. She turned her attention back to her surroundings. As the sky lit up she noticed several wooden planked bridges making their way from the black painted edges of the roof and off towards numerous directions. With the light of Yur shining bright, she quickly saw where those bridges led. One after another, each rooftop became visible to the eye. Each seemed to come alive as the blue stones glowed brightly with the light of Yur. Within seconds the colorful tents and busy people of Fitz began moving about. "Wow..." Was all Robin could say as she let it all sink in. "Is she ready to leave then?" Garabeth's stern voice came from just feet away. Robin turned to see the Commander flanked by two tall young men. Both guards wore the same drab gray outfit as the rest of the Fitz. One's eyes were red and the other had an extremely long nose and pert pink eyes. "I...uh..." Before Robin could respond a loud drumming noise came from far away. "Oh no.... oh no....!" Someone cried out just a few feet away from them. "This late in the morning?" Marin whispered in fear. Robin was about to ask what everyone was talking about when she heard a collective moan come from one of the other roof tops. The sound was breathtakingly sorrowful. It was at once a song and a cry. The sound was soon echoed from another direction, atop yet another roof.

Moments later Robin watched as each of the Fitz stopped whatever they had been doing. Some stepped out of tents and others dropped Akwo stones to hang their heads back and howl their song of sadness to the heavens above. "What is going on?" Robin began to back away looking for a means of escape as it appeared everyone had gone loony. "It is the Reposer..." Trilly came to stand near her, sensing her fear. "The Reposer. Oh, I met him. What does he have to do with this song?" Robin asked in confusion. "It is not a song but more a cry of lamentation." Marin explained then cried out loudly like the rest. "But why? Why now? What were those drums for? Is that why the cries were coming from the town center all those nights?" Robin asked frantically. She needed concrete answers and she wanted them now. "It's the Reposer... he is preparing to repose..." Trilly said cryptically. "Don't ask too many questions. It is best you and your other strange friend do not anger the wongswited or question their ways. Just return below stairs and act like you never saw us. Forget about what happens in the town center. It does not concern you." Garabeth stared pointedly at Robin then at the red exit door at the other end of the roof. Robin realized she would get no further answers. Wanting to get back to Roami's side and safety; Robin raced towards the red door and made her way down one flight of stairs. She then exited the door to that floor and ran down the hallway towards the elevators. She was definitely taking the easy way down. Stepping into the elevator she could not help but fidget and hop anxiously from foot to foot. She could not wait to tell Roami all that had happened. But more importantly they had to get to the town center right now to figure out what the Reposing business truly entailed. ***

"Wait... so what are you talking about? What is Bunk juice? And why in the world would you drink something without knowing what it would-" Roami shook his head in confusion as he tried to piece together Robin's rushed story.

He was still dressed in his black pajama suits. He barely had time to throw on his black shoes as Robin rushed through the details of her adventure and their need to get to the town center quickly. She had kept her purple pajamas on as well but rushed to collect all of the souvenirs she had picked up from Fitz and Wongswited, excluding the large doll house of course. That had been a tough decision; it was just too big to carry without causing a scene. Robin was sure she would take it everywhere she went if she could. She frantically placed the Flob nuggets, blue Akwo stone and Bunk juice in

316

a black hand bag Tika had been nice enough to give her days ago. "Roami does that really matter right now? Please, we need to focus on what they are trying to hide from us. It definitely has something to do with 'Reposing' and I just pray it's nothing at all like 'Disposing' or we may have another problem on our hands..." Robin said breathlessly as they made their way out of the building and raced across town. They did not stop running until they made it to the small park located at the town center.   Robin and Roami raced back to the same spot they had hid the previous night. They breathlessly hunched behind one of the brightly colored, artificial sculpture bushes which stood just at the back of a park bench.   At first all they saw was the Reposer standing in the clearing next to the marble slab which marked the towns epicenter. He looked just as they had seen him the day before. He wore the same brown suit and arrogant expression. Robin crooked her neck to get a better view of him. He was standing near a copse of sculpture trees while banging a large silver colored drum with one large brown stick. Robin yawned and was beginning to wonder if there truly was a deep, dark secret to unearth. Maybe the Reposer was just part of some corny underground music band that only played in the dead of night and early morning. Their perseverance, however, paid off and after waiting a short while they saw tons of

Wongswiteds slowly begin to fill the small park. Although the hour was early everyone wore their finest business suits, not one person looked flustered, hurried or wore their pajamas with curlers still in their hair. Robin definitely felt underdressed as she and Roami were still in their pajamas and her hair was all over the place. "I guess they had this already planned out. They finally have a party here and we weren't even invited. How rude..." Robin sucked her teeth in exasperation. She glared past the rainbow colored crystal leaves of the bush and the wooden slits of the bench to take it all in. Roami just gave her a warning stare that said, please be quiet for once. When it appeared everyone was in attendance a tall and slender purple woman walked out from among the crowd. She looked very nervous and her sky blue eyes glistened in the blue light of the lanterns hanging above them on the street lines.

Her sky blue hair was short and curled softly against her beautifully sculpted face. She wore a pristine white gown which looked exactly like the gown Boonie had worn during his Birthing in Fitz. It flowed all around her and the bottoms had turned slightly yellow from the golden ground beneath them. A man stepped from the crowd and stood a few feet behind her looking just as nervous. He had fiery red hair and green eyes that looked kindly. He was dressed in a black suit and black undershirt. The woman turned around and stared at him for assurance. It was fair to assume he was her husband. Nodding his head he motioned for her to move forward. She smiled timorously then made her way before the Reposer who now stood beside the silver drum. With a deep indrawn breath he ceased his drumming and dropped the wooden stick to the ground. The Reposer looked her in the eyes and she curtsied respectfully at his feet. "Is it time then?" The Reposer asked. "Yes, it is." She responded robotically. "We must wait for the King to-" The Reposer stopped speaking when he saw a path quickly open within the crowd. King Philtu made his way to the forefront. Two large guards stood at his sides; one with a large golden chair in hand which he placed down right before the swarm of onlookers. The king sat on the proffered chair then nodded solemnly at the Reposer to continue. "Let's just get on with this. This is the latest birthing in history! How could it have come so late?!" He looked incredibly angry. Taking a deep breath to control his rage he just shook his head then continued to speak before the Reposer could begin to make excuses, "Just get on with it quickly! We can't have our guests waking up and seeing this business..." Nodding hastily, the Reposer took the woman by the hand and led her a few feet over the golden cement path towards a patch of manicured ground. Here at the town's epicenter, there was a mound of artificial brown grass and in the center of the small upraised hill a circular piece of black marble. "I saw that the other day when we passed by. I thought maybe it was a monument or something..." Robin whispered to Roami. Roami just nodded as he watched the events unfolding with bated breath. As the Reposer and the woman made their way towards the marble slab, two large purple men followed behind them then leaned forward to pull the oval slab of black marble from the ground. Beneath it was nothing more than a circle of red sand.   To Robin, it felt as if the entire procession had taken a deep breath of anticipation at the same exact time. The tension nearly crackled in the air. At the Reposer's stern nod, the woman walked towards the sand and sat on it gingerly. Her white gown bunched up all around her and soon had red stains from the sands pigment. After a few moments of contemplative silence she stood up and stared at the spot of sand she had left.

Everyone else stared at the spot of red sand as well. As the moments passed the woman began to wring her hands nervously.   The red-headed man who had urged her earlier was indeed her husband. He rushed forward to stand beside his wife. He took her tenderly in his arms. All the while theirs and everyone else's eyes never left the plot of sand.   "I guess they have a similar birthing process after all..." Roami said just before Robin shushed him. Just then a tiny hand ripped out of the sand and a small body pushed its way through the sand to lie across the ground. The newborn babe give a hearty scream out to the heavens above.   "Oh no! Oh please no!" The woman said and immediately fainted in her husband's arms. Grabbing his wife the man grimaced then carried her away quickly. The silence of just a few moments before was a thing of the past. Angry screams erupted from every direction. The crowd began to scream and grab angrily at the couple, who stealthily got away.

When their initial targets were gone the crowd rounded up against the small child, left behind and abandoned by its birth parents. The small green skinned baby looked back at the crowd with large tearful purple eyes and began to scream for its mother. His beautiful golden hair was matted to his head and covered in red sand. "Mama, Mama! Who am I? What is my name? Mama, Mama! Who will protect me?" he cried out frantically. Robin's mouth hung ajar in complete shock as tears began to build up and seemed to drown her from within. "Oh no... How could they?! How could they repeat such an ugly thing and do exactly what was done to them!" Robin said this angrily as she jumped over the bench they had hid behind. Without a thought in her mind, other than the safety of the baby, she made her way to the child's side. She stood before him just as the first gold rocks were thrown its way.

"Robin, wait!" Roami said as he raced to stand

beside her. He quickly positioned himself to shield both the baby and Robin from the brunt of the stones thrown at them. "How could you all do this to a helpless baby? Have you learned nothing from what you went through at the hands of the people of Fitz? This is completely crazy!" Robin screamed furiously at the crowd. However, she grew quiet when something at the edge of the crowd caught her eye. "Oh no... Please no. Not you too!" She said with tears in her eyes as she saw young Brifton dressed in a small white suit, gleefully racing around to gather stones. He then threw each one at the young green child. He was mimicking his parents' actions. For Robin, knowing this did not make the betrayal sting any less. Before Robin could continue her tirade against the town's people the tall skinny man who called himself the Reposer, stepped before the two children and the young green baby. Pushing his white rimmed glasses up against his face he glared at Robin and Roami with distaste. "Move aside strange ones! Move aside so that I can do my job and lead this abomination away from us all!" He said sternly. Before Robin could respond with words or her fists, a loud moaning sound began to canvas the town. Everyone stopped and stared up above. The Fitzian's cries from the rooftops was so sorrowful it crept into the bones of any who heard it. Robin herself could not help but shiver. Roami grabbed up the green baby and held him protectively in his arms as he too looked up in wonder. "I know what that is! That is the sound of sadness. That is the sound of your guilt!" Robin screamed out at the crowd and pointed at everyone. The moans continued as each Quarter on each building reacted to the screams they had heard in the town center. They knew now that one of theirs had been born of the Wongswited and would be killed. "You all think you can profit from the pain and misery you put on those poor Fitzians but you are wrong! Like so many people before you, you will be taken down by your own greed and corruption. Yes, the Fitzians under the sea were wrong to abandon you and throw you away. But to make the ones who were forced here, suffer too, that is just as wrong. You went from the victims to the victimizers!" Robin wiped the tears that fell from her eyes during her speech. She looked at Brifton standing with a rock in his hand and could not stop the moan of pain that fell from her lips. Roami; seeing that Robin was close to completely losing it, took her by the hand and pulled her against him for support. The child was still safely behind them and protected from the crowd. The King stood from his chair and motioned towards Robin, "Do you truly think Strange Ones... do you truly think those heathens...those slaves on the rooftops would not do to us what we do to them if they were given even half a chance?! You know nothing of society... you know nothing of the nature of people if you think they are any better than us! Only the fittest survive...everyone else must be kept down for their own good!" Grimacing he covered his ears as the Fitzian moans grew louder.   "Guards I want each one of those Quarters punished by nightfall. No rations of food for three days for this offense. And if they dare stage another Blue Storm for this, be sure to make that a full week without rations! As for that green abomination over there... Reposer get over there and get rid of it now!" The King bellowed. The two guards beside him moved forward to take action. "No way!" Robin said standing protectively beside Roami and wrapping her arms around Roami and the baby. "Now, no need to get angry. I'm just doing my job, that's all. Have to rid the city of this stain. No harm intended; really, just doing my job." The Reposer said with agitation. He moved towards them to pull the little baby from their grasp. "No!" Robin said simply. "Yes well... Then I guess you two will be going with it then!" The Reposer said this and waving his hand in the air, motioned for someone to come towards him. The crowd moved aside as two large green Fitzian servants in tattered gray shirts and trousers, shorn hair and red sleep deprived eyes moved towards the trio. They did not look all that menacing but it was apparent they would do whatever they were ordered.   The servants pushed at Robin and Roami who remained entwined to ensure they were not separated. The baby snuggled between them and tried to hide his cute face away from the angry and vicious glares it saw all around it.   After a few hefty nudges by the two servants, the trio was forced across the gold pavement and into the gold cobbled street.   There a white truck waited for them. It was the only vehicle Robin and Roami had seen since they had arrived in Wongswited. It was made of wood and was circular in shape, very similar to the water buggies in Fitz. Instead of sea horses it had a thick layer of purple gemstones on its bottom which helped it hover in the air.   Where there should have been a hood and an engine, there was a simple cutout and two sturdy ropes so that the two large servants could pull the wagon along with their brute strength. Apparently their gems were not strong enough to lift such a large structure off the ground without the additional power of water. Not to mention, the gemstones could not navigate such a vehicle. The stroller and shopping cart incidents now came back to haunt Robin and Roami's minds. They realized both had been drawn by invisible servants who were chock full of Bunk Juice.   The servants forced Robin, Roami and the baby into the side door of the carriage. Inside they found there was no velvet or plush pillows. Everything was hard and made out of old wood. Sitting on one of the double benches, they continued to hold on to the small baby to ensure there was no way anyone could take him from them. The Reposer jumped in as well and sat on the bench opposite them; facing away from the front. Robin looked out of the small circular cutout window to see the people of Wongswited still angrily yelling and shaking their fists at them. A few rocks were thrown against the carriage and one made its way inside where it hit Robin in the shoulder. "Ow! You stupid-" Robin made as if to throw open the door and run out to seek vengeance but Roami pulled her back in. He looked at her then pointedly at the small baby in his arms. That calmed Robin down a bit. Roami rubbed at her shoulder to soothe the pain. "Does it hurt? Are you okay?" He asked with concern. "It's not so bad..." Robin said as she began to feel the carriage move forward. Like the water buggies of Fitz, their carriage had a small glass cutout in the front which allowed them to see the road ahead of them. The two servants stood before the vehicle and each grabbed a hold of the hanging strings. Without preamble they began to pull the hulking carriage forward as it hovered slightly in the air. The Reposer hung his head out the window and waved at the crowd. Before driving off he said, "Get some rest my good people! I will take care of this problem and tomorrow we will forget this ever happened. Good day!" He yelled for the servants to begin moving the vehicle forward. They drove past the same shopping centers they had happily walked through days before. Drove through Akwo Tunnels they had slid through day after day. Passed store owners and people whose names they had learned and whose hands they had shook. What a difference a day could truly make, Robin thought. As they eventually left the town limits and moved closer to the forest, Robin understood why she had heard so many of the Wongswited call them "The Dark Forests". The tree leaves were ink black and the trunks were a pale sickly gray. The dirt here was grayish unlike the golden color they saw everywhere else they had been. The few pieces of wild grass and plants were all black as well. Robin looked confused, "Where are all the bright plants and flowers I saw in the Quarter?" "You were in one of the Quarters? You truly know how to put your nose where it doesn't belong Strange One. If you must know there are few if any thriving trees or plants still left in the forest. The blue Akwo stone mined from the ground of the forest gives life to the trees and plants. Anywhere you see trees like these here it is because the blue stone has been completely mined from a location. The plants you saw in the Quarter were taken from seeds of thriving foliage." The Reposer looked annoyed for having to explain even this little tidbit to her. "So...long story short... In addition to enslaving the Fitz and making them invisible with your poison juice... You guys also single-handedly destroyed the forests in order to obtain light which you could easily get from the Planet Yur... if you hadn't built buildings too tall to make any sense. The end." Robin looked at the Reposer sarcastically. The Reposer looked as if he would respond but was so angered by her frank yet accurate account of their actions that he just swallowed hard and made a pointed effort to ignore her. He stared out the window as if she too had drank Bunk and became instantly invisible. As they moved steadily away from the town of Wongswited Robin sighed and whispered "Good Riddance!" The sounds of screams and taunts slowly began to recede as they moved deeper into the black forests. Darkness began to envelope them as the lights from the town became all but a memory. Just as Robin began to get anxious, the servants pulled out large metal sticks. Each stick had a chunk of Akwo crystal shining brightly at the end. They pulled their ropes with one hand and shone these lights with the other. This light beamed into the dark forest and helped them to navigate through the ever growing dark shadows. "See Roami? I wasn't going crazy after all. There were green servants hiding around there and leaving our meals at the door. All that time I thought maybe the town was haunted." Robin knew she must be scared because she was nervously grasping for something to talk about that would get her mind off the extreme danger they currently faced.

Looking over at Roami's worried expression and the openly frightened little baby, Robin could not hide from the reality of their predicament or her growing fear. "Maybe it really is haunted. After all, the evil under the surface in Wongswited will eventually come to haunt everyone there." Roami said while staring pointedly at the Reposer. The Reposer sat stiff and silent. From his expression they could tell he was simply along for the ride to ensure his job was done and the child was taken away. In response to their little jibes he rolled his eyes and yawned in response. "How do you sleep at night? Knowing that you destroy lives every day?" Robin glared at him, her hands just itching to attack. "I sleep just fine, thank you. I have the finest house in all of Wongswited; second only to the king. I have all the pleasures and luxuries a person could ask for. Believe me; I have no problems sleeping at all. You two are so naïve. Didn't you hear the truth from the kings' very lips? If given the chance, every one of those filthy Fitzian criminals we allow to live in our beautiful town, on our lofty roofs...would kill us in our sleep! They would take over the town and enslave all of those who they left alive. We are only doing what the victors; the mighty and the strong are meant to do. We lead. They follow. It is what it is. Now please shush about all of this nonsense, you're boring me to death. Ah here we are, finally!" He noticed the carriage had slowed to a stop. Smiling he opened the door brusquely and made his way out before turning around to motion for them to step out as well. Robin made her way out first, glaring nonstop at the Reposer. Roami came out with the baby lying snug in his arms. "Well now, out you go! I won't get any closer if I can help myself. Who knows what kind of monsters lurk out here and no one in their right mind would step foot near Blindfellow Orphanage." The Reposer looked around fearfully. Robin noticed his body shook slightly and jerked anytime an odd cry or shuffle sounded from the depths of the dark forest.

Once he had all three standing to the side of the carriage, he raced back inside and slammed the door shut behind him. "Let's go! Move it!" He quickly ordered the servants to start making their way back towards Wongswited. Before they moved even a step forward the two nearly identical looking servants looked at the children sadly as if they were fish bait. Shaking his head one mumbled to the other, "Poor kids don't stand a chance. The monsters of the forest will take care of them..." The other nodded sadly, "Yes, just like all the rest..."

CHAPTER 11

"Great, now we're really going to die! Did you hear what they just said Roami? Monsters... Monsters! " Robin whimpered dramatically as

she backed up into Roami's side. Her eyes widened as she searched the shadows which seemed to steadily grow around them. Roami wrapped his arms around the young green child and tried his best to stop its soft whimpering.
"Robin think of all the challenges you and I have made it through already. We made it out alive before and we will do it again." Roami said with determination. She did not look too convinced by his words. Robin searched the ground for a make-shift weapon in the event the stories of monsters were more than just that; stories. She walked in a tight circle around Roami, searching the ground intently. Finally she found a sharp gray tree branch. It had broken off so one end was pointy enough to scare away any potential aggressors. Smiling Robin held it in her hand and made her way back to Roami's side. The baby continued to cry softly and kept repeating, "What is my name and where is my mama?" His large purple eyes looked so sad. Just looking at his agony made Robin nearly fall apart inside.
Heartbroken by its appeals, she said, "Roami, we should give him a name. You know what I think would fit him perfectly?... 'Free'." With a soft smile she ran her hand through his silky golden curls then placed her hand on the side of his face in a loving caress. This stopped his cries a bit and he nuzzled his plump green cheeks against her slender brown hand. Roami nodded and smiled as well, "Sounds perfect to me." "That is

your name little one, okay?" Robin said softly as she patted his head soothingly. The baby nodded and nestled against Roami. Within seconds he fell sound asleep. As Robin looked lovingly at his face she could not push back the visions of a similar abandoned baby she had held in her arms so very long ago. Free's face began to mesh with that of baby Jessica who she had been made to take care of while she herself was no more than a small child. The little Hispanic baby girl with the light brown skin, hazel colored eyes, curly hair and contagious giggle came to the forefront of Robin's mind. She had fed, clothed, burped and loved the poor forsaken child while fending for herself in that particular house of horrors. Every now and then she could not help but call out from her soul to that little girl. She wondered where she was now. Had she ever been adopted; had life hurt her the way it had let Robin down so many times? She could only hope not Robin had been successful in closing off these thoughts but something about Free and his painful abandonment brought those memories back to the forefront for a split moment. As she shook the thoughts away Robin was amazed to realize it had been quite some time since she had been assaulted by her ugly past. Somewhere along her journey through strange and exotic worlds, Robin had lost most of her old self. She was not sure she was in any hurry to find that particular Robin again.

Focusing on the present, she looked at Roami and said, "Okay now that he's resting, we should start moving towards some sort of shelter."

"Yes, but which direction? It all looks the same from where we stand." Roami grimaced as he looked around them hoping they would make the right decision on which way to start walking.

"Um..." Robin squinted slightly, "I was thinking maybe that way... Everything seems to be gray and black and desolate but far over that hill a bit... I think I see something...green." She said as she walked a few steps in the direction she was pointing. Free had fallen asleep in Roami's arms so the two began to whisper. "Okay, I guess we have to start moving at some point. Lead the way Robin." Roami said softly so as not to wake Free. Robin held her wooden stick firmly and began to walk across the black grass and thick gray dirt. The ground seemed as if it were akin to quick sand. With each step they struggled to pick their feet up to make the next step. "Do you feel that Roami?" Robin asked with a frown as she wiped the sweat from her brow. They had barely gone a few feet when she realized how tedious each progressive step was becoming.

"Yes... there is something wrong with the ground here. But it is surrounding us; we have no choice but to push through Robin." Roami said as he struggled with both his and the heavy baby's weight as he followed Robin in the ever growing darkness. Realizing that any traces of light from the planet Yur were dissipating, Robin stopped for a moment to pull the Akwo stone she had hidden away in her small black pocketbook.

"See, I told you some of my souvenirs might come in handy." Robin smiled back slyly at Roami. He could not help but smile a little at Robin's attempt at light-heartedness at such a trying time. Her energy helped rev him up slightly so that he did not fall into the gray sand and simply allow it to suck him under. Roami stared at the passing sea of black leaved trees and saw that Robin had in fact seen a trace of green beyond a small gray hill. Standing before them were three large trees with green trunks and purple leaves which shimmered magically in the wind. "Looks like there is still a little life in this dead forest after all. These trees are so beautiful. It's crazy to think this whole place may have looked like this before those crazy Wongswited started destroying everything for their own selfish reasons." Robin said sadly. She held her hand against the green tree trunk and caressed its smooth surface. "Yes, they said the blue Akwo stone is what kept the forest alive." Roami said as he shifted Free onto his other hip in order to take some of the burden off of his right side. The baby was sweating slightly and his golden tresses were plastered against his head in disarray. "Oh yeah, you're right." Robin looked thoughtful for a moment. "I want to try something out. It may be silly but..." She walked

335

a few feet over to one of the gray trees they had just passed. Lifting her hand, she placed the glowing Akwo stone on the trunk. Nothing happened. Biting her lip she went down to her knees and stuck the blue rock in the dirt at the base of the tree. Within seconds the gray trunk began to turn green. Moments after that the black leaves fell to the ground and shiny purple leaves sprouted beautifully in their place. "Oh my..." Robin turned to look back at Roami who stood with his mouth gaping in astonishment. "How did you know you could do that?" Roami asked incredulously. "I just figured... I mean... It's sort of logical..." Robin said with a smile. She pulled the blue stone out of the ground and stepped back to look at her handy work. "It's beautiful Roami." She said with her brown eyes open wide in awe. "And to think... all they need to do is keep the blue stones where they belong. This forest could be a paradise for them..." Roami shook his head sadly. "Yes..." Robin sighed. Roami sighed as well, "Robin... We have to keep moving. Night will come and we need to have shelter in case there really are monsters or something out here." Roami as usual was the voice of reason. "Okay." Robin continued walking in the direction she had set. The trees and ground turned back to the desolate gray and black they had slowly become accustomed to. The air seemed to become thinner the deeper in they went. They soon felt as if they were walking through even air that had become like quicksand; slowly sucking them into darkness.

Before long, the ground itself changed from gray to a deep charcoal black. Once they hit this piece of land it became so difficult to walk they were soon moving at a snail's pace. "I just hope these monsters are not too fearsome. I do not know how I will keep them from harming you and the baby." Roami muttered aloud to himself. Robin overheard him and turned to shoot him an encouraging smile. "Don't worry about me Roami, just take care of Free. I can fend for myself." She stated simply. "Yes, I know." He replied automatically. He knew of course that she could not and he would never ask her to. Roami could not help but think of Robin as his one true friend. As such it was his responsibility to keep her safe and happy. "Roami do you see that?" Robin squinted again to ensure she was seeing what she thought she was. "Yes. It looks like a house. It looks like the House of Intrigues to be precise but...that's impossible..." Roami also squinted to make out the structure that stood far in the distance. As they got closer Robin spoke up again, "Wait... what was that place the Reposer warned us about? He said something about an orphanage..." Robin wracked her brain for his exact words. "Blindfellow Orphanage?" Roami said with dread. "Yes. Blindfellow Orphanage." Robin whispered shakily into the darkness. "Yes, well I

337

guess he was referring to that." Roami said as he pointed towards the large dark house, now just a few feet away. The large black leaves of the forest trees nearly blocked out the odd looking house but what little Robin could see was scary enough to make her want to run back to Wongswited and seek refuge. The massive wooden house was made in the same fashion of the average houses on earth and did look very much like the House of Intrigues from afar. Up close, however, Robin could see the differences plainly. The body of the structure was pale gray with a slanted blood red roof made of marble. The windows were all blackened with grime and the front porch was barely standing. Robin could see that part of the porch had indeed collapsed in on itself. "Oh no! I'm not going anywhere near that thing. It's way too dark and scary. I can imagine the types of monsters just waiting to eat us in there." Robin said as her lips quivered in fear. "Well just think of all the monsters that are waiting to pounce on us out here in these dark forests." Roami said pointedly. "Good point." She said as she stepped closer to Roami. "At least in there we'll have shelter and four walls surrounding us while we're being eaten alive." Robin said sarcastically. Free was beginning to wake and as they made their way up the three creaky wooden steps of the porch, Robin saw his purple eyes open. They lit up as he lifted his head from Roami's shoulder and looked around curiously. Robin and Roami walked cautiously towards the large gray door. "I don't think I've ever been so scared in all my life." Robin whispered as her eyes glistened in the dark. She gritted her teeth trying her best to put up her bravest front. "It's okay Robin. Be tough, we'll make it through this together." Roami said as he took her hand with his free hand then squeezed it slightly. When they reached the gray wooden door, Robin did not wait for fear to grip her but knocked on it immediately. They did not have to wait long for it to open. As the large door creaked ajar the two automatically stepped back. "Yes, can I help you or what?" A skinny green woman asked impatiently as she stood in the doorway. It was so dark both on the porch and inside the home, they could barely see her. She appeared to be a maid of some sort. Her gray colored dress was dingy and torn with a black apron draped over it. The young maids shoulder length hair was yellow and stringy while her light green face appeared sallow. Her eyes were very small and the pupils looked dark red; Robin could not tell due to the blackness that engulfed the entryway. Overall her whole look screamed creepy. Robin was too dumbstruck by the ghostlike look of the young woman to be of any help at the moment, so Roami spoke up. "I um... We got lost in the forests and need to find a place to stay for the night." Roami said quickly; stammering slightly.

"Yes, well..." She eyed them as if they had completely lost their minds. "Have you never heard of Blindfellow Orphanage then?" She asked with some surprise. They shook their heads. "I must say I don't think we ever had anyone willingly knock as this door before... very strange indeed." The maid stared at the trio as if they were aliens. "Oh well, come in then." She said as she roughly pushed them inside. The entryway was just as dark and sinister as the exterior of the house. Before Robin or Roami could say anything the maid quickly shut the door. The two now saw it had at least twelve different locks and bolts running across it. The maid deftly locked each one. "Yes, well I suppose you should know the headmistress will be making her rounds in a few minutes." Before she even completed this statement the maid disappeared in the dark shadows leaving the three guests standing in the middle of a darkened entryway. They were unsure of where to go or how to get there. "Oh boy, what have we gotten ourselves into?" Robin's breath quickened in near panic. She held onto Roami's hand so tightly he could hardly think past the pain. "Well, let's not just stand here. Come on." He said as he carried Free in the crook of his left arm and pulled Robin along with his right.

"Mama..." Free whimpered. He had had a nightmare while he slept only to awaken and find that reality was far worse at the moment.

They stood on deep yet worn red velvet carpet. The walls were painted black and there were no pictures or furniture to be found anywhere. Robin spotted the stairwell leading upstairs from the entryway. The children made their way up the creaky wooden steps. When they finally reached the second floor they found a single red door standing before them. That was all. No long corridor, no other doors or choices to make.

"Odd…" Robin whispered. Roami grabbed hold of the black knob and cautiously opened the door before them. Robin held her breath, afraid of what was on the other side to greet them.

"Ahhhhh!" A chorus of screams erupted the moment the door was ajar. Littered across the floor of the room were young children; all of whom were various shades of green. Every one of them appeared extremely scared, excruciatingly thin and painfully tired. Roami stepped backwards, keeping Robin safely behind him. He waited a moment for their screams to die down then inched forward into the room.

"Oh, sorry! We thought you were the headmistress!" Someone said from among the crowd. The children were all very small and skinny from lack of proper nourishment. They had bags under eyes which seemed to glow green in the dark room; like small animals lurking in a jungle at night. "No, we are not the headmistress. We just came into the house. Who are you all?" Roami asked. Free was completely wide awake after hearing the chorus of screams. He turned around to eye the children curiously.

"We are 'The Found'. And you will be who we are if you don't find a hiding place soon. The headmistress is set to go on her rounds any moment now." A small boy with a head full of red kinky hair said fearfully. Robin looked him over and realized he and the others were dressed in simple gray outfits similar to the Fitz who lived on the Wongswited rooftops. Their clothes had so many tears and holes they seemed like nothing more than pieces of Swiss-cheese.

The large room did not have a single piece of furniture or decorations. It was just a simple square room with creaking gray wooden floorboards and walls barely covered with chipped gray paint. The windows were completely blacked out by layers of dirt and grime. They did however see two doorways to adjoining rooms. Robin noted this as she wanted to ensure they had a means of escape in case something more menacing than a bunch of children found its way towards them. "Huh? I don't understand. Please explain." Roami asked the young boy since no one else in the group seemed willing to speak up. "We were once The Lost and now we are The Found because the headmistress found each one of us at some point or another. Now if you don't hide you will be like us and will never be able to leave the Orphanage again. You will be like us, forced to live here forever..." The boy said sadly. "And what about now? Now that some of you have been found what does that mean? Why are you still hiding from her?" Robin asked as she thought the situation over in her head. "Once you're The Found... If she catches you again...you just...disappear." The same red-headed boy said with tears in his eyes. "Oh no, that sounds horrible! How could anyone-" Before Robin could properly voice her opinions on the situation, the sharp sound of high-heeled shoes marching across the floor resounded throughout the house. "Ahhhh!" Intense screaming permeated the air as the children began racing about in a flurry of pure terror. They scattered like roaches running from the light. Robin and Roami got swept up in the sea of fear and ran about nervously trying to hide from the sound of what was apparently approaching doom.

Robin led the way. Grabbing Roami's hand, she raced towards the doorway near the far right of the room. This took them to another identical room and yet another doorway. They continued moving through room after room. Sneaking through doorway after doorway with no end in sight. In the back of her mind, Robin wondered if the house was under some sort of spell. She was sure, from the outside, it did not look big enough to have held so many rooms. Each room appeared like the one before it, all had gray wooden flooring and black windows barred shut.   There was very little lighting. The only light came from a single blue Akwo gem lantern hanging from the ceiling of each room. Not one piece of furniture could be found to hide behind.

"This is crazy!" Robin said breathlessly as they realized they needed to hide in a place which offered absolutely no secure hiding spots. Along the way they saw a myriad of small green faces racing past them in panic. They were unsure which children were lost or found and could not stop to find out since they were busy struggling for their own survival.   "That looks like a closet!" Robin screamed as she noticed a light green door in the back of one of the rooms they were just about to leave. She pulled Roami back towards it then threw open the small door. Before Roami could respond she shoved him and Free inside. There was just enough room for her to squeeze in as well. Once they were all in, she stepped inside then shut the door behind her securely. The closet smelled of mildew and moth balls but it was a hiding spot. Therefore, Robin did not stop to note they were sitting on damp wood or packed so tightly her neck was stuck somewhere near Roami's elbow.   They struggled to bring their breathing down to a normal pace. Robin even covered Free's mouth to ensure the small baby did not make an errant sound. A sickening quiet began to settle throughout the house as each moment passed by.   The only sound that could be heard was the fearsome march of sharp shoes across the wooden floorboards of the house. Every now and again the trio would hear the feet stop and the sound of screams as an old woman's voice screeched, "Gotchya!" Robin began to cry silently and shake with fear. Roami tried his best to calm her but to no avail. "Oh Roami, I am so... so sorry." She whispered through her tears. "Sorry for what?" He whispered back while listening intently to determine how far away the steps were from their current location. "I'm sorry for saying you were dumb to pick your skin color. Remember in Source One when you told me that your people were allowed to pick the color of their skin and I said you should have picked something lighter?" She sobbed a bit and waited to feel Roami's nod in acknowledgment. "Yes, I remember." He said softly. Although it was not the easiest feat, Roami found her face and gently wiped the tears away with his hand. "Well I am truly sorry for what I said. It was an ignorant comment and I just want you to know now... that I think you are beautiful and I love your color." She hiccupped then continued, "I would love you; my friend, no matter what color you were..." She said as she hugged him and little Free to her chest. Just then the two froze realizing they had not heard the headmistress's steps for quite some time. Before either could remark on this strange fact the door to the closet swung open with a powerful force. They each screamed as they looked into the face of an old woman with small eyes covered in a white film; blind and squinty.   Her skin was gray as opposed to green or purple and her long straight hair was completely white. She was dressed in a formal outfit with a shirt, dress jacket and skirt all of which were dark gray and looked as if they had been worn every day for a century. Her fingers were large and her long, ragged, brown nails reached out towards the children. "Gotchya!" she cackled as she lurched forward to violently grab at them.   "Ahhhhhh!" The threesome screamed at the top of their lungs. Before the headmistress could get at them however an invisible force shoved her backwards. The closet door then slammed shut.

Robin, Roami and Free remained as they were; screaming, crying and holed up in the dark closet.   They stayed this way; screeching in blackness for what seemed like an eternity...

CHAPTER 12

Both Robin and Roami continued screaming for some time with their eyes shut and their fists clenched. However, even intense fear when repeated nonstop for a long duration could become overrated. Just like anything else they eventually grew tired of it. They stopped screaming and grew quiet with only the sound of their frantic heartbeats filling their ears. "What happened?" Robins' voice had become raspy from all her screaming. The two opened their eyes slowly. Something odd had happened. They could feel it in the air; something had changed but neither could put their finger on it. "Roami?" Robin felt for his face. He took her wandering hand into his to give her a sense of security. "Yes, I'm still here Robin." Roami said. "I thought she was supposed to grab us and make us one of The Found. But we're still here... What do you think happened?" She asked shakily. "I have no idea but I know we cannot stay in this closet forever. We will have to step out and see for ourselves." Roami said. "Roami... I hate to admit it but... I'm scared and I don't want anything to happen to you or Free. Let's just stay in here for a few more days or a month or just until we can-" Before she could finish that thought Roami pushed open the closet door with an exasperated sigh. Both were absolutely dumbfounded by what stood before them. "Oh my god..." Robin gasped in astonishment. Roami too, could not believe his eyes. Handing Free over to Robin for safekeeping he stood up and stepped outside of the cramped space of the closet. "How is this possible..." Roami walked haltingly. His knees were shaking uncontrollably. Roami could not tell if it was because they had sat so confined in the closet or if the shock was making his knees weak. "You've got to be kidding me..." Robin said as she picked up Free. Following suit, she stepped out of the closet to stand by Roami's side. "It's the Nommo tree!" "Yes. Just as we left it in Source One. Robin, we're back in Source One!" Roami beamed with happiness. In his rapture he grabbed Robin's hands; then began to dance around and scream into the air with joy. Free laughed at the two and kissed Robin's cheek before joining in their screaming fit. His giggles and screeches only made them feel even happier and full of abandon. "Wow! How did we get back? What was the riddle and how did we solve it?" Robin said as she turned around to glance at the green closet door. Within seconds it quickly vanished into thin air. "You solved the riddle Robin!" Roami hugged her to him and spun her and Free around in a dizzying twirl. Robin could not help but laugh out loud. Without realizing it she kissed him on his cheek. That slowed their actions and seemed to cease even the flow of time itself. Roami smiled down at her sheepishly and she looked down bashfully. Where oh where had the old brusque and brass Robin gone, she wondered. She could not remember ever having blushed or giggled until she met Roami. Trying her best to brush the odd moment away she spoke up to break the silence, "I guess the main thing we had to learn in those worlds was that color is not important. I realized that whether you were a dark color or light color you are still my friend. This is something the people of both the water world of Fitz and the town of Wongswited, had not figured out for centuries. It's odd something so simple could be overlooked for so long..." Robin sighed. She was at once, ecstatic to have left the two worlds behind but also felt a sense of sadness that somewhere, far away the people of Fitz and Wongswited, all still lived in deep ignorance. "But you got it Robin! You saved us!" Roami beamed with pride for his best-friend then hugged her to him once again. "Oh...." Robin said in awe. "All I can say is... Wow!" She smiled with open delight. It was at that moment they each looked at each other as if for the very first time. They did not see their differing skin colors. They did not think about their varying pasts. Both teens just saw their spirits shining brightly from within. After this life changing moment passed, Robin was hit with a painful realization. While they were free; many were still living in various forms of captivity. The Found at Blindfellow's orphanage were somewhere, in a seemingly alternate dimension, perpetually running for their very lives. Then there were the poor Fitzian rooftop dwellers...still forced to drink bunk juice and living their lives as slaves of the Wongswited. Thinking even further back, she clearly saw the light green Mobbins of Fitz walking listlessly; their heads hung low, as they made their way along gray paths doing the bidding of the Fitzian royals... And what of dear Mirub? Robin could still see the beautiful woman drifting away in an endless sea of gray waters. Was this truly how life was meant to be? Robin shuddered back a moan as she realized how many problems there were needing to be solved and how helpless she was to do anything about any of it. She however did not share her dark thoughts with Roami. His smile was far too bright at the moment to dampen his spirits. She would bring her concerns up at a later time; for now they would celebrate only the goodness life had to offer. Shaking her head and forcing a smile; Robin forcefully pulled away from her heavy ruminations. So what was next? Apparently at that very moment, Roami was asking himself the same question. They each took a look around them and began to settle back to reality. "Roami," Robin laughed, "Can you imagine what we must look like to outsiders right now?" Both Robin and Roami were still dressed in their silk pajamas from Wongswited and their slippers were caked with black dirt. Free on the other hand was just that; free and naked. Robin held the naked baby to her side and tried unsuccessfully to cover him with parts of her own robe. They both had to get changed and get Free some clothes as soon as possible. "My parents must be so worried. I have to get back to my village... I mean we have to get back to my village right away! You will come with me won't you Robin?" Roami looked unsure of himself for the first time since she had met him. "Of course I will! Where you go, I follow. We're friends... besides... you still haven't shown me all of Source One." She smiled as she linked her arm in his and let him lead the way toward his village.

Roami took a moment to gauge their current location. With a short nod of his head he started walking past the Nommo and towards a familiar sky-blue forest path of Source One. Robin looked up at the blue leaves swaying in the breeze and smiled up at the minty green skies

351

above. They were back "Home" and while even this world was alien to her, something about being where Roami was made her feel safe and secure. She had never felt this way on earth. A smile crept over her lips. With Free in her arms and Roami at her side she felt part of something worthwhile, for the very first time in her life. Roami looked over at her in wonder. He had never seen Robin as happy as she looked at that very moment. It was as if the hardest parts of her past had magically washed away over their adventurous journeys. He smiled as he watched the green light of day caress her beautiful brown skin and light up her brown eyes. His smile faded as a question popped into his head.

Looking over at Robin he said, "I wonder how much time has passed here in Source One? I guess we will get the answer to that question when we make it back home. I just hope time stood still or my bearer will punish me for getting lost in the blue mists." Roami said fearfully. He looked more afraid of his mom's anger than the cold stare of the headmistress at Blindfellow Orphanage. "Don't worry. I'm sure she'll be too busy being happy you made it back to be too angry with you." Robin said. She felt as if she wanted to skip through the blue grass. Or perhaps even dive into it and make grass angels. Robin was giddy with their accomplishment and so happy to be back. She was sure she had never felt so happy in all her life. Not only had she made a true new friend but they had single-handedly made it out of a maze of worlds that many would have been unable to solve. Part of her whispered the obvious; that she was still in an alien world and did not know what to expect with each second, but she ignored that voice. She knew that home was where your heart was and hers felt safest wherever Roami was. Earth had never been a place of love, warmth or refuge for her. Robin obstinately dared the butler of The House of Intrigues to call her back when she did not want to return. She would stay here in Source One; here with Roami no matter what. She was pulled back from her thoughts when Free nuzzled his little face into her neck and sighed happily. Robin smiled then looked at Roami as a thought dawned on her, "I think we'll have to explain Source One to Free. I mean it is his new home now. Roami, you know this place better than me so I guess you can teach him everything." Robin said. "Yes, of course." Roami smiled and carefully pulled the big cuddly green baby, with soulful purple eyes from Robin's arms. With Free in the crux of his arms, Roami began to show him Source One. Roami named each and every plant and type of creature they met on the way. Free excitedly repeated everything Roami told him. "Tree." Roami said. "Tree!" Free giggled then wrapped his pudgy arms around Roami's neck in a sweet hug. Roami laughed in response. "Molby Flower." He picked one up to show Free it's red and black striped petals and glowing white center. "Moby Bower!" Free grabbed at the flower, brought it to his nose and sneezed. Robin laughed at Free's baby talk and said, "He'll get it in time." Robin was surprised to see how quickly Free had developed since the moment he was born. However, having witnessed some parts of little Brifton's rearing she had guessed she could not assume theirs was anything like human development. Roami was about to point out something else when they all stopped. Loud sounds were coming from some feet away. Robin instinctively moved closer to Roami for safety. "It's my village..." Was all Roami said as he quirked up his ears to determine the source of the racket. "Sounds like... a party, I think." Robin whispered. They continued to move forward but at a faster pace. When they finally drew nearer to Roami's village they could hear it was in fact the sounds of a great celebration. The noise was a symphony of people chatting, singing and laughing. It echoed throughout the forest.

Robin had missed the idea of parties after their dreary stay in Wongswited. There everyone was too focused on business and domination to throw a party every now and then. When she heard the beat of drums and the lilting sounds of flutes floating through the trees she stopped in her tracks. "Oh my God! Yay! A party!" She jumped up and down with enthusiasm. Robin could hardly recognize herself. She had never had cause to feel so carefree and happy. It almost felt as if she had been stuck under a heavy weight or walked beneath a small rain cloud most of her life. But now she was liberated and had her Free and her Roami. Together she was sure they could do absolutely anything they put their minds to. She turned to look at Roami only to find him frozen in place and frowning slightly. Robin automatically grew tense; wondering what could upset him to such an extent. Roami turned to her and looked almost paralyzed by his emotions. "What is it Roami? What's the matter?" Robin asked anxiously. His looked at her blankly and said, "There is a festival…" "Yeah, I know I hear it too. How Cool?!" Robin said with a smile and a quirk of her brow. "No. You don't understand. That could only mean one thing…" Without another word, Roami placed Free in Robin's arms and raced towards his home with a fevered look on his face…

To Be Continued…

The Saga Continues…

QuestMyre

Book Two

"The Land of Mists & Mirrors"

ABOUT THE AUTHOR

HaaJar "Hajee" Johnson has won numerous awards for her poetry and essays from such organizations as the Peace Corps, National Black MBA Association and New York Times. She wrote and produced two off-Broadway plays; the first of which was developed for the African Burial Ground Project and was entitled "Don't see my bones and think I'm dead". In 2001, this play was also developed into a short-film and broadcast by PBS channel thirteen. Hajee's second play was entitled; "Tweetadopplin" and was performed at Galli Theater during the Summer of 2009. Hajee was both Theater Director and actress for Galli Theater throughout 2009, as well. In her heart, Hajee has always been a writer first and foremost. Her total literary collection consists of: 3 adult fiction novels, 2 books of poetry, a 5 part young adult book series and 4 children's book series. In 2011, spurred on by her desire to initiate positive change, Hajee founded a non-profit organization; Tweetland Inc. The organization's mission is to support holistic child development with a focus on at-risk youth. Their current "Fun To Run" campaign is centered on eliminating childhood obesity. Hajee hopes to use her management expertise, people skills and proclivity towards community service to make this initiative a major success.